MURDERS

IN A SMALL TOWN

MURDERS

IN A SMALL TOWN

BARRY WOOD

ISBN: 978-0-9826168-8-8

Published by Fiction Publishing, Inc.
5626 Travelers Way
Fort Pierce, FL 34982

I want to thank

Carol Peecha,
a best friend
and final editor.

Leona DeRosa Bodie,
my editor, for her endless hours
bringing sense to sentences.

Christina,
my wife, for willingly going to play golf,
while I stared, befuddled, at a
blank page.

Author Gene Hull,
for too much to list.

Chapter

ONE

Town of Barretton, Massachusetts 11:00 PM, Saturday night, September 12, 1966.

He stared at the fireplace until the logs burned to dimming embers. There was nothing left for him now. He took a deep breath, and braced himself. All that remained was to pick up the phone ... and dial.

"Barretton Police, Connie Johnson speaking. May I help you?"

"Yes ... this is Parker Sinclair, I ... ah ..."

The last time Connie had heard this voice, the man had been a speaker at a seminar she attended. Connie quickly drew a mental picture of Parker Sinclair: tall, slim, known, half-jokingly, as the owner of Barretton. The moment continued too long. Again, she asked, with a touch more respect, "Sir, may I be of help?"

"Ah yes, I'm sorry. I've ... I've shot my wife."

Connie held her breath and signaled her supervisor, Lieutenant Ken Collin, to pick up the other phone, "Is your wife all right, sir? She asked, "Should we send an ambulance to Great Hill?"

"No need, Miss Johnson. My wife is dead. Please send an officer here."

"Mister Sinclair, this is Lieutenant Collin. What's happened? Are you all right?"

Another silence before Parker Sinclair responded, "I told Miss Johnson I shot my wife. Please come up here."

Collin shook his head, bewildered. There hadn't been a murder in town since the Puritans killed a few Indians long ago. Murder didn't happen here. Something was wrong, damn wrong.

"We'll be there in a few minutes, sir."

He radioed Tom Starr, the officer on night patrol, to pick him up as soon as possible. Collin wanted assistance, and a witness, for whatever they were going to find at the Hill.

Telling Connie to say nothing about the call, he hurried out the front door.

Sixty miles to the east, Homicide Captain Detective Ray Polo, sat alone and frustrated in his office at Boston Police Headquarters. He felt his face flush, muscles tense. His fist slammed onto his desk as he clenched his jaw. He'd been warned once again.

Fellow officers in the room drifted to other areas of the building, Polo had a legendary temper. His friend, the Police Commissioner, told him emphatically that yes, he was a great detective, but his form of swift justice was going the way of the dinosaurs. No more excessive force and no more complaints. An order. It was okay thirty years ago, when Polo started with the police and skirted the law. Even five years ago, he could get away with it. Now however, he was jeopardizing his pension. Back off until he retired. Coast, he was told. Avoid the endless skirmishes with felons *and* his fellow officers.

Polo couldn't back off, or coast, it wasn't in his blood. That drive, and his brain, was the reason he was considered the best of the best. Soon, again, those abilities would be tested.

In Barretton, impatiently waiting for Patrolman Starr, Lt. Collin thought of the impossibility of the situation. He pictured Sinclair's sun-weathered, handsome face. Probably, what people called upper crust. What words described the man? Contained, sure of himself, yet without conceit. He remembered everyone. The townspeople admired him. Of course, his bank and his wealth added to their esteem. Lt. Collin envied Sinclair's easy manner, wishing he could have that same approach to people.

Despite the circumstances, Collin smiled, even when *thinking* of the man; he could never address him as simply Sinclair and certainly not Parker.

Patrolman Starr pulled up, "What's up, Ken?"

Collin jumped in, staring blankly for a few seconds, "Parker Sinclair called, said he murdered his wife."

"You can't be serious."

"You heard me. Mister Sinclair killed his wife. Get going."

"Where?"

"Where the devil do you think? Great Hill for Christ's sake!"

The car shot forward, spraying the station door with pebbles as they headed for the house on Great Hill, the home of Nancy and Parker Sinclair.

More of a hillock than a hill, Great Hill was formed by the last glacier, which ground its way through New England thousands of years earlier. The forty-acre site, which rose sixty feet above the surrounding countryside, was the highest elevation in the valley and given its name by a farmer in the early 1700s. Laden with oak, birch and elm trees, every outlook was a masterpiece with rolling hills, lakes, streams and farms, filling the landscape. Even more remarkable were the sunrises, sunsets, and the black snow or rainsqualls, seen for miles before they struck.

Sinclair had kept this site in mind and, when he sold his mills in Manchester and Lawrence, he bought Great Hill from a farmer who found the land of little use.

The police cruiser left the country road, coasting onto the entrance below the Hill. With the headlights off, the vehicle climbed the steep moonlit driveway. The Georgian estate, previously hidden in a copse of trees, began to emerge, and after they rounded a sharp curve the residence loomed above them.

Light spilled from a room upstairs and one room down. Before reaching the main entrance, the cruiser stopped. Collin got out and walked along part of driveway that ran straight past the right side of the house. To his left, attached to the house, was a two-story atrium. To his right, a large detached garage. Dark, doors closed; no one about. He stopped and listened, eyes darting left and right. In the scant moonlight he squinted down to the paddock, stalls and outdoor riding arena. Not a soul. A horse in the paddock, head down, standing on three legs, one hoof raised slightly, a sign it was sleeping. Collin knew the horse belonged to Emily, Sinclair's daughter. He noted the animal remained calm; all was quiet, no light anywhere except the front of the house.

He walked back to the police cruiser.

Starr questioned him, "Anything?"

"Nothing. Drive to the front slowly. I'll walk along beside you. Stop before the steps."

He looked through the front door sidelights, seeing an empty hallway. Starr stood ten feet away, his hand on his revolver. Collin pressed the bell, hearing chimes inside. Looking through the glass, no movement. Again, he rang. Still nothing moved inside.

Collin tried the latch; the door swung open.

"Mister Sinclair, Police!"

Silence. The silence became disturbing. Collin shouted again, "Mr. Sinclair!"

"Yes, in here." The voice barely audible.

The two officer's eased into the room. Sinclair had his back to them, staring into the fireplace. Wood sap crackled as it touched still warm embers. That, and the ticking of clock were the only sounds as the two officers glanced around.

"Sir, you called us?" Collin asked, "Is there a problem here?"

No answer.

Satisfied no one else was about, Collin approached the rigid figure that continued staring at the fireplace. Through the years, he had spoken with Sinclair many times. Collin's mind flashed to a portrait on the wall in his bank: a firm jawed man dressed in the starched dress-whites of a naval Lieutenant Commander, battle ribbons and the Navy Cross on his chest. The engraved brass plate on the frame stated, PARKER ROBERTS SINCLAIR, WWII Pacific Theater, 1941-1945.

4

Collin's thought drifted from that image to only two days earlier when he had seen Sinclair. Suit and shirt perfect ... tie matching ... hair graying and groomed, perfect ... demeanor and manner, perfect. An important man, engaged with life.

The officer couldn't believe this once vital sixty-years-old man was now a watery-eyed senior, sitting in rumpled pajamas, staring, tears damp on his cheeks.

A flash of silver caught Collin's attention. Beside the phone, on the side table next to Sinclair, lay a nickel-plated Colt, .45 caliber semiautomatic. Too far away if the suspect lurched for the weapon. Collin signaled Starr with his eyes.

The officer noticed the weapon. His eyes widened as he misunderstood Collin's next gestures. Although Sinclair couldn't see the patrolman draw his revolver, Starr's unease churned in his gut. He was nervous, a small town cop, on the force only a year and had never even drawn his revolver on duty before. Did Collin really want him to shoot Sinclair? Was he serious? How could he do something like that? Starr waited.

With a restrained voice, Collin told Sinclair he was going to go walk in front of him.

Now Starr understood. If Sinclair went for the gun, shoot him. Nauseous at the thought, he held steady. Since Sinclair didn't react to Collin's statement, he stepped to the man's left, reached the side table and took the weapon by the barrel. Sinclair never blinked. Patrolman Starr took a deep breath, wondering if he could have pulled the trigger.

Collin held the weapon by the barrel. A sniff told him the gun was fired recently. He cleared the chamber and released the clip, making sure not to touch the grip. Counting the bullets in the clip, he found one missing. Collin put the Colt on the mantle, then pocketed the clip and bullet from the chamber.

He turned to Sinclair, "Now, sir, what happened here?"

No answer.

"Sir, you said you shot your wife. Where is she?"

At the word, wife, Sinclair looked up. It took a moment to comprehend, "Nan's upstairs ... in the bedroom."

Collin felt his belly twist into knots. The phone call was true. The man had killed his wife. Now all that was left was to confirm it. "Starr, go upstairs and check." A glance showed the rookie frozen in place. Collin couldn't blame him, having had the same fears a dozen or more times during his two tours in Vietnam. It was his duty; he knew it couldn't be avoided.

"Watch Sinclair, Starr."

As Collin mounted the stairs, scanning for evidence, he shuffled, subconsciously moving as he had in combat. At the top, he moved toward the glow from an open door. Glancing in, he turned away. Bile touched his tongue, his breath quickened. He finally got himself together and stood in the doorway.

Nancy K, known by that name since her Regis College days, lie on her back, her head resting on a pillow, eyes open. Had Collin looked closer he would have seen she wore a quizzical look, as if questioning what was happening. Blood spread a circle across her breast and, as Collin knew only too well, another red pool would stain her back. Flesh and bone couldn't stop a .45 caliber slug. He checked his watch, 11:35 PM. Thirty-five minutes since the call to the station. He noted the blood appeared nearly dry.

Chapter

TWO

Heading downstairs, Collin knew a terrible wrong had occurred, not to mention the uproar it would cause in the community. Sinclair, a war hero, sole owner and chairman of his bank, a family man with two children and a wife he appeared to love so much, *had killed her*!

Collin knew he must handle the circumstances as discretely as possible until his responsibility ended. He wanted no part of the media storm that was sure to follow.

"Starr, call Dispatch on this phone. Tell Connie what we've found, and ask her to call the county coroner and an ambulance. She's to do it by the station's telephone, not the Police Band. Tell her to make sure whomever she speaks with to keep their mouths shut and destination quiet. No sirens. Have them get to Great Hill as fast as they can without causing attention along the way. There's no houses around here, so they might not be seen."

Collin stood in front of Sinclair, "Sir, your wife is dead. I'm placing you under arrest."

Again, at the mention of his wife, Sinclair woke from his stupor long enough to say he understood that was necessary. After getting clothes from a bedroom closet, no belt, tie or shoelaces, Collin told Sinclair to dress and turned to Starr, "Tom, after I take Sinclair to the station, you're to stay at the bottom of the drive. You know who to let in. If anyone else stops, say there's a meeting going on, and to go about their business. Right now, stay with Sinclair while I look around."

7

With his flashlight, he checked each of the fourteen rooms and the cellar.

In the atrium, his high-powered light on two stories of plate glass, half blinded him, although he managed to scrutinize the room. Around the periphery, there were benches with potted plants by the score. Despite the constant glare, Collin could make out that the pots held orchids. They didn't matter to him. His priority was in determining windows weren't broken. He turned away from the glare to check every lock on the building's ground floor. As expected, nothing inconsistent.

It was almost midnight when Sinclair was brought into the station house. Connie jumped from her seat in surprise. She knew they were due in, but part of her shock was what happened at Great Hill. The other shock, Sinclair looked ten years older, she thought, the sagging clothes doing nothing to help.

Collin led him to one of the cells in the station, and then asked Connie, "Can you stay longer."

"Yes, yes!"

Her quick response told Collin she was far too excited to leave. He went to his office, dropped into his chair, and started the paperwork. His shift was the same as Connie's, 2:00 PM to midnight. There were going to be a few long hours before he left this night. Then again, no one was at home, what difference did it make? He felt stressed, contemplating his to-do list of what came next. He had to get the coroner's report to confirm the time of death. The dried blood bothered him. What about the body? The coroner would take care of that. Have the prints on the gun checked. Call the county and. state prosecutor's office. Call the State Police and County Sheriff. Call the town selectmen first, then Springfield and Worcester Police Captains; they would be closest.

Collin wanted help. He never dealt with a high profile murder case. Should he call their children? They were twins, a boy and girl. Paul and Emily. Nice kids, about twenty-four he guessed. Calling them will be hell. Let the selectmen decide. However, talk with Sinclair about the motive. Other than not giving a reason for the crime, he was being co-operative. Something didn't seem right.

Interrupting his thoughts, he heard Tom Starr call in on the Police Band.

"I'm still at Great Hill. All I want to know is can I head home after the coroner and ambulance leave with the body?"

Collin was staggered, grabbing the mike out of Connie's hand, "Where did you find Sinclair's PB and why in hell are you using it? Any insomniac can monitor it!"

Starr was speechless from the shouting. All Collin could do now was hope the call was too brief for anyone to pick up, "You're not going anywhere you Goddamn idiot! You don't have a car. If anyone gets up to that house I'll have your badge!"

Collin threw the mike down, catching his breath. Connie's eyebrows rose. She had never seen him this angry.

"I'm sorry," he mumbled, going back to open the cell. Sinclair was more focused after washing his face and hands at the sink, and straightening his pants and shirt. He looked at Collin with sad eyes, "Hello, Ken, I heard what happened with that officer. Still, it's going to get out anyway. No real damage done."

Then, changing the subject, "I'm sorry about this."

"I know it's going to get out, sir. I simply wanted to get everything in order first. Do you understand what happened?"

"Yes, my wife is dead. I did it."

Collin held up his hand, "Don't say anything further. You have a right to counsel; that's my suggestion."

"I know my rights, and I *do not* wish to exercise them."

"Mister Sinclair, I strongly suggest that …"

Parker waved his hand as if there would be no further discussion, "Give me a confession form or whatever you call it. I want this over."

At first, mystified by Sinclair's impatience, Collin realized the man's style was to formulate a plan, stop the talk, get it done.

"Connie, bring a legal pad, pen, and date stamp. Mr. Sinclair, there are no forms available here for this sort of thing, write your confession on this pad."

Sinclair's, left-hand gripped the pen; his script flowed firm and unique:

9

I, Parker Roberts Sinclair, on the date listed below, without duress or coercion, having refused my right to any type of legal counsel, wish to make the following statement: That I, on the night of September 10, 1966, at approximately 9:30 p.m., shot and killed my wife, Nancy Katherine Sinclair, in our home at Great Hill. I will plead guilty at any trial, and will not claim any extenuating circumstances.

Parker R. Sinclair, 9.10.66

So frank, so blasted, maddeningly straightforward. And uninformative.

Sinclair gazed at Lieutenant Collin, "Do you need more?"

"Yes, please state why you did it."

He shook his head, the *why* left unanswered.

"Then Connie and I will witness and date-stamp it. Please sign your name again, this time across the date, sir."

It was finished. However, Collin had a question or two after Connie left.

"Mr. Sinclair, you wrote you shot your wife around 9:30 this evening."

"Yes, about then I would think."

"But we didn't receive your call until 11:00 PM."

"Your point, Lieutenant?"

"My point, *sir,* is we're missing one and a half hours."

Sinclair stared at Collin and shrugged, "Now I see what you're getting at. I don't know what I was doing or even if I told you the right time. I guess nothing … I don't know what … I'm lost as to what I did, probably just sat where you found me."

Collin decided to try a different tact to find the reason why the man murdered his wife. It would complete the case. He decided on a ploy; get Sinclair talking about her.

"How'd you meet your wife?

"Odd question at a time like this, Lieutenant. We met at a dance in Marshfield, Rexham Beach.
She was so beautiful I stared at her half the night before I got the nerve to ask her to dance. The first words out of my mouth were to apologize, for staring."

"What did she say to that?"

"She said my name's Nancy Katherine Thomson, let's start by you telling me yours."

He recalled her exact words, lost in the past, losing his grip on the present.

"When did you get married?"

"We were married two years later, in Hawaii, December 27, 1941."

"That was right after the Japanese attack on Pearl Harbor. Were you in it?"

"No, I was X/O, Executive Officer, on the cruiser *Hampton* out of San Diego Naval Base. On the 20th we were part of task force, Taffy 14, sent to relieve Wake Island. Unfortunately, we had to come about and never reached there. The Japanese had two carriers, two battleships and support vessels off Wake. All we had was the carrier *Saratoga*, a couple of cruisers and tin cans, I mean destroyers. If you recall your history, our battleships were on the bottom of Pearl. We got to Pearl the 24th, to a God-awful mess. Our vessel had burned a shaft bearing, but they squeezed us in and had us repaired and out by the 30th."

Collin had him talking, "You got back to Pearl on the 24th and shipped out on the 30th"? That's not much time to get married. Was your wife living there?"

He saw Sinclair's eyes glaze; a wisp of a smile cross his lips, "No, I called Nan in Boston and asked her to marry me. Thank God, she said yes. Then I used my father's pull with the War Department to have her flown to Hickham field. She arrived two days later. We were married, and I returned to my ship the night of the 29th. I wasn't to see her again for almost four years— four years before I saw her and my three-year old twins."

He fell silent, turning his back, hiding his emotions.

Collin knew he had lost him. To bring her up again would only cause resentment. His ploy wasn't going to work. Sinclair wasn't going to give the reason he murdered the woman he loved.

The subject changed, "My only other question concerns your Colt. How long have you had it?"

"It was issued to me in 1940. I carried it throughout the Pacific war."

"Have you fired it, ah … previously?"

"Yes."

"When?"

"I fired it in practice when I received it."

"Any other time?" Collin did not know where he was going, purely fishing.

"Another time? Yes, on my ship … at Okinawa."

Collin couldn't fathom Sinclair on a ship, firing a .45 Colt.

"Do I have to keep asking questions to draw you out, or will you please explain why you're firing a Colt handgun on a ship. Did you have a mutiny?"

"You *do* know we were at war then, don't you?" Sinclair was condescending.

His attitude changed with Collin's embarrassment, "Lieutenant Collin. You served in Vietnam."

It was a surprise to Collin that Sinclair knew.

"And you know how certain events cause you to do something out of character," he continued, "that happened to me. My cruiser and some destroyers were doing picket duty around our carriers. The Japanese Kamikazes were after them, so we interposed our ships between the carriers and the Kamikazes and threw every bit of steel we had at the bastards. Of course, we knew what the top brass wanted, let me say *preferred* rather than wanted, however, it worked out the same. What the brass preferred was for the Kamikazes to hit our ships and save the carriers. We accepted that, it was our duty."

Sinclair stopped; back in the war for the moment, repeating, "It was our duty."

12

After a moment, he went on, "This time we managed to be seriously shot up, many of my men dead or wounded. I was injured and groggy when I saw a Jap plane going to get by us. I stumbled out to the wing of the bridge; pulled out my Colt, and fired off every damn round I had … It would be great to say I shot him down, but no such luck."

Collin was silent. He did not want to take this tact further. He made a mental note this man could get angry and fire a gun. What made him so angry at Great Hill?

The question Collin was going to ask remained stillborn.

Sinclair knew what it was, "And yes, I fired it tonight also."

Colin thought to ask, "Do you want to call your attorney."

"Not right now, thank you."

The realization Sinclair actually killed his wife kept seeping into Collin's brain. He sat at his chair, elbows on the desk, cupping his chin in his hands. His head swung side-to-side. Sinclair actually *did* it … he actually *did* it. He destroyed a life and a *way* of life. What possessed him? Has he realized yet, what he has done? That tomorrow his wife won't be there. This was no bad dream; the truth was his life would never be the same. It would be worse. In essence, it was over.

Connie looked in from the doorway, "How many copies of the confession do you want?"

Chapter

Three

"**M**iranda! I didn't read him his damn Miranda rights! God damn me!"

Connie stepped back startled. Collin was almost sick as he rummaged through his files for the notice from the Police Chief's Association of Massachusetts. What a blunder he'd made! He pulled out the form and started reading, "You have the right to remain silent. Anything you say can, and will be, used against you in a court of law. You ..."

Collin stared at the form, issued to police departments the beginning of July earlier in this year, 1966. At that time, there had been no need for it in his quiet, little town and he carelessly filed it away. You don't read rights to someone speeding, littering, jay walking, a family dispute or an underage kid buying a pack of cigarettes. A drunk you dumped in jail for the night and called his house to pick him, or her, up in the morning. That was all that happened in Barretton. Collin had filed the document and forgotten it, until now.

Everything Sinclair had said, done, and written, could be off the record. Did he know? Was he laughing this very second at Collin's stupidity? Only one way to find out. He headed back to the cell, feeling stupid and furious at the same time. He hadn't the slightest idea of how transparent his face appeared when he stopped at the barred door.

Sinclair looked up, "What's wrong, Lieutenant?"

It took all of Collin's reserve to admit, "I forgot to read you your Miranda Rights."

Sinclair lowered his head, then nodded, "I can see that now. I forgot also. Yet please think back to when you told me I had a right to counsel. I knew my rights and waved them off. Doesn't that cover it?"

"I don't know."

"Lieutenant Collin, I killed my wife." Sinclair blinked a number of times, then continued, nearly gasping, fighting for control, "I will state that anytime to anyone you wish. I stated it in front of Connie. I will shout it from the front door if you wish."

He took a deep breath, exhaling slowly, "Please understand Lieutenant, I want this over as soon as possible. I took a person's life, my wife's, for Christ's sake. I'm guilty and expect to be punished to the extent I deserve. No one could do anything near the punishment I'm giving myself."

Collin pondered that. The reserved Mr. Sinclair had revealed himself, if only briefly. Somewhat relieved about his oversight, Colin returned to his office, pushed his chair back with his legs and locked his fingers behind his head. He intended to ask the Town Attorney if it would be legal to post-recite the Miranda and have Sinclair write out another confession.

Sinclair sat quietly; his thoughts focused on Nancy K. Collin could read it in his face. Whatever happened to him didn't matter, not in the least.

Promising himself to stay more up to date with his paperwork, Collin thought his oversight trivial to this disaster. Mister Parker R. Sinclair, Chairman of the Board, owner of the National Bank of Barretton, philanthropist, and former Master of the Lodge, was liked by everyone, an all round decent person. Oh, and by the way, a murderer.

Collin wrestled with the case. Not able to get it out of his head, he wondered what in hell happened. He couldn't recall a whiff of scandal about either of them. Did he catch *her* fooling around? Did *she* want to leave *him*? Was there something *he* had done that *she* had caught *him* at? Was *she* going to ruin *his* reputation?

Whatever it was, there had to be a damn good reason. A person doesn't shoot their wife without a reason. Perhaps the why would surface from their friends and children. The unanswered question made Collin's head swim. At least things couldn't get worse, or could they?

Twelve-year old insomniac Jimmy Mercer liked to wander the house while his parents slept soundly. They were always tired from work, so Jimmy wasn't afraid to put on the television in the den and switch on his father's Citizen Band radio. He noticed his father left the Police Band on and gave it not another thought.

Jimmy watched TV, subconsciously listening to the occasional trucker who clicked the CB, looking for someone to talk with and while away the night. The Police Band his father had didn't reach Springfield or Worcester so there was next to nothing ever on, other than a cop asking another cop to bring over a cup of coffee.

Jimmy's jaw dropped. The Police Band came alive. "... at Great Hill ...when the coroner leaves with the body ... can I go home ...?"

Jimmy heard someone shout, "... Sinclair's PB ...why in hell he was using it ... any damned insomniac could monitor ... stay there ... idiot ... I'll have your badge..."

Great Hill? Coroner? Body? ... Stay there or I'll have your badge? The PB went silent again. Jimmy couldn't contain his excitement.

He ran for the bathroom before he wet himself, not quite finishing before rushing for his parent's bedroom. "Dad! Dad! Dad! Dad!"

Rudely awakened, Frank Mercer shouted, "What the devil's your problem?"

Jimmy was gasping, "There's a body ... a body, Dad!"

Their loud voices woke Jimmy's mother, "What's all the damn racket about?"

"Jimmy's seen a body."

"He's watching that damn TV again. Make him go to bed!" She rolled over, pulling the pillow over her head.

"No, Dad, no! There's a coroner and a *body* up at Great Hill! Up at the Hill, Dad!"

Hearing Great Hill got Frank Mercer's attention, "That's Mr. Sinclair's home, where'd you hear that?"

"On your Police Band, you should have heard it, Dad!"

Frank Mercer was wide-awake now, "I *can* hear it."

"How can you do that? They've stopped talking."

"Let me get up and I'll show you, and you'd better be telling the truth or you've in deep serious."

Frank dragged himself out of bed, "I have the PB on sound record. If there's sound, it records. I do that so I can listen when I'm doing the books."

Jimmy thought this was the most incredible thing he had ever heard, even better than TV. He ran through the house as Mercer stumbled behind. In the den, his father hit Rewind, waited, then hit Play. All they heard was occasional static.

"You didn't get it! You didn't get it, Dad!"

"For crying out loud, take it easy! When there's noise, like thunder, like yesterday, it's picked up as static. Just be patient, it will come up, if anything's there. Until it does, hit the bathroom. Stop dancing around here like a dimwit!"

Jimmy went, returned. Still, the intermittent static continued.

Seconds later it started, obviously a police officer speaking. Mercer didn't recognize the voice, but he recognized Connie Johnson's in the background, then the words, "... coroner, ambulance, *body* and ... can he go home?" Another voice, angry. Mercer knew Lt. Collin's voice. "... Sinclair's PB ... stay there ... God damned idiot ... I'll have your badge."

Mercer knew for sure someone at Great Hill died. Who? He hadn't seen the kids, Paul or Emily around lately, that left the Mr. or Mrs. Did Mr. Sinclair have a stroke? That could be likely. But why all the secrecy? That didn't make any sense, no sense at all.

Frank glanced at his watch, 2:00 a.m. Jimmy only heard the conversation live a few minutes ago. What was happening was happening now. When Mercer told Jimmy to get some clothes on, he raced to his room yelling at the top of his voice.

Now, Mercer thought, let's go see what's afoot on The Hill. He scribbled a note for his wife, grabbing the keys to the car. Within ten minutes, he and his son coasted to a stop at Great Hill's driveway. Frank Mercer had his own business and was a capable, assured speaker. When patrolman Starr flashed a light into the car, Mercer flatly stated, "We know about the body."

Starr tilted back on his heels, stammering, "How?"

Mercer thought fast. He knew this cop hadn't been on the force too long, "I just saw the coroner at the Four Corners Inn. He's a friend of mine."

If officer Starr was not tired and had more time to focus and ask where the Four Corners Inn was, perhaps he would have reacted differently. However, this articulate person in the car knew what was going on. The coroner told him. That the man didn't say the coroner's name, was lost on Starr. Instead, he stood there, weary and mystified.

Mercer led him on a bit more, "So, what's your take on it?"

That was all it took. Starr scratched the back of his neck, "Well, she was dead when we got here and Mister Sinclair says he did it, so there's not much take, left to take."

Starr was pleased with his play on words. His flashlight was not on Mercer as he blanched, pressing his hand over Jimmy's mouth. After a breath, Mercer guessed, "So, Mister Sinclair must be at the station."

"Yeah, he's a wreck."

"Possible it was an accident?"

"No way, .45 cal, right in the boobs."

"Anything else?"

"Just that I'm tired. Been a long night."

Frank Mercer drove off shaking his head, "Son, you've just listened to a true idiot. Sure as hell, Collin will definitely be taking that badge."

"I bet mom's brother would like to know this, Dad."

"Great idea, kid. I'll bet giving Jeff Pike this information could get us a couple of tickets to the Sox or Celts."

Chapter

Four

Lieutenant Collin was weary. For the second time, he told Connie she could go home, but she wanted to stay. Collin figured what the hell. Overtime at a time like this was no problem. Besides, he had her compiling the telephone numbers of the people he was going to call at 6:00 AM.

Murder was as much new ground for Collin as it was for the town. He thought again of the people he had to notify. The selectmen, Mr. Sinclair's attorneys, prosecutor for the county and state, police commissioners, State Police, County Sheriff and, whoever else managed to stick their nose in to get themselves involved. After that, he would fade into the woodwork, go home to bed and stand aside from the media blitz.

Perhaps a better idea might be to call the selectmen now. Let them take care of the other calls, or a least have them tell him what they wanted, and in what sequence. He was a lowly police lieutenant in a dinky town; let them take some responsibility.

Too worn out to handle much more, he knew he had done a good job. He had handled a high profile murder, had the murderer and a signed confession. It had all been done quietly. Once the selectmen finally woke, they could decide how to handle it properly. That was not his job and they were welcome to it. Instead

21

of calling them at 4:00 AM, Collin opted to wait to 6:00 AM. He didn't want to wake the town fathers too soon.

Patrolman Conroy Besch started his shift with a morose hello, as he signed in, "How come you're still here, Connie?"

She pointed to the cells, then waited for him to return.

"What the hell is going on? That's Mr. Sinclair."

It took repeating until he finally understood. Collin got his attention. "Besch, forget your regular route tonight. Go to Great Hill, give Starr your patrol car and tell him to go home. You take over. If anyone's curious, tell them there's a meeting and to leave. That's what I told Tom to do. Both of you are to keep your mouth shut. I need two more hours to be off the hook."

Collin was sure he could dump the whole mess in the selectmen's collective laps.

5:55 a.m. The moment Lt. Collin approached his office to start the calls, the front door to the station pushed open.

"Hello! Jeff Pike here, Channel 17, Springfield TV!"

Pike shoved his way through the door. Connie stopped in her tracks. Jeff Pike, in person! Collin couldn't believe it and blurted out, "Jesus Christ!"

Pike was quick, "No, I'm not, however I am one of the lesser gods."

Collin was yelling at him, "Who let it out? "Get out! Get the hell out of here!"

The newscaster was astounded; "No one treats me like this. I'm here to cover the murder! You'll be interviewed on TV!"

"Take your TV and shove it. Get out!"

Pike froze in place.

Grabbing him by the arm, Collin pushed him out the entry. As he reached to lock the door, he saw a large, red van pulling up with SPRINGFIELD, TV/17, emblazoned across the side. A few local cars and pickups followed behind.

Collin's strategy crashed. Jeff TV, as he referred to himself, projected across the airways in the early morning Breaking News bulletin. One of the selectmen, caught it, and called the others. The lights on the only two phone lines at the station never stopped flashing. Scores of people gathered in the parking lot. Collin glared beyond the entrance, watching the disaster unfold. The Barretton Police Station was under siege. The Lieutenant used his Police Band to contact the Worcester sheriff's office. He asked for assistance and for them to contact the State Police. He needed assistance at the station, and troopers at Great Hill. That was where who knows how many people would be going next. Officer Besch would be overwhelmed.

The news unfolded that morning and all day. Even when everyone had taken a second breath, the excitement didn't ease. At gas stations, barbershops, grocery stores and most street corners, the townspeople devoured every bit of gossip, adding to it. Each time Channel 17 aired the tape, the community laughed as they saw the Police Station, TV camera pointing at the locked door with Lieutenant Collin staring out, mad at the world.

Of course, many Barrettonians loved seeing themselves repeatedly waving and jumping up and down, for the camera. After the State Troopers arrived on the scene and took control, the party time atmosphere petered out.

Detectives from other law enforcement agencies and state officials took over the proceedings. Sinclair moved to a larger cell at the Franklin County Detention Center and Jeff Pike, Channel 17, waved goodbye to Barretton.

The Sinclair twins said they learned from television of their mother's death and their father's arrest. The police slipped them secretly into the Detention Center that night where they kept their composure for less than a minute before breaking down. When their father cried, the guard left them alone.

The selectmen were furious. The town and its people, especially the selectmen, came across on television as foolish and inept. Having the State Police take over their town was embarrassing enough, but added to that, Jeff TV's mockery continued unabated. He intended to get even over the manhandling by that little tin badge, Lt. Collin, he said. On his daily show, Jeff TV stated his arm was badly bruised and he just might sue the Barretton Police. If the police would rough up an anchorman of his caliber, who would protect other newsmen from police brutality?

The selectmen apologized. Lieutenant Kenneth Collin was suspended without pay.

The funeral for Nancy Katherine Sinclair was September 14, 1966. Police personnel had removed any evidence from the house and released the body to the family.

No notice was posted and the service, held in a private chapel on the cemetery grounds, had few attendees. The three selectmen, Sinclair family's minister, the Great Hill handy man, and the two children were only those present. Mrs. Sinclair's will stated her organs to be donated for medical research. However, the Sinclair children disagreed to that. They could not accept the thought. Her body was cremated, the ashes placed in a vault behind the chapel.

Business associates and friends struggled with a proper response to a terrible incident—a friend murdered, a friend, the murderer. All who knew them settled for flowers. Scores of bouquets ringed the inner chapel, each one with a sympathy card and their name, nothing more.

Emily and Paul Sinclair were clearly distraught, and sat holding hands with their heads down throughout the service.

Outside, the State Police restrained curiosity seekers. Only Jeff Pike's chatter on Channel 17, along with news anchors from three other channels disturbed the somber mood. The forming crowd, which waited expectantly to see Mr. Sinclair, was disappointed; Parker R. Sinclair's request to attend the service was disallowed.

Chapter

Five

Captain Detective Ray Polo was the lead detective now assigned to the Nancy K. Sinclair murder case. Boston Police Commissioner Walter Kearney ordered Polo to find a plausible motive to assist a judge in recommending a sentence if a trial convened. Polo was adamant. He did not want the case, did not care what the motive was, or who Sinclair was. The guy killed his wife. Throw him in jail, lose the key, or better still, lethal injection would save the Commonwealth room and board for another murderer.

Despite Polo's attitude, he read the confession then met with Sinclair. Polo was hard on him, roughing him up verbally. He disliked Sinclair's demeanor; too composed, too courteous. He did give Sinclair credit for admitting the crime, refusing to have an attorney present, and pleading guilty. Polo wished more murderers went that route; it would free up the courts. "Nevertheless," he mused aloud to no one, "this guy is in *too* much of a rush."

Polo's competence with the Boston Police Department was highly regarded and known throughout New England for his ability to solve murders. Prosecutors for the state often furloughed him to help other towns with sticky cases, such as finding the circumstances, the reason, behind the Sinclair murder. Commissioner Kearney firmly reminded Polo; a motive was the loose end that needed tying up, "Just don't smack too many people around, Ray."

Polo was a hometown cop. Born in Dorchester, 1911, Boston Latin High School, class of 1929, Boston College, class of 1935. He had decided on a career in the Army Air Force, but knee injuries received in his senior year, after four seasons of varsity football as an offensive lineman, resulted in his flunking their physical.

When Polo applied to the Police Academy and passed *their* physical, there were those who whispered his football reputation and being from Boston College, allowed little doubt of his getting into the Academy. So many of the college's graduates became city police officers that the two capital letters of the college, 'BC', became synonymous with Boston Cop.

Whatever Polo's physical weaknesses, no one mentioned them. He was 6 feet, 3 inches tall, and two hundred and fifty pounds of pure muscle, at least in the beginning of his career. He was physically intimidating with an incisive mind, a combination that got results where other officers failed. Most of his successes came from tenaciousness; he would worry a case to the bone, then gnaw on it until he found the solution. As the years passed, Polo's citations grew, although tainted by reviews of the Police Board of Overseers from accusations of excessive force. The sole reason Polo avoided censure was his bulging case closed file and common knowledge that nearly all of the complaints were from people found guilty of the crimes. His reputation grew when he made detective. However, Polo refused advancement to any supervisory position, stating he had reached his level of competency. He felt if he rose any further, he would reach a level of incompetence, a point, he thought, which many supervisors had reached.

At fifty-five, Polo was weary and cynical, though still at his peak mentally. His weight remained the same from his college days, when crashing into opposing linemen. Yet most of that muscle now sagged—too many beers at night and too many cigarettes through the day. His gruffer demeanor emerged when; overhearing two young detectives formerly assigned the case, complain that Sinclair was not cooperating. The old Ray Polo responded, "For Christ's sake! The guy confessed, what more do you want? Get the hell out of here, God damn incompetents."

The detectives packed and left quickly, without another word. Polo's moods, often foul, were legend in Boston law enforcement.

Like any good cop with a funny feeling about a case, he decided to start from scratch, and called Ken Collin. Collin was still under suspension and, Polo thought absentmindedly as he met the Lieutenant, that the poor son of a bitch, an okay person, messed up. That's the breaks. At the meeting, Collin methodically explained the events of that night. At the end Polo asked, "You're unsure of something. What is it?"

"I don't know. It's the time difference of an hour and a half from the time he said he shot Mrs. Sinclair, which was pretty much confirmed by the coroner, and when he called us. Mr. Sinclair said he was bewildered. Still, it seemed a long gap in the time."

"Anything else?"

Collin shook his head, "Not really I guess. I heard through the grapevine it was Sinclair's gun and his prints. Left hand, he's left-handed. They found the slug. Just one shot came from the Colt. Didn't hear anything else."

"Any other prints, smudges?"

"I don't know. Does it matter?"

"I don't know, maybe yes, maybe no."

"Why should it, Polo? It was his gun; he kept it clean."

"No prints on the slide?"

"Only mine … that I know of."

"Which would mean he kept it loaded with a shell in the chamber. I don't know about you, to me, but that's strange."

"Look Polo, he shot the gun a number of times in the past, and he could get angry. He said so in his own words. I don't know what you're getting at."

"I don't know either. But until I know the motive, there could be another story."

"The way I think, something set him off, something that had to be really bad. That could justify what happened. Isn't that what you should be finding out?"

"Collin, your problem is you respect the guy too much. You're not looking past his façade and into what makes him tick. That makes for a lousy cop."

Nevertheless, Polo was impressed with Collin. For a small town cop he had done well. The cat got out of the bag before he was ready to let it. The officer should have called the selectmen immediately. Get off the hook as fast as possible. He didn't.

"So tell me, Collin, who knew, and who do you think let the information out?"

"I don't know"

They started to eliminate who knew what, that night.

"What about this Connie Johnson?"

"Connie knows how to keep her mouth shut, Polo."

"All right, Ken, don't get your bowels in an uproar. What about Tom Starr? You said he was at Great Hill."

"He said he didn't talk to anyone except the coroner and the ambulance driver."

"Conroy Besch?"

"He replaced Starr at Great Hill. He wasn't there long. Said he didn't talk to anyone until the reporters rushed him."

"So that leaves Mike Green, the coroner and the ambulance driver. What's his name, Rocco?"

"Green said they were together for three hours. Didn't give anything out."

"Jesus, Collin, anyone else? This list is damn short."

Collin looked blank, "None that I can think of."

"How about that TV guy?"

"He stands behind getting an anonymous tip. Probably came from when we blurted it out on the PB."

"Think Collin, that's not too bright. Pike knew it was murder, not a heart attack or stroke and you said the word murder wasn't mentioned on the PB. I'd put money on someone on your force lying. That's for God damned sure. My bet says Starr or Besch, that is unless there was a skunk in the bushes."

Collin nodded, "Good bet. Although I can't prove it, I'm off limits."

Ray Polo smiled wickedly, "Yeah, but I'm not."

They parted, Polo turning back to shout, "I'll look into it. Not part of the case, still I'll bet you a fiver I find the lying son of a bitch!"

He sat in Collin's office making out his own list. No one was there at the time of the murder, save for Sinclair. No one alive knew what happened, or why, only Sinclair, and he won't say. That meant fitting bits and pieces of information together with the hope he'd arrive at the damn motive. In his opinion, Mrs. Sinclair did something wrong, an argument got out of hand. How simple could it be? Still, he had to prove it, which appeared not as simple.

The list:

Lori Forrest. The housekeeper. They know everything.

Federal C. Wheelwright. The handyman. What the hell kind of name is Federal?

Patrolman Tom Starr. The other cop with Lieutenant Collin at the scene.

Patrolman Conroy Besch. He was at Great Hill also, later.

Mike Green, the coroner and Tony Rocco, the ambulance driver.

Polo already knew Mike Green. Doubtful he would say a word. Maybe the driver shoots his mouth off.

Emily and Paul Sinclair. The kids. Not going to be pleasant. Both still extremely saddened She's taken a leave of absence. However much he disliked it, he had to find the *why* and they looked the best bets if all else failed.

He would also nose around town to find anyone who could shed some light on this. What a waste of my time, he thought, inject the guy.

Polo started at the top of his list. He wanted to put off facing the twins until the last. Then, they may be less likely to be upset by his manner. He was known to get carried away when questioning someone, even if they were only minor witnesses. He couldn't help it, and didn't try. It was his style.

He found Lori Forrest a chatty little thing. Yes, she was the housekeeper, three days a week. There was little upkeep except when the kids were around. There was a bit more cleaning up then, but not much; the kids were good. Everyone was always friendly. Mr. Sinclair was the most courteous person you would ever meet. She couldn't believe he shot the lovely Mrs. Sinclair. It didn't …

Polo held up his hand, "Please, Mrs. Forrest, was there anything that wasn't perfect on Happy Hill?"

"Well, now that you mention it."

Polo waited.

Lori started in again, "It seems there was *something*. I'm not sure what, except when they forgot I was there, or they were upstairs and didn't think I heard."

"Mrs. Forrest, you were eavesdropping. We all do it. Just tell me what they said."

Lori Forrest tensed, embarrassed.

Polo cursed himself for his comment, putting his hand gently on her arm. She jumped.

"I'm sorry I spoke like that, Mrs. Forrest. Please, go on with what you were saying."

A stream of miscellaneous facts, assumptions, and guesses blended into a disjointed stew of little substance. Mrs. Forrest was queen of the trivial.

Once Polo digested the facts from assumptions, it appeared Mr. and Mrs. argued now and then over the same subject. Lori didn't know what, except it might be over a *person or money.*

Man or woman? She didn't know.

"What are the kids like?"

"They're wonderful. Stopped and talked to me all the time when they were there. A close family; the children were there a lot. Paul not so much, now that he's in college."

"Anything else you can think of?"

'I don't think so."

"Are you sure?"

"Yes, quite sure."

Lori seemed talked out.

Polo dropped his card on the table, "If you think of anything else, call me."

"I will."

Lori Forrest swore a blue streak as Polo's car left the driveway, "Call me an eavesdropper will you, you son of a bitch." His card, torn up, thrown in the wastebasket.

Polo jotted down, Sinclair's argued a bit. Who the hell didn't?

Mark Green, the coroner, was next on the list. Polo knew Green from other cases and the conversation was far shorter than with Lori Forrest.

"Mark?" Green knew the voice, and knew Polo could be abrupt, "I'm on the Sinclair case. Did you or that Rocco kid talk to anyone that night?"

"Ray, I don't know how the news got out. We drove straight to the morgue. You probably don't know it's on the other side of the county. We dropped the body, did the damn paperwork, then Rocco and I went to the all night diner across the street. Rocco's a funny kid, going days to Worchester Tech, working nights driving ..."

"'Yah Yah, Yah." Polo interjected, "Funny, terrific kid, great. Tell me, did he talk to anyone?"

"Jesus, Polo, you're an impatient bastard!"

"Only when I'm in a hurry."

"Then, you're always in a hurry!"

"Even funnier, Mark. Now tell me straight. Did the wonder kid spill this?"

"No!" Green hung up.

Polo laughed to himself. Mark is *pissed.* I'll have to kiss his ass and make up with him some other time. Still, when Mark gave a flat no, it was gospel.

The Great Hill handy man was Federal C. Wheelwright. They met at the Hill, Polo thinking Federal a strange name. As they shook hands, Polo couldn't help asking what Federal's middle initial stood for.

"Census."

"Federal Census Wheelwright. I'll bet you get a lot of kidding."

"Why?"

Polo felt foolish, and then saw Federal's lips curl into a sly smile.

"Okay, Federal, you got me, a Yankee joke."

"How'd you know I was a Yankee?"

"How? You talk Yankee." Polo was referring to Federal's northern New England accent, or twang, as he thought of it.

"Mr. Polo, let's put my accent and name to the side, I figure with a Boston accent like you got, and a name like Polo you shouldn't much be throwing snide remarks my way."

"Touché."

"What?"

"It means …"

"I know what it means, Mr. Polo. I been to France and didn't just fall off no turnip truck."

Polo shook his head. "Can we start over?"

"Waste of time, let's start from this point."

Federal began jabbering on. It turned out he was born in the northeast kingdom of Vermont in 1890, making him seventy-six. Their best crop was rocks, he said. His mother was illiterate. From the story Federal heard, his mother asked someone to spell his name on the birth certificate. Instead of writing Franklin Charles, the unknown jokester printed Federal Census, mainly because the US Census was happening at the time. The prankster thought it would be a big joke and someone in authority up the line would catch and change it. No one did.

"If that's what occurred," Polo asked, "why didn't you change your name when you grew up?"

"I liked it; helps break the ice when I meet someone for the first time. Like you."

Federal served in the Great War. It was, "The War to End All Wars," he laughed.

"I would have served in the second one, too, if they drafted me. They didn't, and I sure as hell wasn't going to volunteer again 'cause mother didn't raise no dumb kids."

In the Great War, his duty was to shoe horses, "Must have shoed two thousand of them, I figure, and remember, that was times four hoofs."

When the Krauts, he called all Germans, Krauts, started shelling he saw horses killed by the dozens.

"Horses don't fit in shelters, Polo."

Federal got out of the war with a wound from the shin to the thigh by a shell fragment. He pulled up the bottom of his pant leg and showed Polo the start of it, a gnarled white scar snaking up and under his pant leg.

He started to undo his belt, "Like to see it from the top, detective?"

Polo didn't know what to say.

Federal laughed, "Just funning you, kid. The army doctor wanted to take the leg off. I told the doc if he did, I'd come back on one leg and beat him to death with my crutch. Then I said if I died without the amputation, well then, he was safe. The doc was no fool, he walked away."

Polo had no comment; he knew he was talking with a tough old bird. In addition, like the doctor, he was no fool.

Federal, with a hitch in his step, walked along with Polo. The reedy little man was a one time flyweight-boxing champion of the American Expeditionary Force in WWI. "And what the hell," said Federal," it's a long way from the hardscrabble Northeast Kingdom, so worth every damn minute I lived through."

Federal thought for a second, "To make a long story short, Polo, I froze my arse off in Vermont when I came back from the war. Came down here to get warmed, and stayed put."

As Federal talked, he showed Polo the garage with a Chrysler Crown Imperial, Oldsmobile 98 sedan, Oldsmobile 88 coupe, and surprisingly, a Red, XKE Jaguar. Federal called it an E Type roadster.

There were three neat rooms in the garage, one a bedroom, the second a kitchen with a sitting area and the last holding equipment for grounds maintenance. Federal said he often slept in the garage apartment to watch the house when the Sinclair's were away or sometimes when he had more than a day's work around the property.

Polo saw his opening, "You didn't happen to be staying here that night, did you?"

Federal shook his head.

They looked towards the paddock, "That's Emily's, their daughter's horse. She's a good kid, a bit strange about the horse; won't let me shoe him. I've shoed thousands of horses and she won't let me shoe that one. The horse is a Kraut warm blood, whatever the hell that means. Emily gets some swanky farrier to come up from Connecticut with fancy shoes for the horse."

Federal took a breath, Polo cut to the chase, "What do you think of Sinclair?"

"*Mr.* Sinclair is a gentleman."

"What did you think of Mrs. Sinclair?"

Federal was downcast, "She was a lady, Mr. Polo."

Polo rubbed his forehead. A northerner will talk forever, until you're trying to get *information* out of one. Then, it was a different story altogether.

He tried anyway, "Why do you think he did it?"

Federal bristled, "Don't know that he did."

"He said he did, I asked him."

"Why would he say a thing like that?"

"Maybe because he did it."

Polo turned away from the dejected gaze, trying a different tack, "Look, Federal, I'm trying to find out why he did it, okay? The way it stands now, Sinclair is going to prison for life. If I can find some mitigating factor, some reason, a judge might give a lesser sentence."

Polo couldn't believe what he said. He stopped in his tracks and closed his eyes. Was he starting to believe *that crap*? Because everyone was saying Sinclair was such a great person? Great people kill people; they kill their girlfriends and *they kill their wives.*

He turned to Federal, "Have you ever seen Sinclair angry?"

"No."

"Have you ever heard Sinclair and his wife arguing?"

"No."

"Have you ever seen Sinclair leave the house in a bad mood?" Boy, Polo thought, I'm reaching with that one.

Federal hesitated then, "Not a bad mood exactly, although he was really irritated once."

At last Polo hoped, maybe he was on to something, "Do you know over what?"

"Sure do, forgot his car keys, had to go all the way back inside to get them."

Before Polo got in his car and gunned it down the driveway, Federal's face cracked into a toothy smile, "Temper, Mr. Polo, temper."

Polo was angry. Federal had set him up, "That little bastard led me perfectly." He cursed. But he knew exactly where to channel his anger.

Chapter

Six

Patrolman Tom Starr left his shift at the police station early, walking through the parking lot to his car. No officer was in charge, other than Corporal Gene Munson and he didn't care who did what, as long as no one reported him for snoozing behind one barn or another. He was working two jobs to buy a new Corvette, and needed the sleep.

Starr himself cut out two hours before the shift change, figuring the town took care of itself, so why shouldn't he? Connie Johnson had no authority. All she could do was lay a disgusted look on him and that didn't hurt.

Polo slammed on his brakes in a blur of dust.

Starr dodged the car, "For Christ's sake, watch it!"

Just the remark Polo needed to get even angrier. When he lurched from the car with a purple complexion, Starr's eyes bulged and he backed up, unfortunately not far enough.

"You son of a bitch!" Polo grabbed the shirt, ripping off buttons, "You lying piece of crap! You told someone!"

Polo was faking the whole scene. He was mad in general, but also guessed Starr had lied about giving out information on the murder. No one else was alone long enough that late into the night. He had met Starr during a previous investigation and felt he wasn't

37

using too many brain cells even then, so, added to his being on the Hill alone, it had to be him.

Perhaps this wasn't the correct way to get at the truth. In Polo's mind, however, if Starr is guilty, it would frighten him into confessing. If he wasn't, Polo owed him a shirt, no harm done.

But it was all it took. Tom Starr folded, admitting he told a friend of the coroners that night at the Hill. It didn't make sense to Polo. Mark Green wouldn't lie.

"Who was the friend of the coroners?"

Starr said he didn't know the person; only that he said he was a friend of the coroners.

"Some guy comes along and cons you into spilling your guts."

"I was tired, Detective Polo, I thought he …"

"You lied to the detectives when you said you didn't tell anyone. You lying bastard, you cost Collin his job!"

"I'm sorry, I didn't …"

Polo cut him off, "Start looking for another job. Now get the hell out of here before I punch your lights out!"

Starr couldn't get away fast enough. His hustle suggesting he knew Polo wasn't talking about headlights.

Polo lurched into the stationhouse smiling. It had been so easy it made his day. He was a detective who made it look that way.

Connie watched the encounter from the window. When Polo came in, she had a look that asked, "What? What?"

Polo laughed, realizing she had seen the show.

"Starr's the idiot who shot his mouth off about what happened at Great Hill. I'll talk to the selectmen and get him fired, then see about getting Collin off suspension."

In her excitement, she asked if Polo could possibly grab Corporal Munson by the scruff of the neck and do the same to him. Polo thought it over for an instant. If Connie said that should be done, it probably should. Still, he figured it might be pushing his luck with the force depleted as it was.

"I'll leave it for Lieutenant Collin to fire him." He went into Collin's old office and made some calls.

Malcolm Slocomb was the leader of the three town selectmen. Polo told him Patrolman Starr had been the source for the leak concerning the murder and suggested, quite firmly, Starr be fired. Slocomb agreed to speak with the other selectmen first, although he believed Starr would be released.

Polo insisted Ken Collin deserved reinstatement. Slocomb responded he personally thought Collin should have notified the selectmen immediately after he had incarcerated Mr. Sinclair. That would have saved the selectmen embarrassment. Despite this, Slocomb offered to follow up with the others and inform both Polo and Collin of the group's decision. Polo agreed Slocomb was right, Collin *was* in error, but the selectmen couldn't let Collin swing in the wind forever. Slocomb reminded him it had only been a week. Polo responded it didn't seem like only a week to Collin.

The second call went to Boston Police Commissioner Walter C. Kearney, Polo's superior. In his natural, blunt way, Polo declared he had yet to make headway.

"Walt, I haven't found the motive. Sinclair's a saint according to most people here. About all I'm doing in Barretton is hanging around waiting for him to be canonized."

Kearney smiled. Typical Polo, he thought, as his best detective continued, "For Christ's sake, I've even listened to a person named Federal Census. That's right, Walt, Federal Census!"

Kearney smile ended when Polo asked if Sinclair's motive was that important.

"Ray, straight out, the reason is extremely important to us."

Polo wondered who the *us* were.

Kearney continued, "So every t must be crossed and every i dotted."

Damn, Polo thought, he hated that statement.

"So what's your next step, Ray?"

"My next step looks like my last. I'll interview the Sinclair kids. They haven't volunteered any reason yet, so I don't hold out much hope. I've waited as long as I can to see them, Walt, and I hope to hell that they're able to control their grief. If I can't shake anything reasonable out of them, I'm at a dead end."

"Look Ray, I know it has to come to that, but take it easy, they've been through a lot."

Kearney wondered why he wasted his breath

Polo's third call was to tell Collin about Tom Starr, and Collin owed him five bucks for the bet Polo would find the squealer.

Collin laughed, "I didn't take that bet because it was so obvious Starr was the culprit."

"You a welching bastard, Collin."

They both laughed. Ken thanked him. Polo said forget it, mentioning his conversation with Slocomb. Starr, Polo told Collin, was sure to be gone. The only commitment concerning Collin was that Slocomb would speak to the other selectmen. Ken thanked him again.

Polo's fourth call would be to Emily Sinclair. Before calling however, he reviewed Collin's notes on her and her brother Paul, along with Emily's phone number. They were twins, born September of 1942. No one had mentioned that to him. It would make them twenty-four now. Emily was supposed to be extremely pretty and a graduate from Regis College in Weston, MA. Class of 1964. She was single, a teacher at Thorton Academy, Polo never having heard of the place.

Paul attended Brown University. He hadn't graduated and had taken a sabbatical. Polo frowned; typical kid, he thought, a sabbatical lasting how long? Off and on three years?

It seemed after traveling for over a year, Paul now worked part time in an industrial photography plant doing high contrast film positives and negatives for military contractors. Collin's note added Paul was also taking night courses for enough credits to return to Brown. Polo read the rest of the notes on Paul, "This kid's a real loser."

According to Collin and Federal Wheelwright, neither of the Sinclair kids was married and they were close to their parents, seeing them often, at times staying overnight on weekends.

Paul, they said, was away more over the last couple of years, although never really a homebody.

By now, it was evening and, figuring Emily would be at her condominium, Polo called.

It was answered on the second ring."

"Emily Sinclair?"

"Who's calling?" She sounded on guard, Polo thought.

"My name is Raymond Polo; I'm a detective working for the Barretton Police. I'm calling about your father. I would like to meet with you."

There was no response. Polo asked, "Are you still there?"

"How do I know you're a policeman and not another damnable reporter?"

Polo expected this, telling Emily to, "Call the Barretton Police Station and check on a Detective Polo."

"Okay, suppose I believe you. Now what is it you want?"

"I'd like to meet with you."

Again, she didn't answer. Polo sensed a stall, but still spoke calmly, "I want to meet with you and Paul to go over anything you might know about the events at Great Hill."

"We don't know anything more than we've already told those other detectives."

Polo noted that she was speaking for Paul as well as herself.

"I'm not interested in going over this again, Mr. Polo. Paul and I are tired and heartbroken. We are not going to relive this every time someone wants to talk about it."

"Look Miss, it doesn't matter if you've spoken with other officers. My job requires me to interview you both. It can be at a place of your choosing, or I can have you come to the police station. It's your choice, which would you prefer?"

Emily understood the implication of the question, "I guess we could meet next week sometime. I'll call you with a time I'll be free at school."

"That's not good," Polo muttered. "That's not good enough, Miss Sinclair. This is Friday. I want to meet today. You should have an hour or so available."

This time the lag was longer, Polo wishing he had her right in front of him. She's dodging. This broad knows something, and I caught her unprepared. But damn, if not today, she'll have time to prepare.

"Mr. Polo, I can meet you tomorrow, definitely not before. I have an appointment tonight. I don't know if Paully can make it."

"Fine, I prefer it that way." Polo didn't prefer it that way. Only saying that to make Emily more uneasy.

Saturday, 10:00 a.m. On the dot, Polo pulled into her condominium parking lot by a lake in Weston, Massachusetts.

Expensive place, he smiled, must be paying teachers pretty well. Of course, a rich father doesn't hurt.

Emily Sinclair met him at the door after the first ring. As they exchanged introductions, he thought what a handsome girl. Great shape, athletic body.

He showed his badge as requested.

She interrupted his thoughts, "Are you coming in, and what do you want?"

Brief, he thought. Two questions in one sentence, kind of like, ask your questions and get out. Who could blame her? Polo decided on a different tact.

He entered, sitting down uninvited, "That's a nice horse you have at Great Hill. My ex had one. What kind is yours?"

Caught off guard by the question Emily answered, "It's a Trakhaner, a German warm blood. I use him for dressage. You've been to the Hill?"

"I didn't go inside. I talked with Federal Census, He said you won't let him shoe it."

Again, she was off guard and answered while trying to get her bearings. Showing a slight smile, "FC is a great old guy, but my horse is a far cry from what he was used to shoeing fifty years ago."

"What's the nag's name?" Polo asked with a grin.

"The *horses name* is Bismarck," she said with agitation creeping into her voice.

Polo acted as if impressed.

"That was the horse's name when I bought him, Mr. Polo, I didn't name him. I bought him in Germany and had him shipped."

She stopped talking, then added, "To you, Mr. Polo, I must sound condescending, but women and horses have an affinity for each other, which males don't understand. It also helps to have a father with money who likes to spend it on his darling little girl's whims. Does that satisfy you Mr. Polo?"

"I really didn't need satisfying, Miss Sinclair."

Emily looked at him quizzically, guessing something.

"What kind of a horse did your wife have, and its name?"

"Don't remember either, probably never knew."

"And that's *probably* why she's your *ex-wife*. So, now detective, with the pleasantries over, will you please get to the reason you're here?"

That shoots rapport to hell, Polo thought, realizing he hadn't even asked any tough questions yet.

"Call me, Ray."

"I don't think so, *Detective Polo*."

"Miss Sinclair, I'm not trying to be a wiseass here. I'm simply trying to find out why your father killed your mother."

Emily visibly winced, tears filling her eyes. Polo had been intentionally blunt. He had to get the question on the table or they would be circling forever.

No response.

"Is there anything you can think of that will help us find out why he did it?"

"No."

"Miss Sinclair, you've got to understand. My experience says your father will be charged with second-degree murder. In other words, meaning it was not premeditated. Still, if there are no *extenuating* circumstances, your father could go to prison for twenty or thirty years. At his age, he could die there. Do you understand what I'm saying?"

Emily sat with a hand over her mouth, listening with an intense expression. She straightened, suddenly distracted, "I can not think of a reason. Please leave."

"No reason? There is nothing? No hint, on what caused him to kill your mother?"

"*No!*"

This time the 'no' had a sharp edge. Was she really on the brink? Polo pondered. A little more push will tell.

"There must be something!"

Jumping to her feet she screamed, "Get out! *Get out!*"

The door, thrown outward, collided with the wall. Polo realized he couldn't do more damage, and Miss Sinclair wasn't going be much use. He walked out. Had he pushed Emily too far over the edge or was she faking? Didn't matter. Nothing would calm her, except his leaving. As he left, a man stopped him, asking what was going on. Polo was going to deck the person right there to ease his own anger, but flashed his badge instead. He told the man he asked the wrong question and walked off.

As Polo heard the door slam shut, he looked back. The man was standing in front of the doorway as if it had closed in his face. Then a movement caught Polo's eye. Emily Sinclair, a fixed stare at him through the window curtain. She ducked away.

Polo knew she had learned something, something she didn't think of before.

He sat in his car for a few minutes trying to figure her out and came up empty.

"There's a lot going on in that pretty little head, and I don't know how to get at it."

44

Chapter

Seven

Though it was Sunday, Polo made more phone calls to Federal Census and Officer Besch, then reviewed his results with Collin. His last call was to coroner Green.

"Mark, are you talking to me? No? Okay, anything more you can tell me about Mrs. Sinclair's death? No? Okay, talk to you later."

He's still ripped, Polo smiled.

Mary Wells, one of the selectmen, was asked if she might be able to shed any light on Sinclair's motive. Wells commented, "No, Mr. Sinclair was courteous, reserved, yet not the most forthcoming person."

"Neither is his daughter." Polo commented.

"I'm not surprised. Courteous, not forthcoming."

"That's it." Polo said into the mirror in his bathroom after Colin left, "If they can find the other Sinclair kid I'll come back. Right now, I'm leaving. There's almost enough light to make it back to Boston, get a good nights sleep and be at my office Monday morning and put this damn case behind me."

He anticipated Commissioner Kearney's disappointment. Too bad, even Polo didn't win them all.

His packing was almost finished when the phone rang. A reprieve, he laughed aloud, "Someone coming to solve my problem."

"Polo here."

"Detective Polo," He instantly recognized the voice. "it's Emily Sinclair. We'd like to meet with you."

"Who's we? You and your attorney?"

"No. Paully and I."

Polo's mind churned. What the hell is this? She sounds too pleasant.

"Well?" she asked tentatively.

"What? Yes, sure. When, Where?'"

"You've been to Great Hill haven't you?" More of a confirmation than a question.

"I've been there, to meet with Federal Wheelwright. You want to meet there?"

Miss Sinclair asked again, "You've never been inside?"

"No."

"Then follow the drive to the front door. Paully and I didn't want to come here and then realized we had to. So you'd understand what we're sure happened that night."

They were at Great Hill right now.

This has to be it. Polo felt it. "You and Paul are there now?"

"Yes, we have keys. The police released the house to us. We came here to think. About everything."

"I'll be right over."

"It will take you about twenty minutes. We'll be waiting."

Polo hung up, Unbelievable! The break he needed. And, she had called him. They knew what happened. All this time denying she knew anything. Paul's there too. Good or bad ending, this will resolve it.

The lights were on as Polo approached. The last time he had been there was meeting Federal Census. FC, Emily called him. It was strange he hadn't gone in. Then he recalled FC setting him up

46

about Sinclair being irritated over forgetting his keys and he angrily drove off without entering.

His thoughts dissipated as he stopped behind a Chevy Impala convertible, blocking the drive in front. Maine plates. Emily Sinclair stood at the door, unsmiling. Nevertheless, to Polo she looked great as he followed her in.

Loose silk blouse, stovepipe Levi's, black flats. In the hall light, her blond hair glowed. Polo thought she looked dynamite. It made him wish it was another time, another place, and he was twenty years younger, better looking, more personable, with a ton of money, then he might have had a chance. Oh well.

She walked him down the corridor until they came to the den. "This is my brother, Paully."

Polo held out his hand and as Paul rose, checked his surprise at the wreck confronting him. "How long you been on drugs, kid?"

Paul's face, at one time must have been as handsome as his sister's. Now worn, cheeks too boney, body too thin. Polo had seen scores of young people like this in Boston. It was the same everywhere.

No one moved except Paul, turning to his sister.

"Emi, you didn't tell him? You didn't tell him I've been in rehab and I'm clean now?"

"No Paully, I didn't tell Mr. Polo you were on drugs before, and didn't tell him you were clean now. I wanted him to see you as you are."

"Why?"

Polo spoke up, "Yes, Miss Sinclair, I'd like to know too. Why?"

"Because Paully's been to hell and he's come back, I wanted you to see him. And for the simple reason that we know what must have happened here, and you need to hear it from both of us."

"How long have you been clean?" Polo asked.

47

"Nineteen months. Cop's picked me up stoned, and my father got me probation. I spent four months in a detox facility, Palton House. I've been straight since."

Ah, the joy of having a rich string puller, Polo muttered under his breath. "Can you prove it? Because you look pretty wacked in my book."

"Mr. Polo, if you think I look bad now, you should have seen me before. Emi can tell you that. Now I'm working as hard as I can to prove myself to my boss, and I'm going nights to get enough credits to go back to Brown University."

"Who's your shadow?" They both knew that Polo meant. Who's the parole officer assigned to him?

"Samuel Washington." When Polo shook his head Paul said, "He works between Springfield and Worchester. I'll give you his phone number, and I'll give you my boss's as well."

Polo pondered for a few seconds, then told Paul to write them down. He wasn't about to let the kid off the hook, "And while you're at it give me someone important at Brown."

While Paul was writing down the contacts, Emily whispered, "Please don't be too hard on him Mr. Polo, he's telling the truth. It took a lot to get him to this point. Even more to come *here* to talk to you, and me, for that matter."

Polo decided to follow Emily's advice, keeping his reservations to himself. When Paul finished, he said the Brown University contact was for the Dean of Admissions.

No one spoke. Polo abruptly looked up from reading the card, "All right, tell me what happened here that night."

Miss Sinclair spoke, "First, Mr. Polo," Emily said, "Dad must never find out we gave you this information."

"What the devil are you saying?"

Emily looked frightened, yet stood her ground, "If you're going to tell Dad we told you, we won't say what happened."

Polo's eyes narrowed. He stared at her and kept his temper, an effort that surprised him, "Miss Sinclair, you've got to understand where I'm coming from. Number one, I *will not* receive information with any conditions. Number two, I can't guarantee what you've got for me won't get back to your father."

Emily averted her eyes, Polo felt impelled to continue, "I will say this. If not informing your father of your involvement does not affect the case in any way, then I'll do my best to see he doesn't learn the source. However, that's all I can promise. And I'll be frank about this, if what you know affects your father positively or even *negatively*, it is your obligation to disclose it, or you both could be charged with obstruction of justice."

Polo laid it on the line. Emily Sinclair looked at Paul with a what-can-we-do expression. Paul nodded.

Polo could tell that they both wanted to talk, had to talk.

"Come with us, Mr. Polo."

They walked to the far end of the house, stopping at a dark entrance to another room. Paul went ahead. In the shadows, Polo could see it was the atrium he remembered from outside. Paul threw the light switch and the two-story glass walls glowed from the lights, briefly blinding Polo. As his vision adjusted, he lowered his head from the glare and saw what they wanted him to see.

Shattered urns and vases lay strewn across the entire floor of the atrium. Dead and dying orchids of every imaginable hue were mixed with soil and fertilizer into a corrupted heap of mud, among shards of pottery and broken wooden benches. The carnage bewildered Polo, as did the reason they wanted him to see it. Only along the outer glass wall of the atrium were a few remaining upright benches with half dozen potted orchids.

Polo was bewildered at the carnage. He thought the house had been broken into. What could this possibly have to do with their father?

"What happened here? Who did this?"

Emily glanced at Paul, becoming resolute, "Our mother."

"What the hell are you talking about?"

"Let's go back and sit down Mr. Polo; it's a sad story."

49

After one more glance at the atrium, they returned to the den. Emily and Paul sat, facing Polo. Tears streamed down the twin's eyes.

'Please let me start, Mr. Polo."

Chapter

Eight

Emily began, "A few months ago, mother acted forgetful or would simply stare at nothing for minutes on end. I had taken a course in basic health in college, and I could see the signs every time I stopped by. Our mother was deteriorating. I finally spoke to Dad. He wouldn't accept something was not right. She was only fifty-nine he said. It had to be something temporary. He kept saying it was a passing phase.

Most of the time mom was passive. Then there were two flare-ups. She got angry with Dad. He couldn't understand it. He couldn't reason with her. He didn't know what to do. At last, Dad finally agreed to have Mom see an expert about her actions, a physician, Doctor Goodman. He was in New Haven, away from anyone who knew us. The diagnosis wasn't good."

Emily hesitated, tears forming in her eyes, then continued, "I'm sure you realize what I'm saying, Mr. Polo. Mom had an early form of dementia, Alzheimer, if you prefer. The doctor gave us a prescription to help calm mom when she got upset. He also recommended we look into putting her into a facility that could handle this sort of patient. He didn't mean right away, of course, only that we should prepare. Dad wouldn't hear of it. He became incensed at the thought of her not being home with him. I even checked with doctors in my school system. We work with traumatized children. The answer was always the same; mom would become too much to handle, perhaps to the point of becoming violent. Dad couldn't accept it; he wouldn't let her go. "We tried to help her, but we weren't experienced. Dad couldn't understand why mom wouldn't listen, and she got more and more distraught. Paully was traveling, and I didn't know what to do. Dad gave mom more and more pills to calm her down. They didn't work all the time. Only when she was on drugs and quiet, would he let people see her, and even that became less and less frequent.

"The night … it happened, Dad told me he was on the phone and thought she was asleep. When he hung up, he found mom had destroyed nearly every one of the orchids you saw in the atrium. She went to bed; that's when ..."

Emily got up, going off a few feet, blowing her nose. When she returned, she sat, making a steeple of her hands at her chin.

"Mr. Polo, those orchids were Dad's prize possessions. They were more than a hobby; they were his only contact with sanity. The worse Mom got, the more he turned to them and, God, the more mother hated them. He didn't let her go near the atrium unless he was with her. He wouldn't have a guardian to watch over her. He didn't want anyone to see her like that. Dad had always been able to control events, but he couldn't this time. I begged him to get her treatment in an institution. He wouldn't. He said people in her condition were just stored there until they died. Maybe he was right, but mom was wearing him out. I was afraid Paully and I were going to lose both parents. Dad was so frightened he wouldn't see anyone for himself, or her. The day before it happened … I'm sorry, I'm so confused."

She started choking up, her hands wet from tears. Polo wanted to help, although more than that, at the moment he wanted to know the ending.

"Please go on, Miss Sinclair."

"The day before it happened I told him on the phone I would take the next morning off, come over and help. I wanted to try again to make him get help. That morning I made my breakfast and turned on Channel 17. Some idiot ranted about my mother's death and Dad being the murderer. I called Paully and..."

Emily was spent, reliving the past. Polo signaled Paul to go to his sister and they huddled together crying. Paul babbling, "I'm sorry, Emi, I'm sorry what you've had to go through without me around."

Polo pitied them both, especially Emily.

He left them alone in the room and walked back through to the atrium smiling, "So, that's it, the motive. The fool was so protective of his wife's reputation, he confessed. It's so apparent now, if there were a trial, all this would have come out about her. He couldn't allow that. There's the reason. What are the top dogs going to do with it?"

He'd find out when he reported in to the Commissioner.

Kearney sounded pleased; emphasizing Polo's report would certainly change the sentence. Since Sinclair had confessed, there probably would not be a trial. Of course, there would be an arraignment on the charges followed by a hearing with the District Attorney and Prosecutors of Franklin County with the designated judge.

"Ray, we're going to need everyone involved, including the Sinclair twins."

Polo winced, "That's going to be a trick if their father's present."

Kearney acknowledged, "I understand their concerns. If there's a confrontation, it's too bad; I'll talk it over with the Prosecutors to see what can be done. I'll also have an attorney represent Sinclair, even though he's refused. You stay in charge as the case progresses. Follow legal protocol to the letter, and keep communications open with the legal gang."

What peaked Polo's curiosity was he's a Boston cop with no authority in Franklin County; yet strangely, no one questioned his involvement.

"How can I still have overall charge, Walt? This is out of my jurisdiction."

"Trust me. You unequivocally run the show, period. If anyone, and I mean anyone bitches, call me or Judge Butts."

Polo had heard of Butts. It dawned on him Kearney and this Judge Butts were handling this case themselves and, without question, for others. Polo had not only revealed an acceptable motive, but they knew he was also discrete enough not to ask any more questions.

"You slipped up on one thing, Ray." Kearney sounded smug, "While you were wandering in the wilderness, I found out Nancy Sinclair has a sister, living in Chicago. Do you realize the ramifications of that, my friend, if she decided to get an ambulance chaser to raise hell over this?"

Polo felt his shoulders droop.

"Don't worry, Ray, I told this Chicago broad her sister died and, unbelievably, she wasn't the least bit interested. Said she was out of the country and didn't even know it happened. She asked me if there was anything else and when I said no, she hung up! Can you imagine? Must have been a hell of a lot of love in that family. Anyway, I dug deeper with my contacts and found this broad is married to Milton D. Campbell and that's spelled money with a capital M. I don't think she's going to raise any ruckus about her sister's death, or money. Talk to you later. Keep up the great work!"

Polo inhaled, slouching back into his chair. There's a game in play here and I want to know what it is and why I'm in it.

Kearney was too what? Pleased? Even happy? Hard to say. The very least, he was satisfied. Polo wasn't a new kid on the block, although this case had baffled him all the way. A fix is going on, the good old boy network in action. Sinclair is a part of it and it's doubtful he even knows. But, what if he did know? What if he thought he would get special treatment from his friends?

"Son of a bitch! If he did, I've *really* been had."

His instinct said no, too farfetched. Still, stay with it; think some more. No one could pull off a scheme like this; too many players. However, it then came to him; he was not *a* player he was *the* player … an outsider in Franklin County and more importantly, a problem solver who knew how to keep his mouth shut. The nebulous *they* used him to find a motive and he did. Now they had something to work with. Of course, Sinclair won't get off Scot-free. That would be going too far. Nevertheless, they'd been given a reason for pleading second-degree murder, extenuating circumstances. A lot of finagling was possible with that plea. A temporary insanity plea by itself wouldn't work. Too many pitfalls. Yes, a charge of second-degree murder is just the trick. With the right judge and prosecutors, a remorseful defendant, Sinclair's son and daughter supplying the extenuating circumstances … Hell, a good attorney would be a waste of money.

Bit by bit, Polo's smile broadened until he burst into a raucous laugh, "I've been faked out all along. Where were my brains? I didn't simply deliver *a* motive they could work with, I delivered *the* motive. God bless me!"

The laugh stopped. His eyes vacant, "Do I give a damn?'

When it started, he wanted to inject the man. Now there were no regrets over what he uncovered. Let Sinclair off the hook easy if that's what they wanted. He turned out to be not such a bad guy, just got sucked into a situation where he couldn't cope. Couldn't live without his wife being with him, he winds up killing her. What a distortion of love. Almost a mercy killing. Mrs. Sinclair was gone mentally; her mind messed up, angry, lost in a place impossible to understand. Sinclair knows *what* he did. Does even he know *why*? Orchids pulled the trigger, not Sinclair. How does anyone explain that?

Even if he gets away with it, he will never get away *from* it, "I guess I wish him luck."

Polo tried, with little success, to bury a nagging feeling, about Emily. Is she the reason he changed his mind over injecting her father? Had she influenced his thoughts from the moment he saw her?

Chapter

Nine

Polo's report put dormant gears in motion. Judge Morgan Butts, now the obvious go-to person, faxed Polo to acquire affidavits from various sources and witnesses.

That list included Parker Sinclair's written confession He also needed Emily and Paul Sinclair's *opinion* of their mother's mental state, her behavior, and their father's state of mind leading up to the fatal night.

Doctor Carl Goodman, Nancy Sinclair's doctor, was needed to provide sworn testimony to collaborate the Sinclair twin's statements on their mother's condition. Connie Johnson and Lieutenant Ken Collin, stating Mr. Sinclair's physical appearance and actions on the fatal night, and the Selectmen, for character statements.

All potential witnesses should be ready to testify at a date specified.

Polo realized his list was short. He assumed Judge Butt's would order sanity tests and other experts, apart from Polo's assignments. Acquiring the affidavits was straightforward, but took time. The only hitch was a query by Doctor Goodman who was mildly interested that Mrs. Sinclair had deteriorated so quickly. Not unheard of though, and he communicated that information to the Judge.

Emily and Paul's statements entered into the record. Again, they asked that those statements and their appearances in their father's defense not be brought to their Father's attention.

For a change, Polo's meeting with Emily Sinclair went well. The tension had eased considerably. She was relieved the decision to tell all was over and she appeared resigned to her father going to jail. Polo wanted to tell her the fix was in, but refrained. He did say she shouldn't worry too much. From his experiences, things would work out. This helped and they talked for a while longer.

As he was leaving, she smiled, "Thanks a lot … Ray."

"You're welcome … Emily."

After Polo submitted his reports to Judge Butts, he had little to do on the case. The Commissioner said to take time off, although to stay local until he called.

Bored with two days of down time, he went up to Barretton to congratulate Ken Collin on his conditional reinstatement. The selectmen realized most of the error in judgment lay with former Patrolman Starr. Collin found Corporal Munson sleeping behind a barn while on duty and removed him from the force, then asked Polo if he would be available to help screen the new applicants. Polo responded positively, and went back to his apartment in Brookline, picking up some clothes and miscellaneous items. While there with the Commissioner, Kearney said events were moving at a rapid pace now, while Judge Butt's office reviewed the affidavits. Polo gave his new phone number, saying he would stay available.

He worked with Lieutenant Collin reviewing new applicants for two positions. Collin winced at Polo's severe interviewing techniques, despite which, they found two good prospects out of ten applicants; One, a police officer from Holyoke, looking to be closer to his family and the other, an officer wanting to transfer from Worchester to a small town. Both were good, experienced men.

To fill his time Polo drove around looking at towns in the area. In the back of his mind was retirement. It wasn't too far down the road, and he didn't plan on retiring to Brookline. Finding himself driving past Great Hill, he drove up to the house. Two cars and a truck blocked the drive in front.

Federal Wheelwright was standing by the garage as Polo walked over.

Federal looked over and smiled, "Been a while, Polo."

They shook hands. Polo's anger at Federal was long past. He looked at the open garage doors. All the cars were gone except the XKE Jaguar.

"What's going on?"

"Emily said sell them, except the Jag. That's Mr. Sinclair's favorite. She wants to keep it pristine. That's her word, not mine. You know, for when he comes home."

Federal glanced about, nobody there, "Do you think she's okay, Polo? 'Cause she's having the house all cleaned up, you know, the atrium and that bedroom being all gutted from floor to ceiling. Spiffed up all over."

Polo guessed what was going on, "Emily's trying to keep busy. You know, keeping her spirits up. Between you and me, she probably wants to keep your spirits up, too. He'll be home someday, not soon, but he'll come home."

Federal brightened, "I sure hope your right, 'cause Emily's said that she wants me to move here to watch the place for as long as Mr. Sinclair is gone. For good, if I wants. Told me she'd even enlarge the rooms at the garage if I liked. Hell, Mr. Polo I live in an old trailer down by Miller's Farm, this is a big step up."

Polo smiled, "I'm sure they get their money's worth out of you, Federal."

As soon as he spoke, he realized it was the wrong comment to make, and Polo wished he could take it back.

"I don't think that way, Mr. Polo, and I don't think they do neither."

Glossing over Polo's comment, Federal offhandedly mentioned, "Do you know Miss Sinclair's in the house?"

Polo rang the bell. A cleaning woman answered, saying Miss Sinclair was in the sitting room.

When he spoke, Emily looked up, then turning away quickly, tears running down her cheeks.

She tried to brush them away, "Hello … Ray."

It seemed so unnatural to see her this way. He choked hello before reaching for his handkerchief. He handed it to her, wanting to wipe away her tears. Not daring.

Emily turned and blew her nose, telling him she would keep the handkerchief, if he didn't mind.

There was an awkward lag; both of them stared. Emily spoke first, "It's nice to see you again." She smiled to herself for saying that.

She looked so forlorn he wanted to hold her, to tell her everything would be all right. Instead, he said, "You look terrible. How about making a cop a cup of coffee?"

"A cop wanting coffee? Of course! How could I have been so impolite not to ask?"

The lighthearted question and apology broke a barrier between them. They lingered for the better part of an hour talking about his past and hers. Both felt Polo's life far less boring, and they kidded about it. After a while, he saw her slipping into the present. He couldn't have that. He had to perk her up again.

"Emily, I want you to know something you must never repeat."

"What?" He had her attention.

"Give me you word you'll never repeat what I'm going to tell you."

"Of course I'll give you my word."

"All right, I'm going to trust you on that."

Polo checked, no one could hear, "There's a good-old-boy network working for your father."

"What does that mean?"

He hesitated, this was something he had never done, "It means there are people going to help your father with the, ah … situation."

"Excuse me for being so dumb, Ray. How are they going to help my father?"

"Well … these people kind of *arrange* things. In your father's case, although they cannot get him off scot-free, they can arrange a lighter sentence. When you gave me your father's motive, I passed it on to these people and that was all they needed to grease the wheels of justice."

"You did this for my father?"

A tough question for Polo to answer, he started to say he did it for her and stopped short. "My job was to get the motive."

Emily's gratitude lit up her face. Her smile melted him.

"What does all this mean, Ray?"

"In my opinion, your father will be charged with second degree murder."

She wilted.

"Listen to me, Emily. *Now* it will be with extenuating circumstances. That means the prosecutor, the judge, and your father's defense attorney can huddle together; and I'll bet they come with a more than fair sentence."

"What do you think it will be?"

"My guess is between six to eight years; time off for good behavior."

"My God." Emily blanched, "Even that's too much."

"Emily, think. You must realize your father could have received a sentence of thirty or forty years. He would have died in prison. What you and Paul told me saved his life.

"You must believe what I'm saying. He won't be seventy when he gets out. Without you, he would have been a hundred. Think of it."

Emily struggled to relax, "You helped too, Ray. You knew how to get the information to the right people."

"As it turned out, I did. That's just how things turned out."

"Without you it wouldn't have happened."

Emily got up and put her arms around him. Polo held her as if she would break, while she cried softly, "Thank you, Ray, thank you."

Polo was guilt-ridden, He was the person who wanted her father injected, wanted to get rid of him, "Don't thank me, It was my job."

Emily pulled away, "We've got to tell Paully!"

"No. You can't."

"Ray, we've got to. He feels as bad as I do … as I did. We must let him know!"

"Emily, I would like to. We can't."

"Why not?"

Ray took both her hands in his; she didn't pull away, "Look. It's difficult to say this. You know Paul's been on drugs. I know he says he's clean now, but ex-druggies can have recurring anxiety, kind of like flash backs. That could happen. If he should say, or even look like he knows something and someone asks him, he'll talk. And, if he talks I could loose my job and my pension. You *can't* tell him."

"That's why you had me give my word? Why did you do it?"

He looked down and seemed to shrink physically, a big bear of a man ill at ease.

Her expression showed she understood, thinking how blind she had been, "Ray, I appreciate what you've done more than I can ever say. I won't tell Paully."

"Okay," He said gruffly, "I don't think Paul will have too long to wait."

They were inept in covering the moment. Another cup of coffee neither of them really wanted helped release some of the tension. A few other meaningless subjects later, Polo said he had to get back, explaining there may be phone calls from his contacts.

He cursed himself all the way to his motel. How stupid, stupid, stupid. How God damned stupid could he be? Standing there like a tongue-tied retard. Christ! How stupid, stupid …. Entering his room, Polo stopped cursing, the phone ringing.

At the house, Emily sank back into her chair, thinking how strange. She hated him when they met, and now she liked him. He'd helped them so much. Helped her father. Not only that, she liked him for what he is, a great big person with a decent streak in him a mile wide. And my God, she thought, he'd trusted her with his job and pension!

Their relationship has turned into something she hadn't expected. "Geez, Ray," she was talking to the mirror, close to crying again, "we can only be friends. I hope you realize it must be that way. Please don't make me have to bear another problem."

Chapter

TEN

Judge Morgan Butts got Polo on the phone. After introductions, getting the feel for each other, Butts felt that Commissioner Kearney's assessment of Polo was correct. The detective could be trusted on things he needed to know.

Butts came to the point, "On 14 October, at 11:00 AM, I want you to escort the Sinclair children to my chambers at the Dedham Courthouse. Walt Kearney told me about them not wanting their father to know what they told about their mother. We can work around that, although their testimony will be the key. Actually, the way I see it there may not be the need for Parker ... Mr. Sinclair, to be there at all. The Prosecutors, Bill Matt and Michael Hancock and District Attorney George will meet at my chambers with two or three other people. No need for you to know who they are, excepting James Temple who has been designated Mr. Sinclair's defense attorney."

Polo interrupted, "Should I go down and pick up Doctor Goodman?"

"We have his deposition, the affidavit. There's no need for him to come here."

Judge Butts then spoke confidentially, "Read into what I'm saying, and follow me on this, okay, Polo? We have all the affidavits we want or need. This meeting will be held in my chambers, in camera. I assume you know what that means. We will meet with the two Sinclair children for a few questions, mainly to confirm your report, after which they will be excused. In this case, we want justice tempered with mercy. You'll wait with them if a question or two should arise, although I doubt that. You will not discuss their testimony. After that, we will confer in closed court, as I said, in camera. As Mr. Sinclair has confessed, we will only be deciding the classification of the offense and the retribution the Commonwealth of Massachusetts demands. You'll not be present at either meeting, Mr. Polo. I mean no affront, not even a stenographer will attend. We will longhand the findings ourselves. This process sounds unorthodox, but we want the verdict kept confidential until Parker is informed. After that, the Court's decision will be entered into the public record. If anyone reads it, I'd venture a guess some court reporter might make a few niggling remarks about it. So be it.

Detective Polo, you have done us yeoman service. Two other detectives got nowhere with this mess. Walt Kearney said if the motive could be found, you'd be the man and you proved him right. This will not be forgotten. We've thought this over and we would be most pleased to offer you the position of Detective Supervisor, Homicide Division.

I understand you turned this rank down previously. However, should you reconsider, you would be positioned to become Deputy Superintendent and then, say in five years, Walt might be retiring as Commissioner. If Johnny Collins is still Mayor there's a good chance you … well, you see what I'm driving at. Naturally, the decision is yours. Discuss it with Walt, and let us know what you decide. Now, do you have any questions?"

"Judge Butts, I'm not a slow thinker, but my brain is so swamped with what you've said, my thoughts are incoherent right now."

"I understand. Take your time and work it out. Oh, I forgot to mention, baring the unforeseen, our decisions on the verdict and retribution will be finalized the day of the meeting. We will inform Parker the following day, after which, Walter or I will call to inform you. So, by the 15th you should know, and thank you again. You are everything we were led to believe. Goodbye."

Polo's mind was racing. Me! Boston Police Commissioner. Gad! Wouldn't ex-wife Colleen have liked that? Police Commissioner's wife. I bet she'd have put up with more of my guff if she ever thought that would happen. Emily would be glad for me, I'd bet.

So what? So nothing, I'm not taking the job. Talk about rising to my level of incompetence. That would take the cake. No to that, thank you … then all this other stuff.

I was right; the fix is in, and in spades. Judge Butt's thought I was more of an insider than I am. What he said about "read into what I'm saying … two or three other people will be there … meeting in closed court … my chambers in camera."

Christ! Butts should have simply come out with it, instead of swanky words to hide the truth. He could have said, Mr. Polo, this meeting is a sham. Parker is a friend of ours. We're hiding behind closed doors to contravene the truth and help a buddy. One of our good old boys has gotten himself into a bit of a jam by killing his wife.

Don't worry, Polo, with the information you dug up we're going to work some magic. Wait until the 15th, you'll see. Butts should have said that.

Polo's mind flitted back to the offer. His payoff: the prize to keep quiet.

His mind delved deeper. The offer was bogus. Bogus! Kearney must have told Butts he could offer Polo any position. Kearney knew he wouldn't take it. Kearney knew him better than he knew himself. Kearney knew Polo felt he was at his peak of efficiency and would refuse any advancement no matter how lofty. And damn, Kearney's right on the money, right on the God damned money.

He toyed with the idea of accepting the offer, perhaps become Detective Supervisor, if only to bug them. Yet then he would be uncomfortable in a position he wouldn't like, and stuck there. Then, if the Deputy Superintendent opening somehow didn't happen, where would he wind up? In a dead end position he couldn't stand. Therefore, in reality, they've offered him nothing.

Then again, why should he be offered anything for doing his job? Why didn't they simply say thank you and let it go at that? That was all he needed, instead of all this crap about this phony job offer. They knew what they were up to wasn't straight, bending the rules. So what? Happens all the time.

Polo had seen this sort of deceit countless times. It riddled the lower courts. This was simply the same. Granted on a more elaborate stage, nevertheless the same. Then it dawned on him. Although they bent the rules, they actually must have felt a touch of guilt. They hoped he'd fail to see the sham for what it was. When he turned it down, as they expect, they'd say, when we offered the deal, he said no. We don't owe him.

Debt paid.

The saddest part? He knew the process and was content with it. More than content, he was pleased. Mrs. Sinclair had lost all sense of reality, making life hell for herself and those around her. Her husband, driven to desperation in his bewilderment, shoots her, then he's left racked with guilt, only wanting to be punished. The two children? Paul's not too swift, probably will regress to the druggie he was, or still is. And Emily? God ... he liked her. Everything has been dumped on her; mother dead, father going to jail, a brother whose dependence on drugs will ruin him and cripple her.

He shook free of his thoughts, I'm going to help her. Father and brother can damn right well help themselves.

Calling Emily, he let her know the date she and Paul would meet at Dedham Court. He also set a time to see both of them at a coffee shop in Sudbury the Saturday prior. He'd go over the events he thought would unfold in Dedham.

Polo and Emily arrived early at the coffee shop. They small talked for thirty minutes. Paul never showed. After an hour, they gave up waiting and Polo, hiding his aggravation because she was there, reviewed the court proceedings. As there was just the two of them, Polo implied the Dedham session was more formality than sentencing process. What he told her previously about the network was confirmed. All she and Paul had to do was authenticate their story about her mother's condition and the violence in the atrium. Polo showed her a copy of his Confidential Memorandum to Commissioner Kearney, regarding their statements. Emily nodded yes, and Polo returned it to his jacket, stating it was privileged information. Don't tell Paul or anyone else.

Polo looked at her seriously, "Tell me about Paul."

"I don't know why he's late.'

"I don't mean today, Emily. In general, what's going on with him?"

"What do you mean?"

"Come on, Emily. This is no time to beat around the bush. That kid's as nervous as a pregnant fox in a forest fire. He's got guilt written all over his face."

Emily stared, not denying what he said. She took a deep breath, "Paully thinks it was his fault."

"What's his fault?" Polo was impatient, leaning forward on the table.

"Give me a minute, Ray, I want to be precise. I don't want to make things messier than they are."

Finally, she whispered, "Paully thinks he caused mother's breakdown, for what happened to her."

"That's foolish; Alzheimer is something that just happens to people. Can't he see that? Or is there more?"

"I think it may have been the drugs he was on."

Polo said nothing.

"A couple of times Paully heard them arguing about his drug problem. He thinks it started her slide."

Chalk one up for Lori Forrest, the housekeeper, Polo thought. She knew the parents argued, more than once.

Emily continued, "Mom wanted Paully to be home where she could look after him. Dad wanted him institutionalized, at Palton House, the one Paully mentioned to you. It wasn't a *house* believe me, Ray. It was a boot camp. Stricter than you can imagine and he got through four months. As Paully told you, it's been nineteen months, and he's still clean and I ..."

Polo interrupted, "Emily, I don't believe he's clean."

"Please, Ray, please believe it! Look what he has been through. He kicked his drug habit, then started believing he caused mom's breakdown. Now that father's in jail, Paully blames himself for that too. Can't you see how he feels?"

"I'm sorry, Emily, I'm not buying it. He's wallowing in self-pity, that's what addicts do."

Emily's face reddened as if she'd been slapped. Nobody had ever spoken this bluntly. Tears filled her eyes and she tried to stop them and failed. Polo saw she wasn't angry; she simply couldn't speak. She was at the breaking point, and he was thoughtlessly pushing her over. He threw money on the table and took her by the arm. She followed blindly. Even before they reached his car, the sobbing began. A little girl lost, unable to stop. In Polo's car, it got worse. Her shoulders shook, through bursts of tears. He held her in his arms and she clung to him.

When she finally could sit with only a hiccup now and then, she turned to him; her hair matted, what little makeup she wore, streaked down her cheeks.

Only then did Polo speak, "Boy, you sure are a wreck."

She gave a few, low laughs, "Ray, subtlety is not your forte."

"I've been told that a few times."

"I'm not surprised."

"Emily, we've got to talk."

"That sounds like a well rehearsed break up line."

"Yeah, with me always on the receiving end."

They laughed, though Emily guessed Polo wanted something off his chest.

"What is it, Ray?"

"You're not going to like it, but here goes. I know your problems seem insurmountable at present; however, I have faith that you'll overcome them by getting back to work. Once you start helping kids again, you'll get back on an even keel. After a few years your father will be okay and the two of you will work though it together.

Paul's a different story. I know the truth is going to hurt, and believe me, that's the last thing I want to do to you. Your brother is *not* clean. I spoke with his parole officer, Sam Washington, and he said Paul's always away, unavailable when it's time for a urine test. Sam's going to request a hearing for parole violation if Paul does not respond shortly and positively."

"What are you saying?"

"Emily, when he's caught he'll be looking at some serious jail time."

"Oh God, Ray! Don't tell me this!"

"I know he's your twin, but you can't take on his problems. You can't be his keeper forever. He's going to take you down. Don't wreck your life and your father's, trying to save Paul's. It's not going to happen."

"I'm going to keep trying forever, no matter what."

That hurt more than he wanted to admit. He wanted to say he cared for her. He held back. The foolishness of such a remark would rank up there with some of the most asinine comments he ever made. He also realized continuing the subject of Paul further would only create a chasm between them.

"Okay, Emily, I understand. Let me see what can be done for him."

"I appreciate that, Ray. Thanks a lot."

Polo called Samuel Washington to see where things stood. Washington was of no help. He had no idea where the Sinclair kid was. Washington hadn't heard from him in over two weeks. Next week, he would charge Paul with parole violation. Washington wasn't going to cover for him, even for a fellow officer.

Polo contacted Emily again, asking if she might know where Paul could be. She was devastated by the news and no help, saying Paul could be anywhere from Truro on the Cape to Quebec. "Paully's a wanderer, Ray. Always has been, even when a kid and only had a bike he'd be gone all day, wouldn't come home until after dark."

Emily started reminiscing, "I remember when he was seventeen. Dad bought him his first car, a used XK120 Jaguar roadster. He took off for a week. We didn't know where he was. Later, he said he went all over Cape Cod, every twisty road he could find. A few years later, Dad liked that Jag so much he bought a new red, XKE Jaguar roadster for himself. He still has it and we ..."

Polo interrupted, Emily had drifted into happier times. Although he did not want to stop her, there were other things on his mind. Paul's whereabouts; he was needed for the Dedham Court meeting. Should he put out an all points bulletin for a 1960 Chevy Impala, white convertible? Maine plate, first three numbers 633. Then again, if Paul is out of the country, forget it; and if the authorities found him, he'd be arrested.

"Emily, get me a recent photo of Paul and I'll file a missing person's report. I know he's driving an Impala, Maine plates. I'll trace the number through the ME Registry."

No one knew where Paul went, he wasn't found before the meeting. On 13 October, Polo called Judge Butts with the news he only had Emily Sinclair.

The call was short. When Polo gave the news, Butts asked in an understated tone, "You don't know where your witness is?"

The question had already been answered. Silence for a few seconds. Polo held his breath. Butts continued, "Blast it! All right, we won't need him, bring Emily Sinclair. That is if you can keep track of her."

The morning of 14 October, Polo drove Emily over to Dedham Court. She was anxious over Paul's disappearance, saying he had left for parts unknown before, although never when his presence was necessary, such as now. Except for Emily's concern, Polo couldn't have cared less. He figured Paul had reverted to drugs, which inevitably made a person irresponsible. Fortunately, turned out Judge Butt's said they could do without him; and in Polo's mind this reinforced his belief the judgment and sentence were predetermined. Everyone involved going through the motions for appearance's sake and sentencing.

"Listen to me," Polo told Emily as they drove, "I'll see what might be done with the Parole Board. Right now put Paul out of your mind, he'll show up eventually. You have to concentrate on this meeting."

Polo knew where Paul was concerned, there would be precious little not already written in stone.

While he was thinking of Paul, Emily glanced at him. He had on a suit that looked new, nice matching tie. He'd shaved and had a haircut recently. This couldn't be solely for the meeting, she thought, he wouldn't have bothered. This must be for her. Emily didn't realize she wore a thin smile.

Polo saw her looking over, "What are you putting the peek on me for?"

"No reason, Just keep your eyes on the road."

James Temple, Defense Attorney for Emily's father, met them at the courthouse. The attorney was a surprise to Emily. Polo kicked himself for not mentioning Judge Butt's appointed Temple. She looked at Polo. He nodded that was okay. She relaxed, then shook hands with Temple.

Polo was to remain in the antechamber, the attorney said, while Temple escorted Emily in to see the panel. Although Polo had told her this would happen, she appeared apprehensive, looking again to him. He smiled and said knock them dead, kid. They laughed as the door closed behind her.

Polo sat, analyzing the look Emily gave him in the car. It was enigmatic. What did it mean? For sure, a typical woman's expression. Whatever, no question it added to her allure. Another thought bothered him. When he first met her, she appeared self-assured. He was amused at her attitude and liked that in her. Now, she was changing. Although he understood why, considering the recent dissolution of her family, she was no longer the strong woman he once thought. Had it only been a front because she had to cover for Paul, had to be strong to keep him going? Whatever it was, the face she put on was dissolving. The insecurity she showed when meeting Temple, and then having to leave Polo couldn't be hidden. She was leaning on him for support. It wasn't the way he wanted her to be. Where in the devil was all this going to lead? It sure as hell would end in disaster for him and ….

Not twenty minutes had passed. Emily walked up to him, "Let's get out of here."

Her expression, inscrutable. She walked ahead of him, giving no sign whether she was angry or frightened. Polo couldn't read her walk, either.

Chapter

Eleven

Emily got in the car quickly, "Let's go, Ray." Looking through the window she said, "They sentenced Dad. Four to six years."

For a mile or two, he left her with her thoughts, and then asked, "How do you feel?"

"I guess after you told me what Dad could have received, I'm happy that's all he got. He's strong. I know he'll get better, and we'll be together again after this."

Polo left her to find her bearings while he contemplated. Four to six. Damn! Good behavior and he'll be out in maybe three. Talk about almost getting away with murder. Great having friends in high places.

"Ray, I didn't mean to walk off without you back there. I was afraid someone might be looking and I did not want them to think we were friends."

"Why not?"

"Because they told me not to tell anyone, even you, until after tomorrow."

"Emily, they told me before, that you wouldn't know the sentence today. I was to tell you tomorrow, after I was told."

"You're not upset about this, are you, Ray?"

"Me? Christ, no! I'm glad that the damn waiting is over for us, I mean you."

She reached over and took his hand, "You did this. You're the reason they kept his sentence low. They told me that."

"They told you what? Why? It was you admitting what happened, that's what did it."

75

"Yes, except you got it out of us where the other detective's couldn't. They said they were offering you a top position for your help."

"Jesus Christ, Emily! Don't you see how I helped *them*? I gave one of their friends, their own class, a way out. The only thing is, it turns out I did it for you, so you wouldn't be hurt, because I …"

"You're shouting. Please, calm down. I know what you're saying, and know what you're not saying. Damn! My mind is too scrambled to think straight right now. I've depended on you, probably unfairly; you eased my fears about my father and made me realize you were the only person who could help. So I lean on you now because you're strong, you know where I should be going and how to get there. I don't know Ray, let's stop talking about it."

She brightened, "How about dinner tomorrow, to celebrate?"

"Sounds fine and to change the subject, how about telling me what went on back there in the inner sanctorum?"

"When I went in, you knew I was shaking. I counted nine men, when I had a second to breathe. Mr. Kearney introduced himself and actually asked how my father was doing. Then, he said he thought the world of you."

Polo raised an eyebrow.

"He did say that," Emily stressed, "He couldn't have been more complimentary. Then, he introduced me in the strangest way; these are the County Prosecutors, didn't give them names, this is the judge, no name, and this is your father's attorney, who you and I met in the corridor. And these other gentlemen, he said, waving a hand in their direction, are interested parties. There were five of them. He didn't introduce them, just acknowledged they were there. I don't know who they were, but believe me Ray, they were suits."

"I'll bet they were suits and friends of the family, Emily. I'd sure like to know their names. Did they look like good fellers?"

Emily laughed at Polo's slang, "No, God no, these were Boston bluebloods through and through. At least two of them had on Masonic rings like my Fathers. These were movers and shakers. I was around my Dad long enough to recognize them when I see them, and I was looking at a covey.

"Were you sworn in?"

When Emily said no, Polo simply shook his head. Not the least surprised.

"So what happened next?"

"Not too much really. I sat down at a table. The two prosecutors and Temple, Dad's attorney sat on the other side and they slid across two identical forms. As I read them, I could see your report to Commissioner Kearney on Paully and my conversation that night at the Hill. You were very accurate, Ray. Anyway, I said they were correct and they asked me to sign each copy and to sign Paully's name and write my initials by his name, which I did. Was that legal?"

Polo smiled at her, "Who cares? Those documents will never see the light of day."

Not understanding, she continued, "That was pretty much it. A few, "Thank you Miss Sinclair", and Mr. Kearney walked me to the door and ordered me not to speak to anybody about this, including you. I could see him almost wink when he said you. That was when he said you had been offered a top dog position in the Boston PD. Congratulations, Ray."

"Congratulations, hell. I'm not taking them up on the offer, it's bogus."

Totally perplexed, Emily asked, "Why do you say that?"

"I don't want to talk about it. Maybe another time."

The harshness in his voice stopped her from delving.

They drove on in silence, each mired in their own thoughts. Emily turning her attention to Paul, hoping he was safe and would be home soon and okay. Polo's mind a jumble, wishing he had written down the license numbers of any expensive vehicles around the court so he could check them out. Despite wondering who the Dedham 5 was, he concluded sometimes its better not to know. Unidentified people can get irritated when you ferret out their names. And where is that dimwit, juice-taking junkie, Paul?

I've got to chase that dope head all over New England to bring him home for Emily? Christ! Damn, damn, damn!

"Where do you want to eat tomorrow night, Emily?"

"Why don't we go up to the Bedford Inn?"

"I'm not from these parts, where's that?"

"Bedford, New Hampshire. I don't think anyone will recognize me up there."

"Do you worry about that?"

"Yes, I do. Even when I stop over to work, people take a second look at me."

"That, Emily, is your great looks."

"Sure, Ray, I'm the queen of the May."

They were dressed to the nines. Just short of formal. Ray in another new suit, fitting as well as a suit could fit a fifty-five year old, six foot three, two hundred-thirty pound man. A man with a gut he was doing his best to suck in.

On the other hand, Emily turned heads when she walked past the restaurant patrons to their table. She wore a silky black dress, which enhanced her figure. With perfect light makeup and long blond hair flowing over the dress, she was simply flawless.

Polo shook his head, following behind her, not caring one bit if he was thought to be her father. Didn't matter to him at all. He strutted along. She was his date and every one else could cry in their beer.

After they were seated, Polo relaxed and Emily seemed at ease. It was their night to kick back, and enjoy the moment.

"Hey, ain't you that *Sinclair* broad?"

The person with the loud mouth was big and he was drunk. Emily was shocked, watching, the scene as it unfolded seemingly in slow motion. Polo, in one upward flowing motion, his fist cocked, delivered a crushing blow to the drunk's chin. Open-mouth, Emily watched the stranger's legs turn to rubber. The back of his knees slammed into a half wall behind him, pitching him over backward, his body crashing onto a table where four patrons were eating their meal. Food, silverware, glasses and plates flew everywhere, the table collapsing. Men yelling, women screaming, the area a shambles.

Polo and Emily didn't stay for the end. He grabbed her and they were out the exit into the parking lot. Polo scooped her up then ran for the car. Opening her door, he tossed her in, looking back to see if he was being chased. No one. Polo pulled off his jacket, jammed it over the car's number plate, and jumped in, started the car and burned rubber out of the lot. Emily was stunned, totally disorientated. The last thing she actually recalled seeing was Polo's fist flying through the air. After that, a collage of images as she was pulled, lifted, tossed, Polo jumping in, the car racing away.

She sat, staring at Polo. He drove like a lunatic. And laughing? How could he be laughing? What's going on here?

He stopped the car on a side street, jumped out, retrieving his coat off the Police plate; the jacket frayed; it had done the job of hiding the number. Emily was more composed, speaking calmly, "Ray, may I please quietly ask, *what in hell was all that about*?"

Though still laughing, Polo managed to get out, "Emily, I haven't decked a guy like that since college. It felt great!"

"You must have hurt him."

"Damn right! That jaw will be wired for a while."

"What was it all about?"

"Two things. Actually three, as I think of it. One night when I was in college I was waiting for friends in Michael O's Pub, a beer joint near Boston College and this big guy, a real wiseass, kept ragging me about what a lousy game I'd played. So I got sick of his crap and decked him. Unfortunately, he had friends, and they banged me up a lot. From that point on I swore if it happened again, I'd be gone before anyone could react."

"Tell me," she asked innocently, "did you play a lousy game that day?"

"That, young lady, is beside the point."

"You said there were three things. What are the two that made you run like hell out of there?"

79

"One, I could lose my badge, a Boston cop wrecking a joint in New Hampshire, and the second reason, I didn't like what he said to you."

"Look, Ray, things like that are going to happen and you can't go breaking jaws each time anyone says something you don't like. I thought by going up to Bedford we would be far enough away and I wouldn't be recognized. Wrong again. This is the reason I don't date. I guess I'll have to go south of Connecticut not to be recognized or north to the wilds of Maine."

Polo, who didn't know she wasn't dating, offered, "The wilds of Maine sounds good. Maybe you could date some of those Maniacs I hear about."

"You're maniac enough for me, thank you."

They both laughed. Awareness, an appreciation of each other crept into their minds.

Polo drove on without speaking, comfortable they didn't have to chatter on about nothing. Seeing a MacDonald's he pulled into the drive-through.

"I don't believe you're doing this, Ray."

"Hey, we can't go in dressed like this and have someone recognize you. I'd have to break another jaw. Besides, my knuckles are sore.

"Your poor little knuckles are sore? I'm so sad thinking about them."

"What do you want to eat?"

They ordered. As they left, Polo drove back the way they had come. He had seen a lakeside parking area and pulled in.

"You know, Ray, this isn't so bad. Comfortable leather seats, great view over the moonlit lake, excellent food, soft jazz on the radio; nope, not a bad evening after all."

"Talk to me, Emily."

"I am."

"No, I mean tell me more about you."

"We all ready discussed this and decided your life is far more exciting."

"I don't mean excitement; I mean what do you do? You know, who are *you*?"

"God, Ray, you ask me at a time when my life is so fouled up. If it wasn't for you, I'd be ready for the loony bin."

"That's nice to hear, but not true. You're too strong. You'll come back. Tell me about your school and your horse."

"You're hitting me with the two subjects I love, so prepare yourself. At school, I teach traumatized and brain damaged children, mainly to speak and write, if it's at all possible for them. At times, it's heartbreaking. There are kids who have been so badly treated or beaten they can no longer function normally in life. We try to coddle them, but they shy away, frightened. We give and give ... I'm sorry. Ray, it's too much to get out of me right now."

"Tell me about Bismarck then."

She smiled sweetly, "You remembered my horse's name! How nice of you. As I recall, you couldn't remember the name of your ex-wife's horse."

"Yah, yah, yah, get on with it," Polo said, giving a disgusted sigh.

"Ray, Bismarck's a darling. Everyone loves him everywhere we show. He's bulletproof; nothing bothers him. He knows so much more in dressage than I."

He gave her a questioning glance.

"Sorry, Ray, I didn't realize you aren't as knowledgeable as us upper crust horsy set."

He rolled his eyes, "You're losing me."

She ignored him, "Dressage is a discipline in horsemanship, a way of showing the rider and horse are one, to be precise in specific movements, hopefully with elegance. I reached the Prix Saint George level, although I'm not a good enough athlete to advance to the next level in dressage."

Polo stared at her, "Athlete? Isn't all you do is sit on a horse and point it."

"My God, it's hopeless trying to teach you some couth."

81

He laughed, "No, no, really, go on, I'm listening, I'm listening."

Emily glowered, "I don't think so, *Mister Polo*."

"Oh, God, we're back to *Mister Polo* again? Gone too far, have I?"

She couldn't help herself, "Yes you have, you unrefined, jaw-breaking hooligan."

"Thank you, Emily! I never realized you were that fond of me until now."

She stared over at him in the dark. "You're pushing your luck, fella, although I do admit to a little fondness for you."

They spent the rest of the drive discussing the next day's meeting with her father. Sinclair would know by then his sentence was four to six, with time off for good behavior. As far as they knew, her father did not know Emily and Paul's information was the justification for the light sentence. If Sinclair learned what his twins said about their mother, Emily felt he would disown them. Since her father was terribly protective of his wife, his daughter knew she had to hope for the best, while preparing for the worse. Then again, how could she prepare?

Polo was surprised when Emily asked, in fact insisted, he accompany her. At first, he was against it, until she said that if her father knew the truth, she couldn't face him alone. Polo needed to support her, especially since Paul wasn't there. Even if Paul was there, she told Polo, he was her backbone.

"Emily, you've got to understand where I'm coming from. When I met your father, he was in jail, admitting to murder. I was absolutely against what he had done. I was very hard on him because my job was trying to find out his motive. I'll be frank with you. I did what I was ordered and that's all I was after, the motive. I felt anyone who killed their wife should get life in prison at the very least, and I told him that straight out."

Frightened, she put her hand to his mouth to stop him. She never knew, "Don't tell me about then, Ray. What do you feel now?"

"I never believed there were two sides to a story when it came to murder. Then, when I listened to you and Paul up on Great Hill that night, I understood what a sacrifice your father was willing to make to protect your mother's reputation. Did he think Alzheimer was something to be ashamed of? Yes. Was he wrong? Yes. Your father is too vain and too proud concerning his family. Yet he did admit to what he had done. The problem I have is, he will never accept what he did was wrong. Despite that, he would have spent the rest of his life in jail for her. That thought struck me so hard, later. How do I feel now? I still have trouble with what he did, but the fact you still love him, makes me wish him the best."

Emily put her hand into his, "You're coming with me tomorrow, Ray, and that's that."

Chapter

Twelve

When his phone rang, Polo was leaving to pick up Emily before visiting her father. Paul Sinclair's parole officer was on the line.

"What have you found out, Sam?"

"Found your boy."

"In a gutter somewhere?"

Washington smiled, "Quite the contrary. He's at Palton House, ever heard of it?"

"Hell yes, the kid's been there before. How'd that happen?"

"Steven Napier, he's Superintendent at the House, called and said Sinclair checked himself in. The kid asked Steve to call me."

Polo mulled this news over for a few seconds before answering. "Sneaky little bastard, isn't he?"

Washington laughed, "You got it right there, Polo. Kid knows he's broken parole, checks himself into rehab and figures the state won't touch him in there, and he's right. If he comes out clean we'll probably reinstate his parole. Good trick."

"Napier figure that out, too?"

"Yep, just as we did. We're all on the same page about the little bastard."

"What condition was he in when he showed up?"

"Semi-stoned," Napier wouldn't get technical. What do you think, Polo?"

"That kid will blight that family the rest of his life."

"Yeah, you're right. But it's not your worry anymore."

Polo grimaced and without thinking blurted out, "Easy for you to say."

"Why do you say that?"

"No reason. Give me the superintendent's phone number. I'll check in with him."

Washington gave the number, not asking why Polo wasn't back in Boston by now. Polo was still involved? Something else must be going on. But what the hell, he's got his troubles, I've got mine.

"How long is the little shit going to be caged, Sam?"

"Napier says four months. No phone calls, visitors, packages or letters, unless there's an emergency. That's gospel. Talk to you later."

Four months. Polo couldn't help smiling; Paul was out of his hair for four months.

On the way to the Franklin County Detention Center, Polo told Emily about Paul checking himself into the Palton House. Polo was on the verge of telling *why* her brother checked back in until he saw Emily was relieved Paul had returned to rehab. She felt he was intelligent enough to know he needed help and Polo couldn't ruin her mood. How blind people can be, he wondered.

Parker Sinclair was in the visitor's area standing at the window. He heard her voice and turned to welcome her. As she and Polo walked across the room, Parker's, smile faded, trying to place Polo. He recalled the confrontation with the detective and was utterly confused. What was his daughter doing with this person? Was he going to badger him again? Did he know something? Sinclair was cautious, waiting to see how things developed.

Emily hugged her father; tears in her eyes. Polo stood aside, feeling his being there a blunder. He walked to a bench, aware he was a complete ass. From the corner of his eye, he noticed Sinclair was not as haggard as their meeting in the county jail. He also caught Sinclair staring at him while Emily spoke forcefully to her father. Polo rose, starting for the door when Emily called over. No pleasantries exchanged, though the men were courteous enough to shake hands.

Parker Sinclair spoke first, "Emily tells me Paul had been, shall we say, erratic once more and you have taken it upon yourself to track him down and see that he is safe in Palton House again."

Not true, Polo answered quietly, "Not quite that way, but he's there, sir."

"Although, Detective Polo, I must say my recollection of your interrogation has left me at a loss as to why you would do this for us. May I ask why?"

Polo was in a bind. He could see Emily behind her father shaking her head not to reveal what he knew. This left him absolutely no reason as to why he helped. Sinclair was being blunt.

After moments that felt like minutes, Polo came up with an explanation he hoped would work, "Sir, I wished you had not asked that question as my answer might embarrass you."

Polo's mind raced as Sinclair looked at him questioningly, unspeaking. "My job was to get the motive from you ..."

Sinclair cut in, self-satisfied, "And I did not inform you, did I?"

"No, sir, you did not." Polo was annoyed, kept in check and continued, "Since I *did not* find the answer, my superior instructed me to continue searching; so I began with people who knew you. Your daughter and son were of no help. They only kept saying you were a great father.

So, then I went on to Federal Census, Ken Collin, Mary Wells, Mr. Slocomb, and a number of other people. Everyone kept saying what a wonderful person you were, a pillar of the community. Anyway, although your daughter hadn't known of my *conversation* with you, she knew I was a detective with contacts.

87

She asked if I would help in finding your son. I was hesitant to help. Nevertheless, here I am."

Parker Sinclair's eyes were flicking back and forth between Emily and Polo, all the while concentrating on Polo's words. At first, Polo saw Sinclair's doubt, which dimmed until he appeared satisfied, abruptly changing the subject, "Mr. Polo, Morgan Butts told you my sentence, what are your thoughts on it, light don't you think?"

"Yes, frankly I do, and to answer your next question before you ask, I am not privy to the machinations of the Superior Court about lengths of a sentence, and I do not ask."

Sinclair read between Polo's words, "You know Walt Kearney and you've talked with Morgan Butts. I know you have. You must be well trusted with intrigues performed on my behalf."

Polo didn't answer.

Sinclair waited a moment, then continued, "I can see why you're trusted."

Again, Polo didn't answer.

"I'm being transferred to a prison in Concord, Northeastern Correctional Center. Do you know it, Mr. Polo?"

"Yes, it's minimum security, kind of a nonviolent, pre-release prison."

"An odd place to send a convicted murderer?"

"Not if the murderer has friends in high places … Mr. Sinclair."

Through this conversation, Emily was fascinated by the wordplay of the two men. Very few people had held their own against her father's intenseness. Polo, she felt, had done well under difficult circumstances.

Sinclair digested Polo's last remark, then asked him to leave for a few minutes as he and his daughter had business to conduct. More than happy to oblige, Polo walked back over to the bench, found a National Geographic, and thumbed through it, glancing over at Emily and her father.

Parker Sinclair, Polo mused, sure lives up to what I've heard. Seeing him in jail before is nothing compared to his appearance now. What a transformation. He knows some unspecified *thing*, is going on. He's incisive, no fool. He had me on the ropes, yet let me go. Emily and I are going to have to watch our step. He's getting back to what everyone talks about, courteous, but. As far as I'm concerned, it won't be long before he returns to the proud, remote cuss he really is. How he got a reputation for being wonderful beats me.

Emily was still unsure if her father was ignorant of her and Paul's testimony. Although he seemed to be completely involved in the information he passed on to her. He had appointed one of his bank's Board of Directors, Alice Evans, as the new Chairman, replacing him. It would create upset in the Board, he thought, which was fine, a bit of a shakeup was healthy and he would back any move she made, since he owned the majority of stock, with overall control.

For all the uproar in the county over the murder, there had been only two depositors who withdrew their money; and those were free, personal checking accounts. Though Sinclair wondered who they were, he wouldn't ask. From prison, he managed all his other business interests by arranging for each manager to meet with him bi-monthly, once visiting hours were set.

Emily was to receive her inheritance on her twenty-fifth birthday. That wouldn't change. Only a year away he noted. However, he modified his Will to ensure Paul's right to inherit moved into a Trust, fixing a low income limit for him each year. There were to be five members of the Trust and it was thought best Emily not be a member. The plan was that, when or if, at least four trustees judged Paul fit to handle his inheritance, he would receive it with limited restrictions.

This was far from ideal to Emily, who kept her reservations to herself when her father agreed to pay all of Paul's medical expenses. He then mentioned he would pay Emily's tuition if she agreed to return to college and major in economics. His thought was to spin off a small group of companies she could manage, if

89

she felt she might like that. Alternatively, if she preferred, he would buy her a company of her choosing. However, he insisted she get her degree in economics first. These ideas were entirely new, and she needed time to think it over.

Sinclair's next subject was Polo, "Why are you with him?"

Again, Emily explained, "Polo helped with Paul …"

Sinclair cut her off, "There has to be another reason as well, don't try to tell me otherwise."

Emily tensed, she couldn't be as quick-witted as Polo, "He helped Paully, and Mr. Kearney told him to drive me down to the Dedham Court …"

Sinclair caught the remark, "What the devil was down at the Dedham Court?"

Emily thought fast, "They only wanted to tell me in person what your sentence was."

"Who are *they*?"

"You know, the people you mentioned, Judge Butts and Kearney"

Her father relaxed, "All right, Emily, sorry I was harsh. I heard you were there."

Emily's smile was unseen. Only half-truths; far better than whole truths.

"So, he helped Paul and drove you down to Dedham. What else should I ask you about?"

"Nothing else, Dad."

"How old is he?"

"He's fifty-five, over thirty years older than me; if that's what you're asking."

"That *is* what I'm asking. I might add that he's an old fat cop and odds are he's a heavy drinker."

"Cripes, Dad, since when did you get to be so prejudiced?"

"Since my daughter looks with big eyes at a person I totally suspect and reject."

"Big eyes? For God's sake! He helped both of us with Paul. All I am is grateful, as you should be.

"Why did you bring him with you?"

"Because for some foolish reason I thought you might want to thank him, my mistake. Let it go at that."

"I'll let it go at that, for now, Emily."

They walked over to Polo as he got up.

Sinclair looked straight at him, "Mr. Polo, I would like to offer you a monetary reward for helping my son, although you do not seem the type to accept one."

"You're correct. I'd find that insulting, if offered."

Sinclair did not like the rebuff, "Very well, my daughter said I should thank you for what you have done for my son. I do, and I wish you the best in your endeavors."

He kissed Emily on the cheek and walked off.

Polo rolled his eyes, "Lovable guy, I can see why everyone's nuts about him."

"Oh, Ray, it's Dad's way of testing you. He's upset over the way you were before. He's accustomed to respect, not being manhandled, which I imagine, you were with him. And also, he thinks I've got big eyes for you."

"I've been noticing that too, Emily, you really should stop it when people are around."

"I what? Okay, have your little joke, you big creep."

"Now come on, you must admit I'm a fun creep."

Driving back to the Hill, Emily told Polo of her conversation with her father about her inheritance coming in one year, the sanctions on Paul's trust and her father's offer of more education in Economics, offering to have her run some businesses or pick her own.

"What do you think, Ray? Should I do it?"

"What do I think? I think your father is trying to educate another son."

"I'm not following you."

"To me, your father is giving up on your brother getting straightened out. He wants an heir to carry on the family name, the empire. Work it out. Paul's money will be in trust indefinitely, which means, bluntly, your dad has written your brother off. Old

Dad wants you to study Economics and *that* means someday he'll be willing to hand you his empire on a silver platter. So you see, my dear, you will be your father's second son."

Rather than objecting, Emily mulled over Polo's observation. He said nothing further, guessing by Emily's silence, that she realized it could very well be her father's strategy.

She broke the silence, "Ray, you get to the core of an issue quickly, and you're possibly right. I may seem a flighty broad. I'm not. With a degree in Economics and a few years on the job training, I could take over. The question is do I want to be a legacy?"

Polo laughed, "Emily, believe me, I've been around flighty broads in my life and you're not even close. This past month would make anyone manic, yet you're doing great under terrific pressure. And I know you could probably do whatever you set your mind to. You simply need some time to decide whether you want to remain a humble school teacher or, be a top woman executive with more money than God."

Emily listened attentively to Polo's evaluation of the situation until he got to the end of his last comment. Her face cracked into a smile, "Damn, Ray, this must be why you're such a good cop. Once again, you've simplified the analysis of my problem. Boil it down to the essentials: humble teacher, or richer than God."

"You got it, kid, what could be simpler to decide?"

This was one of those times when a succession of comments spurred fits of laughter and giggles. If anyone had heard them, Emily wouldn't have cared. Polo would have been mortified.

On reaching Great Hill, she asked him in for coffee. He said he shouldn't, saying he'd scheduled a meeting with the Commissioner the following day to discuss another assignment. For this reason, he had to get back to his apartment in Brookline and was already behind schedule. Emily knew this time would come and was not prepared.

They spoke of their first meeting and how she wanted to smack him; he said he thought she was a brat who had never been spanked or, if spanked, not nearly enough.

They chatted on until Emily said, "My birthday is the 28th. Would you take me to dinner and celebrate?"

"I'd like that, but are you sure you'd want to after the last dinner date we had?"

"Damn, how'd I forget that? I'll bet your wanted poster wallpapers every restaurant in New Hampshire. Wait, let's go towards Boston. I can stay at my condo so you won't have so far to drive to and from Brookline."

"Sounds great, I'll call you on the 27th."

"I'll give you my number."

"I've got it."

She looked at him in false spite, "Oh yes, from our lovely first meeting."

She was out the door laughing, up the stairs and into the house.

On the way back to home, Polo was puzzled. What am I doing? This girl's just turning twenty-four, wants to be with me on her birthday and I can hardly wait for the 28th. I better get back down to earth, or this is going to end in a mess, for me at least. Gad, imagine being shot down in flames at fifty-five.

Chapter

Thirteen

Commissioner Kearney couldn't meet with Polo until 5:00 PM. His first statement after, "Hello, Ray," was, "Got a stinking job for you."

"When don't you, Walt?"

"Come on, Ray, your last job was a creampuff. Spend some time in the country, find out an obvious motive, see a pretty girl, and come back to the office, a walk in the park."

Polo was leery. Should he read anything into Kearney's comment about a pretty girl?

"Jesus, Walt, it was hell out there. Indian summer heat, dead leaves everywhere, traffic, beating women off with a stick, you don't know the half of it."

"Yah, yah. Like a drink?"

"Sure, the sun's over the yardarm somewhere. I'll have a scotch, ice, light water."

"You want Dewar's or Glen Fiddich?"

"Give me Dewar's. Those single malts taste too much like whiskey to me."

"When did your tongue get such educated taste buds?"

"Since I started drinking your scotch when you weren't around. Except that's another story. You must have a really stinking job for me, giving me a drink."

"Actually, you're going to have a great time. Miami for a week, all at Department expense. What more could you ask?"

"That's the PD Leadership Conference isn't it? That's your job, aren't you going?"

"No, and you're one of the first to hear this ... I'm retiring."

Polo nearly choked on his scotch, "Christ, I can't believe this. Seriously?"

"It's like this, I've been offered the Chancellor's position at U Mass. Stay there ten years, and I retire with full pension to add to my Police pension. Double dip, walk away comfortable in my golden years."

"Yeah, not a bad deal, still, I'm surprised. Too sudden. Something you're not telling me? You being put out to pasture?"

"Things happen. I was offered the deal; I took it. Why don't you do the same? You could get into the Academy as an instructor, then a good chance for Superintendent."

"I guess. I'm just not thinking of doing anything more right now."

"That's your problem, Ray, remember, you're not a kid any longer."

"We'll talk about that later. Now, why am I going to Miami? Any number of stiffs could go ahead of me."

Kearney looked uneasy, "Ray, I'm asking a favor. You're going with Congressman Ed Murray."

"Murray? That Southie Pol? Why the hell is he going?"

"Because Johnny Collin's wants him to."

Polo saw the whole scheme, "Christ, Walt, You're telling me the Mayor is going to make Murray the next Police Commissioner? Is he nuts?"

"No, It's because Collin's has good programs he wants pushed through and Murray's got three relatives in the House and Senate, as well as friends."

"Jesus, why do I even ask? So I'm to babysit Murray." Polo made it a flat statement.

Kearney nodded, "Collin's asked me for someone experienced to introduce Murray around and watch over him."

For the next half hour, they discussed the circumstances heatedly. Polo finally accepted Kearney's request, as a going away present from Polo.

"In any case, Ray, you'll see your old BPD buddy Sal Fanara in Miami. Isn't he a sheriff or something down there?"

Polo smiled, "Not just any old sheriff, he's Director of the Public Safety Department and Sheriff of Metropolitan Dade County. That's different from the Miami Police."

"God, that's a mouthful."

"I know, I kid him whenever we talk. I ask for the DPSDSMDC. Drives him crazy."

Kearney got to thinking about Sal Fanara, "He still have that raspy voice?"

"Yeah. Never lost it after that son of a bitch stepped on his throat that night."

"I'll never forget that, Polo. You'd been on the force what, a year? You and Fanara get jumped by a bunch of South Boston punks after a Celts game. You're being stabbed, yet you still got off a shot and killed the bastard stepping on Sal's neck."

"You know what I always told Sal that if it ever happened again? First I would shoot the bastard stabbing me, *and then* shoot his guy."

They both had a good laugh and Kearney offered, "What the hell, your guy only knifed you three times into blubber before you kneecapped him, and you got two months off to restore to your splendid self. That was your first commendation."

"That's right, from you."

"God, how long ago? Damn, I'm getting melancholy. Lot of water over the dam since then."

"Yeah, lot of spilt milk too. Have another drink, Walt, let's get drunk."

So he did, and Polo did …two aging Boston cops telling stories on each other into the night. The Commissioner passed out, dead drunk on the couch. Polo threw a blanket over him, then called his wife to say he wouldn't make it home. That was okay with her, she said, as long as he was safe with Polo.

He sat, staring at his boss, thinking of the good and bad times they worked together. Then, he hid the keys to Kearney's car in the toilet tank. Polo was now the one becoming melancholy. He fell into his car, and although drunk, somehow made it to his condominium.

The night before his date with Emily, he reconfirmed. She sounded happy, saying she had made a reservation at a small restaurant in Sudbury. Emily wouldn't take no for an answer when she said she would meet Polo there. It didn't make sense for him to drive miles past the restaurant to her condo in Weston, then back track to the restaurant then repeat the whole process when they left. It wasn't the way it was done when he was younger, he complained, but finally relented and set the meeting time at the Sudbury Public House.

Polo had not spoken to Commissioner Kearney since they drained the Dewar's and then finished off the Glen Fiddich. He called to see if Kearney were still alive.

"Who is this? And it better not be a son of a bitch, name of Polo 'cause I'll have him thrown in the tombs for aiding and abetting an old man into drinking his brains out."

"I love you too, Walt. We'll never have a night like that again I'm afraid."

"I don't want another night like that again. And don't go mushy on me, Polo. By the way, I found my keys in the toilet, you bastard."

Polo ignored him. "Don't go mushy on me. I don't like mush either."

"Pick up your itinerary for the trip in the next couple of days, Ray. We'll talk then."

Before Polo headed into the Sudbury Public House, a car pulled in, its horn beeping. He turned and found Emily, driving a new Mercedes.

"What is this?"

"Hi, Ray, it's a brand spanking new 1967 230SL Mercedes Benz, my new car. Five speed stick and everything. Want to go for a ride?"

"Emily, look at me, then look at the size of that car. It's made for midgets, for Christ's sake"

She grinned, "Point well taken."

"A bribe from someone we all know and love, perhaps."

"Yes, it's from Dad, and probably is a bribe," she kidded, "but, after that clunker I drove, it's a pleasure. Eat your heart out."

"Your car wasn't a clunker, you're spoiled. Anyway, let's go inside. I can eat humble pie while you tell me what you decided to do with your life."

They took their seats with Polo looking at her expectantly, not saying a word. They ordered Dewar's. Still Polo waited.

Okay, Ray, what would you like to know? Emily was mocking him slightly.

Polo said straight faced, "This is 1966, how can you have a 1967 automobile?"

"What are you talking about? It was built in 1966, as a 1967 model."

"Think this through Emily; It was built in 1966, and we're in '66, it's a 1966 model."

"God, Ray, you can be exasperating!"

She turned her nose up at him in false disdain, "I'm not having a good time, Mr. Polo, and I'm going to go home if you keep this up one minute longer!"

She tried to keep her tone severe, yet burst out with a belly laugh, "I mean it, Ray; you're really a terrible person."

She spoke loudly, people in other tables turned, "Sorry folks, I was just kidding."

She turned back to him; scarlet faced, whispering, "Ray, this is entirely your fault."

"Me? I'm not the one shouting at the top of her lungs. Typical woman."

"Don't you typical woman me, either."

She was not going to be provoked further, putting on her schoolteacher voice, "Mister Polo, if you wish to have the pleasure of my company further this evening, you will refrain from your boorish behavior and act in a more civilized manner."

"I understand, Miss Sinclair. I will do nothing to further upset you."

"Thank you sir. See that you remember that. Now, what would you like to discuss?"

"I would like, teacher, to discuss whether you have had the chance to, or whether you have not had the chance to, decide your decision … or not."

"Without doubt, Ray, that's the most mangled English sentence my ears have ever had the misfortune to listen to. See, I can mangle a sentence too."

"I'm trying to keep it light, Hon." The Hon slipped out. Polo had no idea how it jumped out, and though Emily took notice, she glossed over it, becoming serious.

"Ray, I've given Dad's offer a lot of thought. It's great offer and I've been pro and contra on it. It comes down to this; I love my teaching job. I'm helping kids, and they need me. It's a wonderful feeling to know you're wanted. I'm that simple. I grew up with money, Ray. Even now, I don't want for it.

When I get my inheritance next year, I'll be well off. That's the straight truth. So all I'm giving up is position and power. I don't need either. My father has given me almost everything I've ever wanted and I'm sorry I can't do what he wants. It would make him happy, yes, but at my expense. Life's a turmoil right now, you know that, Ray, and it's only my job and you that have stopped me from going off the deep end. I know you're not sorry I'm turning down Dad's offer, so I know I'm not disappointing you. I appreciate everything you're doing and I hope I never loose you as a friend, because I'll always be your friend."

Emily hesitated, eyes downcast, "Kind of long winded, huh, Ray?"

"Not long winded, just frank. You don't want to hurt your father. It's your main concern. Apart from that, you're at an age where you're finding your way. It isn't easy to go against a parent. That happened to me years ago. I think you've made the right decision and I hope I've not influenced you too much."

"Ray, you're not much younger than my father,"

Polo didn't need that reminder.

"But you see things more clearly. You understand me and I don't doubt you knew the decision I would make even when I told you about the offer. You did, didn't you?"

"I guess I did. Anyhow, let's celebrate this decision and your birthday."

They talked on about her teaching, the horse, his upcoming trip to Miami and the commissioner retiring.

"See, Ray, you might have gotten that position!"

"I'm sure I wouldn't have. The Mayor has that position going to a politician."

"That's not fair!"

"Christ, don't get me going on what's fair."

"I'm sorry. What else is going on?"

"Well, kid, I done gone and brung you this." Polo handed her a small wrapped present.

"A gift! Gee, Ray; you didn't have to give me something!" The little girl in her opened the gift, a gold charm bracelet with five gold letters dangling from it.

"What do the letters signify?"

"E for Emily. R is for Regis, your college. P for Paul. D for Dad. And B for Bismarck."

Tears brimmed, "My God, that's the most thoughtful gift I've ever received."

Emily continued staring at the bracelet for a few moments, "The R and the P are also going to stand for Ray Polo."

"Thanks, kid."

Polo swallowed hard. Emily could see it, and knew he didn't like being that way. She lifted her head in mock disdain, "The bracelet is very nice, but daddy bought me a silver 230SL Mercedes Benz convertible with a five speed stick."

Polo was startled, then roared, "You *are not* a lady, Emily. You *are* a nasty little brat!"

It was Polo's turn to look at the patrons and apologize.

Emily jumped up, "No problem everyone, this is my sugar daddy. He just bought me a new Mercedes. "

She leaned over and kissed him on the lips. The people around them clapped. One of the women shouting, "Go for it lady!"

Polo felt goofy, whispering, "I didn't buy you that car and I've never been this embarrassed in my life."

"You? I'm the one who should be saying that! God, I hope no one recognizes me."

"I've got an idea, Emily. Why don't we be quiet and eat?"

They talked about Polo's trip. "Watch out for hookers, Ray. They multiply in Miami."

She spoke more of her meeting the day previously with her father to tell him she was not going to go back to college and wanted to remain at Torton, her school. After her father said he understood he handed her keys to the car, having had it delivered to the Correction Center with plates and insurance. She told Ray her father said he would take care of her old car. Someone around the Center could use it.

"And, Ray, you know? I'll be damned if he doesn't seem okay with where he is."

As they stood at Emily's Mercedes ready to say goodbye, she asked, "Nothing about Paul?"

"Excepting for an emergency, he's to have no outside contact of any type for four months. He'll be released at the end of February next year."

"Could you find out anything about how he's doing?"

"Emily, you know better than I. Palton House's boot camp style and that's not the way they like to do it, according to Paul's parole officer. I suppose I could ask Samuel how we find out how it's going."

"If it's not asking too much, would you?"

"Okay, I'll check when I get back from Miami."

Polo opened Emily's car door as three female patrons from the restaurant drove past. One rolled down her window and shouted, "If that's the car your sugar daddy bought you lady, hang on to him for dear life!"

Ray and Emily parted, feeling foolish and laughing.

Chapter

Fourteen

Boston Police Headquarters, Commissioner's office. Coming in to pick up his flight tickets and itinerary, Polo knew Commissioner Kearney would have last minute advice concerning Eddy Murray, the Southie pol.

When a meeting Kearney was holding ended, and the door to the conference room opened, out came the Mayor of Boston, along with the Boston Police Department Superintendent, his Assistant, and lastly, Commissioner Kearney.

No one was smiling.

They gave Polo a courteous hello, and continued to the elevator with, strained goodbyes all around. When they were gone, Commissioner Kearney motioned for Polo to follow him into his office and close the door.

Kearney's face was beet red, "He wants me out in two weeks damn it! He wants me out in *two weeks*!"

Kearney flopped into his chair and stared at Polo for an endless minute. Polo sat and studied the anger clinging to Kearney's face.

"You'll be out sooner if you have a stroke, Walt."

"You're right. No sense blowing a fuse at my age. I understand the mayor's problem; he has an outstanding set of proposals to get through the House and Senate. It's that God damned Murray who can block the bill, and he will in the House, if he doesn't get what he wants, and he wants my job as his payoff. The Mayor's bill comes up in two weeks, and Murray will vote his group yes, *if* he gets a written confirmation in two days and named Commissioner immediately following the bill's passage. It's disgusting what the Mayor has to do to get programs past these little tin gods. I know, it's nothing new. Spiteful cliques hold up government programs that can benefit a helluva lot of people. It's always been this way damn it, except Murray has no command experience. He doesn't know diddlysquat about managing a carnival cop, never mind the Boston Police Department. My sweat rebuilt the BPD over fifteen years and this will take morale right down the hopper. You saw the faces on my superintendents as they left. No matter how I try to prevent it, this information will trickle down through the ranks. Christ, the patronage that guy will spread around. Ah, hell, what's the use of everything we've done?"

Kearney fell back in his chair, "And speaking of Murray, do you know what the little shit's done now? You'll love this, Polo. He changed his flight ticket to earlier today. He's gone to Miami, even though the Mayor wanted you to go with him tomorrow."

Polo saw a glimmer of good come out of this information and smiled.

"Don't think you're off the hook, Ray. Get your ass down there and check on him."

Polo got up, affecting a Jimmy Cagney, tough guy appearance, "I've friends in Miami, what do you say to having him disappear."

"Not a bad idea, although don't say it here," Kearney said wryly, "Murray might have had Internal Affairs bug the joint already."

Polo stared at Kearney with a half smile, half-serious expression.

"You never know Ray, you never know."

Polo checked into The National Hotel in the historic section of Miami. Historical sections of municipalities usually mean worn or seedy. The National however, lived up to a pristine reputation of style. It's Art Deco building and furnishings were flawless, with service to match. When Polo signed in at 9:30 PM, he asked if an Edward Murray was registered. Informed Murray had checked in, Polo asked the clerk to ring his room. As there was no answer, he left a message he was in room 107 or, if not there, look in the hotel's lounge until eleven.

In his room, Polo unpacked then called his former Boston PD coworker, Sal Fanara.

"Is this DPSDSMDC?"

"Polo, you're still a nut case!"

"Hey, Sal, I'm only trying to show respect. How's it going?"

"Good, Ray. When you called yesterday and said you were coming I set up a get together after tomorrow's seminar. Drinks and BS stories. I want you to meet a couple of my men who asked how I got my raspy voice. I told them about the punk stepping on my throat while you were figuring out how to release the safety on your revolver. They want to meet you; said you should have taken longer with the safety."

Polo laughed, Fanara had humor like his own. It was the reason they were together for three years without the blowups between many other police officers. Polo invited him to the National's lounge. Fanara said he was twenty miles away on the other side of Miami, and Polo wasn't that good a friend to drive over at this time of night. Polo smirked, saying Fanara was taking up too much of his drinking time yakking. They agreed to meet after the seminar and hung up. Polo wandered into the lounge and sat at the bar, nursing a scotch. Two other senior police officers from Pittsburg were sitting near him and the three fell into questioning the value of the upcoming seminars. The officer's were there mainly for a few days of sun, booze and getting away from their precinct ... and, of course, perhaps some broads.

At 11:00 PM Polo slid off his stool, stretching to ease his creaky bones. He heard his name paged. A phone call. Polo guessing it was Eddy Murray.

"Ray, its Sal."

Surprised, Polo could only ask, "Yes, Sal. What's up?"

"Do you know a guy called Edward Murray? Says he's a big Boston politician."

"I know him; he's the guy I'm supposed to meet. How do you know him?"

"I don't. All I know is right now he's at Magnolia Street, under arrest."

"What in the hell happened?"

"Look, I'm at home; got the call this guy is yelling bloody murder. Says he's been roughed up and arrested on no grounds. He used your name. The station called me before trying to locate you. I told them I knew where you were and we would be there as soon as we could. Grab a cab right now to Magnolia Street. I'll meet you at the station."

Polo arrived, Sal Fanara already there. As Fanara was Sheriff of Metro Dade, his officers were fully aware he absorbed everything they said and always required accurate reports with no vapid thinking or errors. Fanara saw Polo and gestured him not to come closer as he continued listening to his officer's statements. Signaling Polo two minutes later to follow him, they settled into office chairs behind closed doors.

"Well, Ray, seems your buddy got himself into a little trouble."

"He's not my buddy and how much trouble?"

"Huh. If he's not your buddy, then he's in a whole lot of trouble."

"Tell me."

"First, what's the story? Because I knew him back when I headed up the Framingham PD a few years ago."

Polo delivered the main points. Mayor Collin's needed Murray's voting block in the House or Senate to get his programs passed. Fanara knew Commissioner Kearney, and could see he was getting the proverbial bum's rush, so Murray could take over the Boston PD. That was all Fanara needed to dislike Murray even more, because he remembered Kearney as a straight shooter.

"Okay, Ray, now this is what I got. You know I left the Boston PD to be Chief in Framingham. When I was first getting my feet wet, Murray was arrested for soliciting a prostitute. I found out later two patrolmen caught him. Long story short, the prostitute dumbed up and the two patrolmen transferred to the State House as sergeants. It was too late when I found out, so regretfully, I let it slide, my mistake. If you remember Lenny Robertson on the Boston PD, he went to Attleboro as a lieutenant. He told me our very same Ed Murray bought his way out of a hit and run DWI, when a witness wouldn't testify. A week after that the witness was running around town in a new Chrysler. I'm telling you, Ray, the guy is toxic."

"Tell me, Sal, what can you hang on him?"

"Soliciting, drunkenness, disorderliness in a public place. *And* resisting arrest, with or without violence, take your pick. The reason I say that is Officer Joan Nickels, my decoy, said Murray was slightly difficult to handle until he saw her backup. Then, Murray backed off and allowed the cuffs be put on. When she was placing Murray into the squad car, Nickels *accidentally* smacked Murray's head on the roof frame, so it's a tossup as to who did what. So now, let's get to the point. You don't want Murray as Commissioner and I'm with you on that. You want his votes to get stuff through the city government. So we do what?"

"Threaten him."

"Okay with me. How?"

"What's Murray doing now?"

"Trying to sober up and calling for you and an attorney."

"Tell you what; go tell him I'm on my way. Act real tough. Explain if he wants an attorney, then you'll make sure a reporter will be following along behind. That should stop him from doing anything for a while. Threaten to charge him with everything you've told me as well and send an official Letter of Complaint to the Boston Office of the Attorney General, stating the same facts.

His chewing on that info will give us time to figure out a plan to nail the son of a bitch."

Fanara returned after five minutes, "He's a snotty little bastard, but I got his attention when I mentioned reporters, the charges, and the letter. He's starting to get rattled."

"Good, that's the way we want him. Let him stew a while longer."

Polo stared down, disgusted with the prisoner. Murray, had difficulty focusing.

"Who the hell are you?"

"I'm the traveling companion you didn't think you needed, and it turns out you couldn't last two days without screwing up."

The statement dawned on Murray, "You're Polo, huh? You're a cop; get me out of here, away from these southern shitheads."

"They hear talk like that and you'll be on a chain gang tomorrow, cleaning streets."

"What the hell is going on? First, that other asshole threatening me with all sorts of crap, and now you? Let's get out of here. Bail me out. You'd better wise up fast, Polo, 'cause I'm going to be your boss in a few days and your badge and pension will follow you down the shithole after I'm through with you."

Polo started laughing. "You think you scare me? That other asshole you're referring to is the Sheriff of Metro Dade County. 850 officers, and you're one cheap punk who'd better wise up. Fanara can call any judge right now, and you'll be in a swamp tonight, serving thirty to sixty days. Don't even think of bail, it won't happen. You'll be dodging gators and none of your crony's will be able to do a thing. You're a God damned fool Murray, thinking you can bully your way through this town. Believe me, you're going to find out real fast Miami cops don't like Boston loud mouth assholes coming down here, thinking they're big shots and can get away with anything they want, including propositioning undercover cops and resisting arrest."

Murray was sobering fast, more nervous by the minute, the start of a complete turnaround, "What do we do, Polo? I can't serve time. That would cause me big problems up north. This is crazy! Can't you do something?"

"Maybe, but "we" aren't in trouble, you are, and I don't like you, so why should I?"

Murray's was thinking fast, "I can do big things for you. Get me out of here and I'll make you Chief of the State House Police. You get a lot of pull out of there."

Polo turned to leave, "Not interested."

Murray paled, "Don't leave! What do you want? Name it!"

Polo kept walking, "I'll think of something, First, I've got to make sure the sheriff hasn't called the judge to send your ass to the gators."

Murray was shaking as Polo left smirking.

Polo sat with Fanara, "Cripe, Ray, I heard you shouting. That's one scared ass there."

"Sal, it helps to be big and mean and loom over people. I'm going to let him sweat for a while, then we'll see. First thing is to speak with Officer Nickels."

"I filled her in. Once I told her that jerk wants to be Top Cop in Boston and we're cooking up a scheme to stop him, she's cool with it. It's our call. Whatever we want to do she'll go along, says it sounds like more fun than going to court with him."

"Great. Tell her I said to give her a raise."

"I don't think so, Ray, but I'll see she gets better duty than she has right now."

"Okay, Sal, what I want you to do is to draw up an Arrest Report listing everything you can charge him with. I'll take it from there."

Fanara returned with the charges, signed, dated and stamped by Officer Nickels, Officer Britt, who saw Murray giving Nickels a hard time, and Sheriff Fanara. It was forty minutes since Polo left Murray. When he and Fanara entered the cell, the prisoner was in the initial stages of a severe hangover.

Polo set the general tenor of the meeting, "Murray, this is Sheriff Sal Fanara of the Metro Dade Police Department, Top Dog. He's the guy you called an asshole."

111

Fanara hadn't known what Murray had called him, making a noise strangely like a growl. The growl was involuntary. Startled, Murray shrunk into his chair. Polo then read from the Arrest Report and Charge Sheet. Murray's eyes bulged, he receded deeper into the chair, panic struck.

Sheriff Fanara spat the words, "Mr. Murray, I'm all for sending your sorry ass to Penal Unit Fourteen down in the glades."

Although no such place existed, Murray believed everything in his present condition.

"Polo thinks he can change my mind if he can make a deal with you."

Murray bit at the possibility, "I'll listen I'll listen. Tell me what you want."

Polo laid it on the line, "You're going to decline the Boston Police position, and you're going to fast track the Mayor's programs, ASAP."

Murray was staggered; his mind confused, wondering how Polo knew about the deal. Who else was in on this? He sweated, squeezing his hands. Had he been setup? If Sheriff Fanara spilled the information to Boston television and papers, even with Boston's reputation for keeping dubious politicians in office, it could possibly ruin his career, if not his marriage.

Murray, however, was known as a back room dealmaker. He wasn't going to give up anything easily. Better to stall and try to work out something more to his advantage.

"I don't think so. Let's hear something else."

Fanara got ugly, "You want something else? I'll give you something else. Let's go!"

"Go where? You can't take me anywhere! I'll take my chances with an attorney."

Fanara laughed, "Right now I'm only going to charge you with drunkenness, so no attorney. I've got the judge's writ right here." He waved a paper in Murray's face, "You're mine for at least thirty days! You think I screw around with little weasels like you? You're mine."

Fanara called out to the front office. "Nickels bring a car around to the side door!"

Polo interjected, "Sal, Wait a minute, wait a minute! Take it easy. Let's try to work something out."

Fanara was adamant, "He said no, he's going."

His back to Murray, Polo fought not to smile, "You know he really didn't say no deal, Sal."

"Close enough. He thinks he can play games with me. We'll see how he likes the games the guy's play in the glades."

They heard the squad car screech up to the side door. Fanara grabbed Murray's arm. Polo threw up his hands, hopeless. Murray clung to his chair. The dreadful stories and the movies about Florida's prisons flooded his brain. He was going into shock, scared witless. Being physically pulled out of the chair he screamed, "ALL RIGHT, ALL RIGHT!"

"All right what!" The sheriff still gripped him.

"I'll do what you want! I will!"

Fanara pushed him back into the chair, still acting angry, "Too bad. You like prostitutes? You'd have had a real good time where I was sending you."

Polo and Fanara spent the next hour writing an ironclad agreement, stating all the points: Murray's decision to pass on the Commissioner position and his being assertive in helping the Mayor's programs. Further, he acknowledged and admitted the charges against him, understanding the charges were held in abeyance until, or if, such time he should attempt to renege on the agreement. Last, it stated Murray had not been coerced in any manner.

Polo and Fanara knew the last sentence was ludicrous but threw it in anyway. Who on earth would believe a person signing this agreement had not been coerced?

They went back to Murray's cell, handing him the agreement. They waited. He looked up, "No coercion? That's sort of gilding the lily isn't it?"

When there was no answer, Murray signed. Polo and Fanara read Murray's mind, sign now, get the hell out of Florida, then ignore it when he got home. Therefore, after the signing by all three, Murray was assured that if he even *thought* about changing his mind Fanara would blitz the Boston media with the signed confession and demand extradition. Polo reminded Murray, as if he didn't already know, the Massachusetts Attorney General couldn't stand him, and would be quite happy to generate the needed paperwork returning him to Florida. Fanara added he would welcome him back; he'd have a nice damp cot waiting,

Two officers took Murray to his hotel to pack, then to the airport, where they were to wait with him until the morning flight. The officers walked him down the jet way and stayed there until the aircraft was pushed back. Murray thought their attention typical of stupid cops, he wanted out of Miami more than they did.

Polo, Fanara, Officers Nickels, and Britt relaxed.

"You two should be on stage. Nickels laughed, "That was the finest good cop, bad cop performance I've ever heard. If you have a class for this in Boston, I'll take in a seminar up there."

They were having a good time. When Fanara growled, Polo commented, he almost laughed and gave them away, "What the hell was that sound anyway, Ken?"

"I don't know where it came from. Just a guttural response when I heard you say Murray called me an asshole."

"Just like shooting fish in a barrel," Polo said, "excepting Murray might have asked to see the form Fanara was waving around, which happened to be the laundry list for the patrolmen's uniforms."

Worse, if Murray had called their bluff on taking him to the shadowy Unit 14 in the glades. Yep, they laughed, "Just like shooting fish in a barrel."

They unwound for another ten minutes then Polo excused himself to call Commissioner Kearney.

It was nearing 3:00 AM. Polo wasn't in the least concerned about phoning Kearney at home. After seven rings, "Who the hell is this? Polo? Christ! Do you know what time it is? Where are you, drunk in Miami?"

"No, not yet. I just had to tell you about a great meeting with your little friend, Eddy Murray. We got a lot of things cleared up, which means that, even as we speak, he'll shortly be on his way back to Boston with his tail between his legs. *And,* he definitely doesn't want your job, *and* he's going do whatever he can to help the Mayor get his programs through."

"What the hell have you done for this sea change in Murray? Nothing too far over the line I hope. In fact, don't tell me," a smile seeping through the Commissioner's words.

"I won't go into it on the phone, Walt. Call the mayor so he doesn't sign the appointment today naming Murray Top Cop."

"Sounds like we owe you the big one, Ray. We'll talk later. I'll call him right now; he won't mind being woken for this. You *are* sure, right?"

"Walt, really now. Have I ever steered you wrong?"

"God, don't bring up all those times. Still, I'll trust you on this despite them."

Polo opted to stay another day, deciding to get together with Fanara and some of his friends. He noted there was a seminar on Problem Solving Teams, formed to prevent Latino, black or white gangs from plaguing city housing projects. These seminars assisted other police forces around the country with various gang problems of their own. Although this subject was not in Polo's job description, he was interested, noticing no other Boston task force group was present.

After a few brews and laughs. he caught the last Northeast flight into Boston, drove to his home and fell exhausted into bed at one in the morning. Too much excitement for this old duff, he thought. But, God, it was fun.

He didn't notice the flashing red light on his phone.

Chapter

Fifteen

S truggling out of bed at 10:30 AM, Polo saw the flashing light on his recorder. At the moment, he wasn't up to listening to messages, or answering them. He hit the head, cleaned up, ate some cereal, yawned a dozen times and sat down. One call.

"Ray. Emily. Paully's gone. Samuel Washington called and said Steven Napier at Palton House told him Paully slipped out. He must have had a spare set of car keys because Napier has the original ones. He's been gone two days. I'm frantic and Dad's furious. Said Paul promised he'd go there and stay until he was well. Dad will cut him out of the Trust completely … I'm sorry, Ray, I'm running off at the mouth. Please, call me when you get back."

Returning the call and getting Emily's recorder, he left a message he'd be at home until noon, then at his office by one. She had both numbers.

Emily didn't call by noon, so Polo went to the office. He laid out the whole Miami scenario for the Commissioner, doing as best he could to play the parts of Sheriff Fanara, Murray and himself. Kearney laughed so hard his open door drew in Superintendent of Police Henry Makkin, and Polo had to start from scratch again. At that point, the Mayor phoned, confirming Polo was right. Murray told him he was no longer interested in the job and one hundred percent behind the Mayor's programs. Quote, unquote. The Mayor thanked Polo, "Anything you need, I'm here."

"Mayor," Kearney took the phone, "this would make a great story for Polo's retirement. Too bad we can't tell it."

The mayor was quick to respond, "It *would* be a great story. Don't you dare tell it."

"Polo," Kearney said, shaking his head, "of all the things you've pulled, you will never top this, no matter how hard you try. And please, don't try."

One of the secretaries poked her head in. "A woman on line 6 for Polo. Wouldn't give her name."

Eyebrows raised, Kearney posed an odd glance, then nodded, excusing Polo.

"Ray, it's Emily. Can you talk?"

"Not really. I can get out of here and be at Barretton by around five. Can we meet at the Hill?"

"I understand, yes. See you there."

Kearney told him to take two vacation days off, "That will make four this year, Polo, and it's only November."

Driving towards the Hill, Polo's mind was on Emily, and the cross in her life, Paul.

Federal Census met him, "What's happening, FC?"

"Oh, you've picked up Emily's nickname for me."

"Why not? Anything going on around here?"

"Emily said you'd be coming by and you already know Paul's AWOL."

Polo got out of the car, asking, "What can you tell me about that pain in the ass."

Federal shook his head, "He wasn't always that way, Mr. Polo. He was as nice as Emily when they were growing up. Couldn't ask for nicer kids. A great family. Going off to college, that's when the problem started. I admit Emily was the more responsible of the two. It was her leaving for Regis that left Paul alone when he went to Brown University. First time they'd been apart that long. You could see the change in one year; she was the same girl, he more withdrawn. We didn't know what was happening, thought it was part of a kid growing up. You know, feeling his oats like we used to say. I was that way, you probably was too. That first summer, he'd up and get in that Jag, give a wave and be gone. Come back after a week, be gone again. Mister Sinclair didn't like it. I know he was concerned, but no one dreamed it was drugs at the time, no one."

FC shifted position. His leg was paining more and painkillers were not helping, the leg and thigh worse each week.

"Sorry, Mr. Polo, now about Paul. Sometime in his second year he was at the house and I heard arguments with him. Emily would be away at college. After the quarrels, Paul would come out, jump in his car and race off. Where? Who knows, no one knew. Right after a blowup between the Mr. and Mrs., he got busted for drugs on some yacht, name of *Down Hill* in Cataumet, on the Cape. Sure was down hill for Paul after that.

Mr. Sinclair asked what I thought he should do. Let Paul take the heat, I said. You know what I mean, Mr. Polo? Kinda teach the kid a lesson. Well, Mr. Sinclair couldn't do that to his son and wangled the kid probation. You see the good that did, don't ya?"

"Sure do, FC. I've seen it in my business so many times I'd want to smack some parents alongside the head with a two by four. Still, I don't have kids so it's hard to say what I'd do if it was my kid. Anyway, how's Emily doing? When she called, she was quite upset."

"Mr. Polo, understand what I'm sayin now. She and Paul's as close as cats to milk, and will be no matter what, twins is like that. She's always watching over him. I'll warn you, Mr. Polo, don't you go trying to help her and leave Paul out, or you'll make one big mistake. She'll shut you out. I'm telling you this because I know Emily kinda needs your help. That's okay, as long as you knows your *position*, if ya knows what I mean."

"Back off, FC. I like Emily as a friend and friends should help friends. My job puts me in that *position*."

FC lapsed into northern Yankee, "I'm just sayin' what I'm sayin'."

"Your sayins' are understood, FC."

"Okay, Mr. Polo, okay. Be careful when you see her."

Polo let it go at that, "Jesus, he muttered, "that guy gets under my skin. Trouble is he's right. And what did he mean, be careful?"

Emily met him at the door, "That was quite a conversation you had with FC, Ray, find something in common to talk about?"

"Yes damn it, we did."

Emily couldn't follow the remark and from Polo's look, didn't question further.

There was brewed coffee and Polo appreciated the break from FC.

"Anything new from Paul?"

"Not a thing. I'm worried, Ray. I've taken a leave of absence from the school."

She seemed oddly at ease, almost relaxed. Polo caught on quickly.

"What are you on?"

"What are you talking about?"

"Come on, Emily, what are you popping?"

She dropped into a chair, "Jesus, I can't hide a damn thing from you can I? Ray, I couldn't help it. I was a wreck worrying about Dad and Paul, and you weren't here. I needed something to quiet my nerves and I found some of mum's old pills."

"Damn it, let me see them."

She reached into a cabinet and passed him the bottle.

"This is a prescription drug. I don't know it by name, but whatever the hell it is, its fifty milligrams. How many did you have? When did you take them? How do you feel?"

"Take it easy, Ray, I had one about two hours ago, and I feel fine, a little mellow."

Although he was ready to take her to the hospital, Polo realized it would cause a scene. Thinking more sensibly, he called the number of the pharmacy on the bottle. They verified the pills were a moderate tension reliever and the dosage would simply relax a person, definitely causing sleep.

"Jeez, Ray, talk about Paully being as nervous as a pregnant fox in a forest fire, that's you, maybe you should take one."

Emily laid her hand on the back of his. He didn't feel foolish. He was alarmed. The more she looked at him, the more she realized it, "Thanks for the concern, Ray. I didn't realize how much you ..."

She didn't know how to continue.

Polo shifted in his chair, "Instead of another coffee, would it be too much to ask for a scotch with a splash of water to calm my old nerves?"

She came alive, "Not a beer? Cripe, Ray, and you used to be such a cheap date."

Emily had to talk about her brother, "Anything you can do? Dad and I are frantic."

"Not really, kid, that's up to the parole department, and they're too damn busy trying to keep track of child molesters, ex cons, women beaters and every other nut case let out on early parole. A probation violation by a non-violent ex-druggie won't make the front burner."

Polo could see that as much as Emily tried, she was losing her focus. Before she lost it completely, he sent her to bed after saying he would overnight at a motel and see, or call, in the morning. He doubted she would remember a word, and he took the pills on the way out. He stopped on the stairs, "If I take these, what if she finds her mother's stronger pills?" He replaced them and walked to his car. Lesser of the two evils, he felt. For a moment, he thought of the pills. Strange, Mrs. Sinclair was so far gone mentally; yet she'd been given only moderate level tension relievers. Perhaps they were older pills Emily found, or taken with something else. His thoughts were interrupted finding Federal Census fixing trellis vines in the dark.

"Waiting for me, FC?"

"Wanted to see if Miss Emily is all right, she seemed a little shaky earlier."

"She'll be all right. Took one of her mother's pills by accident, a mild one. Put her to sleep, that's all."

"By accident, huh." Federal Census walked off.

"FC, we're on the same page with her, okay?"

Polo spent part of the next day with Lieutenant Ken Collin, discussing his concern over not bringing his police officers together as a cohesive unit. Polo was curious about him, asking how he became a cop. He was a former Golden Glove boxer, Collin stated, and when the service grabbed him, he became a Military Police officer, sent to Vietnam.

Wounded twice, he mentioned … once, by a knife wielding drunken sergeant. He beat him badly to get even. The next wound, by a Viet Cong sniper, tore through his knee and out his foot; no question of saving it. The blessing was, Ken explained, the wound got him home, even though he lost the leg below the knee. Polo was surprised. He never knew. Collin walked with only the slightest limp, barely noticeable unless a person was looking for it.

Polo mentioned he had some vacation time coming and he'd see if he couldn't help. Collin wanted to hear that.

When Polo met again with Emily, she had not taken any pills. Saying that only under dire stress would she take one again. He told her there was nothing wrong with popping a pill now and then to take the pressure off. They were better than jumping off the Mystic Bridge.

He mentioned there was little he could do until Paul showed himself and even then, if he did show, not much could be done. Polo said he intended to follow-up with Samuel Washington and anyone Samuel might suggest.

By the time Polo reached his condo, it was nine at night. He was weary, feeling the years he had punished his body. He started to climb the stairs. Half way up, he convinced himself he was looking forward to retiring. He didn't give a moment's thought to the vehicle driving slowly past. Two shots, a sharp pain in this arm, then a burning in his thigh. Polo spun around ducking, grabbing the handrail with one hand, his revolver with the other. Hunting where the gunshots came from, he saw a vehicle, with an arm extended from a rear window. Another shot sung past him. As his wounded leg collapsed, he snapped off three rounds in the general direction of the vehicle as it sped away, lurching side-to-side, tires spinning. He lost his balance and fell, his hip striking the edge of the stair as he tumbled onto the driveway. Neighbors saw the vehicle and rushed to aid him as he sat bleeding, cursing a blue streak. Someone called 911. In two minutes, four squad cars screeched to a stop, an ambulance close behind. Clothes cut away, tourniquets applied, drip needles inserted. With difficulty, due to his size and inability to help, Polo was struggled into the ambulance and delivered, over painfully bumpy streets. to Emergency at New England Baptist Hospital.

Within minutes, the hospital's Triage staff stripped Polo, wheeled him into the operating room, and surgeons huddled over him. Despite considerable pain, the wounds were not life threatening. One bullet had torn the outer flesh of his left triceps and exited with little damage, the other lodged in the flesh of his left thigh.

X-rays showed minor damage, with the exception of a hairline fracture of the pelvis, caused from his fall. That explained the severe pain he was experiencing.

With Polo sedated, the remaining bullet came out, the wounds treated. Placed in Intensive Care and sedated even more, the pain in his pelvis was still severe.

The next morning, he woke to the Commissioner staring at him and smiling, "What's new, Ray?"

"Can't think of a thing, Walt." He slurred before drifting off into drug-induced sleep once more.

The following day they moved him to a private room. He spoke haltingly to Kearney, a few superintendents, officers, including Ken Collin, nurses and Emily. He recalled not one moment of it later.

The third day, with the drug dosage reduced slightly, he was lucid. When Kearney and Superintendent Makkin arrived, he could make sense of their conversation. Polo felt lucky, Kearney thought otherwise.

"I don't think they intended to kill you." Kearney explained.

"For Christ's sake, Walt, they hit me twice."

"I know, but when you have time to think about it more, keep this in mind. Number one, if they wanted to kill you they would have ambushed you when you were getting out of your car. Think, shooting at a person from a moving vehicle is not conducive to accuracy. Number two; they used a .22 caliber pistol."

"A lousy .22?"

"That's right, small caliber. Not likely to strike fear or kill anyone unless it's in a vital area. Since it was small caliber, we thought it might be someone sending you a warning, then again, we figured it was more of a get even."

Polo tried to let the words sink in. Too complicated with a mind still on drugs.

"Who'd want to get even, Walt?"

"Good Lord," Kearney laughed, "you must be still whacked out. I'll bet there's any number of guys would do that, however, only one person comes to mind."

Polo's blank expression persisted. Kearney stared at him, almost shouting, "Jesus Christ, Ray, Eddy Murray!"

Polo closed his eyes, unperturbed. "Maybe he helped me make up my mind to retire."

"Man! You *must* be high on drugs. The Ray Polo I know would be raising hell to go after Murray. Although, thinking about what you just said. I didn't know you were giving serious thought towards retiring. Not a bad idea. But wait until you're better, and off drugs. One thing we should discuss though; is the quality of your shooting. We found the car you shot five blocks away. Bullet hole in the trunk. Rear window shot out. No sign of blood. Car was stolen. But hey, at least you hit the car."

"If I recall through this fog, I fired three shots. Either the last one went into the blacktop or into someone."

"We checked the hospitals; no one's been in for gunshot, so who's to say. And now I guess we're leaving; you're off to La La Land again."

After a few days in the hospital, Polo had pills on schedule to stand the pain in his pelvis, yet still allow to him to keep up a decent conversation. He noticed every time he looked there was an officer about, sometimes three or four standing in the corridor or opening his door to let visitors enter. He especially noticed their lingering a moment for small talk when Emily arrived.

So now, Polo thought, Emily had a mother murdered, a father in jail for killing her, a brother on the run for drugs and a good friend in the hospital, shot. Girl, if pills help you through it all, go for it. I am.

The fractured pelvis tormented him more than any past injury. Not one of a dozen other breaks, including a separated shoulder and fractured ribs, came close to matching the pain.

Three weeks of painfully, and slowly, moving from bed to wheelchair to walker to cane, found Polo appreciating the rehab technicians helping him become mobile.

The mayor stopped by to see how he was improving. Sal Fanara flew up to check him out, making a few snide remarks concerning his age and lack of agility. Numerous other officers dropped by along with a few neighbors from his condominium. When Kearney and Makkin stopped in for a chat, they mentioned the police officers. There were at least two present in the corridor at any time, day and night. It was not duty; the officers volunteered, making sure he was never left unguarded. The Commissioner wanted Polo to know. Towards the end of their meeting Kearney questioned, "Okay, Ray, I know you're going to do something to Eddy Murray, what is it?"

Polo gave an innocent look, "Me? What gave you that idea?"

"Come on, Ray, give."

Polo, stalled, finally admitting, "You know me too well, Walt. I got thinking, Murray's got that new Buick Riviera and I thought maybe, you know, just maybe, I'd aerate it a bit some night."

"Not smart, Ray, especially if you're thinking retirement. Don't lose your pension doing something stupid. It could only escalate until someone got hurt, or dead. Then, all hell would break loose."

"Ah, excuse me? I seem to recall someone we all know and love has already been hurt and is now undergoing some God damn painful rehab."

"Who? Oh you? Yes, you're right, can't deny that. But here's what I want. The Mayor's programs are through the senate so Murray can't hurt him. Say we make a bunch of copies of his confession in Miami. Then we write in bold letters, Things could Get Worse and send them by US Mail, UPS and FedEx to his home and office every day for a week. I think he'll get the message, sweat a lot and think twice before trying anything again.

"Christ, Walt, that's boring and really wimpy. We were a little more direct in the old days. We'd pop him. On top of that, he'll think I retired because of him."

"The old days are gone, Ray, and we're going with them. We're dinosaurs. What the hell do you care what the little punk thinks? I'm asking you to do this as a favor to me."

"That's not playing fair, Walt." He grudgingly nodded his head. Over the next few weeks, he rehabilitated his arm. It was mainly the pelvis that pained him constantly. Not much could be done, other than allowing it time to heal. He was not a good patient, and he was big, so naturally his healing took twice as long. He got about with his car, a walker and cane. As it was the left side of his pelvis, he could still work the gas and brake with an automatic transmission. He had scores of sick time accumulated and untaken holidays, so Kearney told him not to work any more, knowing Polo's decision to retire at the end of the year. Kearney was disappointed, although knowing it was for the best. The wounds and debilitation, coupled with Polo's size, weight and smoking, precluded any thought of a leave of absence. Both men considered his retirement simply the best of the few choices.

A bright spot came when Lieutenant Collin asked for assistance training his expanding police force. New officers had been added since the town was growing. The request allowed Polo's placement on loan, for whatever time required up, until 30 December, his retirement date.

Emily slipped in and out of his life during these weeks. She often made his day when she visited, and he knew her sprits lifted as well. She spoke of the transformation in her father. He had become concerned, upon learning of the prisoner's poor literacy level and lack of basic education when released. The foremost problem and where her father felt he could help, was the inability of the men to read or, if they could read, to comprehend. Her father had her list various remedial primers and ordered them fifty at a time, charged to his personal account. The Center gave him meeting rooms and with help from Emily, he learned to setup study courses for the prisoners. Her greatest joy was her father's renewal. He grew with a purpose, a reason to emerge from his lethargy. Going from cell to cell, teaching one person or twenty, he motivated his student's to improve.

The proudest moment, for Emily, had been when the Superintendent of the Correctional Center, Oskar Hines, stated, jokingly of course, he wished Sinclair had received a twenty-year sentence. Then he could teach there for twenty more years.

Sinclair had smiled at the comment, saying perhaps after his release he might return to help.

Polo pondered Sinclair's request for a December 1 meeting. This could be trouble over his involvement with Emily, Polo concluded, and called her. She knew nothing and it annoyed her that her father would impose on her personal relationships. Polo told her to back off, say nothing, until they knew what her father had on his mind.

The meeting was not cordial. The two men barely managed to respect one another. They skirmished, Polo holding himself in check, on edge, awaiting the reason for the meeting to emerge,

127

ready to tell Sinclair off. When the reason came, it came as a shock.

"Mister Polo, I understand you were ambushed and shot twice. I see you are having problems getting about with a cane. I apologize if I have inconvenienced you at this time. However, I do want to pose a question."

Here it comes, Polo thought. Courteous presentation, nevertheless, here it comes.

"I understand you are retiring from the Police Department at the end of the year."

It was not the remark Polo expected, "News travels fast. That is correct."

"I wonder if you would consider becoming the Chief of Police for Barretton."

Surprised, Polo struggled. The last thing in the world he expected. Trying to get his bearings, "Would you please clarify, just what you mean?"

Sinclair smiled, "You've every right to be surprised, although it's really quite simple. I'm asking if you are interested in becoming the Police Chief for Barretton on January 1st."

"No. I wouldn't be interested."

"I thought not, although I felt there was no harm in asking."

Polo remained confused. What was this person asking him?

In other words, Sinclair had the say in offering him the Chief's job. Make sense of it. He's in jail and running the town.

"Mister Polo, may I call you, Ray?"

"If I can call you, Parker."

"Fair enough … Ray. I want to apologize, which is difficult for me. Regarding my daughter, I believe you have treated her in a courteous manner, which I admit, I did not expect. However, Emily has vouched for you. Your respect for her, as well as your efforts in trying to assist my son, has caused me to discount some of my negative, shall I say, impulses, concerning your motives. I apologize for my mistake and hope you will accept my apology."

"Of course … Parker." Polo was mentally shaking his head. This guy's out of 1910, for Christ sake. As far as being a gentleman, I hope he doesn't mention that to anyone. Paul? Hell, if they stuffed him in a sack, they'd be better off. I know blood is thick in family, especially twins, but, Jesus, get over it!

"With that said, Ray," Sinclair continued, "I've had time in here to think about the future of Barretton, where it will be in ten years. It is becoming sadly obvious the town will be a bedroom community for Springfield and Worcester before we know it. That will mean growth. Uncontrolled growth, the way our zoning is at present. Growth is inevitable, of course. Nevertheless, it's our obligation not let it run amuck. I've had the selectmen over here, as well as concerned citizens, to discuss the long-term health of our town. I won't bother you about uncontrolled growth, high-rise condominiums, heavy industry and so on. These are not here yet, but their on the horizon. The fact it has not invaded us by now is an advantage and allows us to get our ducks in a row, as the unique saying goes. We've decided to present the townspeople with a hypothesis on where the population of the town will be in ten years. Then, present a referendum on city management, whether it be Charter Government, Town Manager, Selectmen, Mayor or another type. These referendums will be presented by sources with no affiliation to Barretton. Then it will be up to the people.

The town's nine thousand at present. We project it to grow at a rate of three thousand people a year, a thirty-three percent increase. Think of it. Of course this includes children and they require schools and teachers, pensions plus other services. All this means serious growing pains if we are to prevent Barretton from going through what is happening to other towns. I mean those towns ill prepared for growth, towns overpowered by developers.

The reason for my rather lengthy dissertation, Ray, is all this requires a police force, growing with the town, not just willy-nilly by adding an officer here and an officer there. I know Ken Collin has asked you to give him a hand and that's fine as far as it goes. Except, if you will excuse my being frank, giving a hand is not enough. We must prepare for the future, *now*. I have spoken to Lieutenant Collin. Our hope, and all the others, is if you *will not* accept the position of Chief, would you accept another leadership position? It would be to develop and oversee programs and goals for two years, all of which would be to create a viable police force for the town, now and for the future."

Sinclair paused, waiting for a response. Polo nodded, silent.

"If you agree, I'm sure all involved will concur. It will be a paid position as Superintendent, in complete charge, for one year followed by a consultant position for another year. Your housing and living costs, town expensed. The salary is open for discussion. Initially the offer is a thirty percent increase over your present salary with the Boston Police Department, plus a twenty percent performance bonus each year.

As we hope to be ahead of the curve with our police department, there will be times where we have more than necessary in officers and equipment. You determine that balance. The bank will loan the funds with a no interest bond, payable in ten years. That will include funding for a new police station, vehicles, additional officers, training, and so forth. Of course, this will not happen overnight, but phased in, in stages as we grow and you see fit. You will have oversight responsibilities for personnel, budget and performance guidelines, which you will set for the department."

Sinclair stopped for a moment. Polo gave no indication of his thoughts on an offer so unexpected.

"Ray, you will be answerable only to the type of government the citizen's chose. Should you resign or be terminated, with or without cause, your contract will be honored for the remainder of the two years, minus bonus or bonuses of course. I want you to know I do have one personal concern, which should be on the table. You have a reputation of being fair, although rough. If the, may I say, *edge* could be taken off the toughness, it would help in a small town."

Polo nodded, not the least embarrassed, and still uncommitted.

"Do you have any questions?"

"Not at present, other than when do you want a response?"

"First, I want you to know this offer is not being made to anyone else. If you turn it down, we may look to some other person. However, you come with excellent credentials from your superiors and peers, as well as my daughter. I wish a response within a week."

"I've understood *everything* you've said Parker, and I will say your offer is quite attractive. Surprising, nevertheless, attractive. I'll respond within the week."

"Before you leave, Ray, there is one other thing I want to ask. Is there anything you can do to find my son? I will pay you to help."

"Parker, save your money. If there were a way to find him, I would help without pay. As I've told Emily, Paul is not a heinous person and no one, not even the parole division, is going to put out any sort of bulletin on him. They're simply not going to expend the limited resources they have chasing him down. I can't utilize departmental resources for that and yes, you could spend a great sum on private detectives and they'd only milk you for money, and you'd get very few, if any, results. It's up to you. Emily has led me to believe he's come back before. However, you both must realize, if he does, he'll spend serious time behind bars, and I don't mean in a cushy place like this. Get this straight, Parker, your money isn't going to help this time."

Sinclair appeared distracted, "I see. I imagine then, Emily and I must adjust for that probability. Aside from that Mr. Polo, I'm sorry ... Ray, please give me your decision at your earliest convenience."

Now *that's* an experience, Polo considered, as he signed out of the Center. Instead of leaving, he asked the internee if Superintendent Hines were available. A quick check and Polo was seated in Oskar Hine's office. Hines was so thin; if Polo had seen him on the street, he would have guessed him a drug addict. Despite the appearance, the handshake was firm, the eyes alert.

"What may I do for you, Detective Polo?"

131

"I really don't know, Superintendent, I've just had a most enlightening talk with Parker Sinclair and I'm a bit befuddled. What do you make of him?"

"I'm glad you asked, I think he is a fine gentleman, doing a lot of good for us here."

"Gentleman or not, if you remember, he murdered his wife."

"It was second degree, extenuating circumstances. A Court decision."

"Does that allow him to have the run of the place?"

"Good day, Mr. Polo."

Polo smiled all the way to his car, "Fun now and then, rattling their cage."

He cruised along, reviewing the meeting. Primary point, Sinclair runs the town. Why not? Gangsters run their operations from federal prisons, why shouldn't one of the good people in a correction center try to improve a little town? Sinclair saying the bank will float the bond, that's BS. That money is coming from him. Offering me the Chiefship, incredible. Must admit though, the other offer sounds damn good. What a way to retire: my own police force for two years at a damn good income.

Then again, when you think of it, if the town hired professional consultants, it would cost them more, and get less. I'd be answerable to no one other than town government. Collin is trainable. Start with him as the nucleus, then the two officers he and I approved, they're definites. Get the three of them in training at the Police Training Academy, moneys no object according to Sinclair, I mean my new friend, Parker. Training, training, training. Be the best! Make all the other towns use us as the standard, get an architectural contest going for the new station, look at other stations; listen to their Chiefs. Get their input. Vehicles ... what's the best type for a small town? A Progressive Budget, man, I hate that crap, except must learn it, rent a CPA, rent an attorney, keep everything legal, the Miranda rights will drive new guys nuts, if I don't first. Sinclair asking me to use less muscle: hell, I hardly shouted at him. Maybe small towns don't need it. Not like Boston.

Work with the kids; stop the drugs before they start, if they're not on them already. Do the talk circuit. Christ, I hate that, too. Get the townspeople behind us. What else? Anyway, it's beginning to look like I'm taking the job.

Emily was elated; more so after thinking the meeting would be over Polo's association with her. What a turnabout. Her father's offer of an influential position in the town was more than she dreamed. Telling Polo he could call him Parker was the icing on the cake. They were lighthearted and asked Federal Census to join them for coffee. His insight on the town could help.

They sipped their coffees, each wrapped in their thoughts. Polo stared into space dwelling on the position. FC felt Polo would be an asset to the town. Emily thought how great it would be. She would see him more. Then, distressed, her feelings turned to Paul, wishing he were around. Emily mentioned she was returning to work, which both men concurred to be the best thing by far.

Polo called her father on the spot and accepted the position. Sinclair was pleased and told him to do anything he wished for the last month before he started, officially on 1 January 1967. Sinclair gave Polo a telephone list and the names of nine people to call and meet, if possible before he started. Included on the list were the three selectmen and seven other people Polo had never heard of.

After a good session with Lieutenant Collin, Polo reviewing his action plans along with Collin's. As he left, he told Collin to contact the two approved officers and have them aboard the first week of December.

Back in Boston, he met with the Commissioner and told him of the offer and his acceptance. Kearney already knew from Sinclair. Polo didn't approve of that. He would see to it that no one reported to the Commissioner.

The next item on Polo's list for Kearney was an emphatic *no* to any retirement party, that is, if one was planned. If there were, he wouldn't show up.

133

For both of them, it was a difficult time. Thirty years on the force for Polo, thirty-five for Kearney. They had known, admired, argued, bitched and enjoyed each other for twenty-five of those years.

"Ray, I want you to know I'm not taking that position at U Mass. I'm staying on as Commissioner, thanks to you."

Their body language spoke more than words.

"Hell, Walt, Eddy Murray was fun, a piece of cake. Sal Fanara and I simply dredged up a trick we used in the past."

Kearney eyes were bleary, "Yah, the past. It's gone for us old warhorses. Still, as you say, it *was* fun."

They parted with the knowledge Polo would be in and out for the rest of the month. As he left, Polo told whoever he saw he'd be back before retiring and there was no need for goodbyes at the present time.

By the middle of the month, he had consolidated most of his and Collin's goals. They were laid out in order of initiation, with completion dates set in stone. They had their goal.

Chapter

Sixteen

Soon after the shooting at his condominium, Polo found it easy to break his lease, and by 16 December, he and two Boston police officers were moving furniture from his Brookline condominium to a rented house in Barretton. Being little help due to his injury, he managed, in one trunk load, to carry all the insignificant debris he accumulated since he was thirty-five when his wife left him for someone she cared about more. At the Barretton end, Emily, Ken Collin and FC waited to arrange the furniture and the few accessories encompassing the way he lived.

Polo's place looked exactly as Emily envisioned. Austere. She planned to add much more, curtains for an example. He was a middle-aged bachelor, grousing about, oblivious to his surroundings, careless about his personal environment. She decided to improve what there was to work with, although knowing it would require perseverance getting him to accept change. She had the time.

After finishing, they all had a few beers and sat around, Emily mentioned putting up a few curtains. Polo accepted the kidding that followed good-naturedly. She saw his look and decided curtains could wait. The next time she thought to bring up the subject, she would use the word drapes, perhaps that would be easier for him to accept.

Polo immersed himself into his job. The first two men he hired were already police officers, now he wanted to increase their knowledge. Through contacts, he enrolled them in the Active

Officer Academy Program. Lieutenant Collin, because of his Military Police background, was assigned to the Academy's community outreach programs, designed to convert MPs to civilian law. Both programs were intensive and extensive, one hundred hours, held in Worcester. Polo assigned himself to a specialized in-service course for police veterans, held in Springfield.

The courses were to start 1 January of the New Year, which would leave only three officers on station duty for thirteen weekdays. Polo felt the officers in training's proximity to Barretton would allow for any emergency in the town. He also judged the performance of the remaining officers at the station would help determine their fate.

Police Superintendent Makkin asked Polo, as a favor to the Commissioner, to attend the office Christmas party. As Polo did not want a retirement party, Makkin said it was the least Polo could do for the friends and associates he'd known down through the years. Polo balked until reminded he could slip out whenever he wanted.

Begrudgingly, he went to the party, and had a great time, until he became suspicious. Everyone he knew on the force was there, more people than had ever attended any Christmas party. When Sheriff Sal Fanara showed up, giving him a bear hug and wouldn't let go, it dawned on Polo something was going to happen. The awareness came too late. Strong hands grabbed his arms, pinning them behind, handcuffs clamped. Polo struggled in vain. A blindfold then pulled over his eyes. Cursing did not get his arms free. He stopped fighting. His captors propelled him along as fast as his gimpy leg would allow.

He sensed people running down stairs, his being in an elevator, doors opening, people laughing. He swore, "If I'm being made a fool of, I'll break bones."

He was outside, people murmuring, muffled sounds. The handcuffs removed, the noise increasing.

Angrily, he pulled off the blindfold, unable to see properly from the spotlights. There, in front of him, stood a silver 1967 Buick Electra 225. He felt it happen and couldn't stop ... tears stung his eyes. The people stepped back, letting him gain control of his emotions. It took a long moment. A moment they would never forget. Polo looked around, "The God damned blindfold irritated my eyes and the spotlights caused them to water."

A roar from the disbelieving crowd. They had Polo sit in the car, while camera's flashed and endless comments he would never remember rained down on him.

Then, back upstairs to party more. In the relative quiet of the Commissioner's office, Polo shook his head, still in disbelief, yet coupled with gratitude.

"Actually, Ray, I should thank you. We were so over subscribed with donations that once we had enough for the Buick, I donated the rest to Teddy William's Jimmy Fund, so they thank you also. By the way, it's bigger than Ed Murray's Riviera."

"Damn it Walt, booze is making me all mushy."

"Damn it back to you, Ray, don't you go getting me all mushy."

They all applauded as Polo was leaving. He turned, "I know you're really applauding because I'm retiring." Then, surveying them all, "Thank you for what you've done and I hope you know my feelings about this place ... and the people in it."

Emily saw the Buick and burst out laughing, "Ray, this is *so you* it's incredible. I can *just see you* cruising Miami beach looking for teeny boppers."

"Anything else amuse you?"

"Yes, you told me it was a 1967 and this is 1966 so it must be a 1966."

"Okay, Emily, you're turning my own words back on me. We're even."

FC wandered over, "What in hell's creation is this piece of tin, Mr. Polo?"

Emily responded before Polo could speak, "It's Ray's new *1966* Buick Electra 225."

"Big. What's the 225 stand for?"

Polo winced, "I'm told it stands for the car's length in inches."

FC started to smile, "I don't thinks I'd brag none about that." He continued, "And a '66? The '67s are out, why didn't you get a new one?"

Polo threw his arms in the air, walking off. Emily explained to FC about the car. He was impressed that anyone would think so much of the detective.

The holidays were strange. Emily was emotional, worried about Paul somewhere on drugs. He had always come home to the family from his trips, never missing Christmas together. This time he didn't return. Having her father in jail also depressed her.

Her school had a Christmas party for the children before they scattered to their foster homes. Christmas day she visited her father, the next day returning with Polo, He wanted to keep Sinclair up to date on the activities in the town. He was pleased with all the news and Polo was content, no one was reporting his actions back to Parker.

Polo gave Emily a small opal pin and she gave him an *official* Buick key chain., a Buick hat and Buick T shirt. Her gifts were lighthearted, nothing to raise the eyebrow of a father.

Emily attended the New Year's party hosted by the Management of Thorton Academy and danced with a man named Tom Smith, whom she thought was nice. She figured him to be married or divorced. When he asked her out, she simply said she didn't go out with school employees. Learning this, he reversed course and said if there were no way she would go out with him, would she be interested in his fixing her up with a good friend of his. Tom vouched for the man and thought she would really like him. Emily stalled around until she came to terms with the truth of the matter; she was acting like a shut in and should be getting out more. She named a night; Tom went off to call his friend, a great person named Mike Moore, he said, and Mike agreed. Emily and Tom danced to few a more songs, and then he again tried to date her. She wondered about him, fixing her up with his friend and then turning right around and tried to date her again. That was enough for her; she said good evening, after promising to keep the blind date.

When the doorbell rang, Emily was actually looking forward to a night out and hopefully some adult small talk. Date night. She gathered herself together and opened the door. There stood Tom Smith.

"What are you doing here?"

"I'm not Tom, I'm his twin brother."

"Tell me another one."

"Are you sure I'm not his twin brother?"

"Yes I am."

"Then, how about Mike couldn't make it, so I thought why ruin your evening?"

"How do you know you haven't already?"

"Aw, come on Emily. Give me a chance."

"Is Tom your real name? Are you married, divorced, engaged, or going steady?"

"Going steady? My God, I am thirty-two years old. You don't go steady at my age. And I'm none of the others either."

"I asked you, is Tom Smith your real name?"

"Tom, yes, Smith, no. My real name is Thomas Whitefield Archer Crane, to be exact."

"Come on, you can do better than that."

"This is hopeless," he said.

She smiled at his discouragement, "Okay Mr. Tom WAC, or whatever you call yourself, where are we going?"

They went to a club in Weston, not far from Regis College. The lounge had a five-piece group playing big band ballads from the 1940's. She never paid much attention to that type of music before, yet Tom's interest in the music and his easygoing style blended into an enjoyable evening. Enough so, when at her door, as he asked her for another date, she explained she was still against seeing a fellow employee. She would have to give it some thought.

The way she said *Tom* when saying goodnight, made him say he would quit his job to date her.

That was enough for her, "Okay, I'll go out again."

She asked, unexpectedly, "Do you know who I am?"

Tom closed his eyes a moment, "Yes. You're Emily Sinclair. You lived in Barretton. I know a little about what happened there."

"That doesn't bother you?"

"Only if it bothers you."

"That's a nice answer, thanks. Call me the second week in January."

"Two weeks is a long time," he protested.

She smiled, closing the door. He made her feel good.

By the third week of January, all the officers were back on duty in Barretton. Polo was proud of the men he had sent to the academies. They, as well as he, had all rated high and done so well, that he decided to enter the rest into the Academy. Soon, Polo would add two more officers, and require his entire force to live within the town. As part of Polo's Getting-to-Know-You Program the new officers walked the main street introducing themselves, and socializing so they assimilated with the town. Next, the department carried out seminars at teenage clubs, schools, social organizations, Democratic and Republican Clubs and other groups. Officers were to remain apolitical at all times. Polo spoke at a few of the meetings, although he mainly culled out officers who projected well and pushed them into that job.

Saying he is an Interim Chief or IC for short, gave the impression he wanted, a temporary, not integral, adjunct of the Barretton Police Department. Lieutenant Collin would become Captain on 1 June. On 1 January 1968, one of the two Academy officers would become Lieutenant and the other, Sergeant. The remaining officers would advance as demonstrated by their abilities. Subsequently, the force enlarged and opportunities grew. It was a dynamic time for the force, and the town.

He had a lucky break when he discovered Connie Johnson; the dispatcher, was a Certified Public Accountant. A monetary deal easily worked out as she thought Polo was the best thing to have happened to the force and the town. She worked out well for him, as it served the dual purpose of helping with budgetary projections to goals, plus it gave his officer's hands-on experience handling switchboard communications.

He met with the Selectmen, Town Committee Members, County Clerk, County Commissioners, Country Tax Collector, School Board Members, and Circuit Court Judge, Morgan Butts, of the Sinclair sentencing farce.

After contracting for four police-specifications, Dodge vehicles, Polo met again with the Selectmen. Malcolm Slocomb was the key to building the new police station. Which was best? Add on to the town's aging facility, or build a complete new complex to bring all the town offices together under one roof? After seeing the sad state of the town buildings, Polo's vote was for tearing down everything. However, he told them to plead their case to Sinclair. Polo only had the go ahead for a new station house, the rest was up to them.

Polo liked the Selectmen. They were doing the unexpected. Old school people, they held the purse strings tightly, and Barretton had a lower tax rate than the surrounding towns. Financially the town was well positioned, and by tapping the reserves and speaking with Sinclair, they felt a floating bond could be absorbed with a minimum property tax increase. The unspoken thought for the complex was to create civic pride and this entered into the equation. Polo knew what Sinclair's answer to a bond would be and left it to the Selectmen to find architects and contractors and draw up concepts and costing. Polo deferred to everything they might want, although firmly stating he had the final say concerning the Police Station.

He was proud of his accomplishments. He had confirmed everyone's belief. Everything was going according to plan, no glitches.

He had not spoken with Emily for a week. Now he had the time, and would give her a call to have coffee together.

Ken Collin asked him for coffee first. Ken was nervous, Polo afraid the Lieutenant was going to resign. They sat in the coffee shop, Ken staring at his coffee, fidgety. Polo apprehensive.

"Come on, Lieutenant, for Christ's sake, spit it out."

Ken looked fearful, "I wonder if you would mind if I asked Emily out?"

Polo went blank. Then loud, "What the *hell* are you talking about?"

Ken was nervous, but stuck to it, "Cripe, Chief, Emily and I got to talking back when we were waiting for you to bring your furniture and, I don't know, I thought I'd see if she'd like to go out with me. I'm asking you because you're, you know, kind of like a father to her."

It hurt Polo, considered a surrogate father. What could he say? "You don't have to ask me for permission. Thank you for giving me that respect, but you can call her without needing my approval. I will only mention that I don't know if she is ready to date yet, she's been through a lot."

The answer lifted the Lieutenant's spirits. Though not letting on, Polo's mood sank. Damn. He clenched his jaw, what could he do? This was going to come about someday. He'd had her to himself all this time. Bound to happen.

Polo put on a good face, wished Ken luck, then begged off, saying he had another meeting. Ken watched him head for his car, his face dismayed. Ken was not surprised. He and other associates guessed there was something going on, and Polo's look confirmed it. Now the question: Is the feeling he has for Emily returned? Ken wanted to doubt it.

Emily met Polo for coffee, telling she was having drapes made for his house. He simply nodded, distracted.

"What's wrong? I thought you had everything going gangbusters. The whole town's talking about everything you've accomplished."

"I don't know, Emily, maybe I shouldn't say anything, but I want to make you aware, Collin is thinking of asking you out."

"He is? He told you? Do you think I should, Ray?"

"Hey, that's up to you, kid. My only thought was that I didn't know if you were ready to date, and I told him that."

Emily knew she might as well bring the subject up, "Ray, I've already had a date. I would have told you earlier. I haven't seen you."

Another kick in the gut, "Anyone I know?"

"No, he's not from around here. I met him at the school's New Year's party."

"Good. You've got to get out for a change."

Emily knew he was putting a good face on it, "Speaking of going out, Ray, when are we going out again?"

"I don't really know. You seem busy, and I've a lot on my plate. I can't commit to anything."

"The devil you can't, Ray. We're going out dancing next week so you better learn some fancy steps. And fast!"

He gave in, bad leg and all. No question he would.

Emily and Collin went to the movies on their first date, seeing *A Man for All Seasons*. Afterward they stopped for a drink in Pittsfield. She was relieved no one recognized her. She was surprised Ken had picked that movie, knowing the complexity of the era's historical events. His diverse musical interests from the Tijuana Brass to Puccini's *La Boehme*, also amused her. He talked with depth of the books he had recently read, *The Fixer* and *In Cold Blood*. He was angry with himself for mentioning that book. Emily ignored it.

It was obvious to her Ken was nervous at first, and then, as he kept talking, relaxed. He was easy to listen to and his topics, a number of times, surpassed her knowledge. He had far more substance than she guessed. True, he was interesting when they waited for Polo to bring the furniture and now, she didn't find their conversation awkward. He listened attentively, responding with comprehension.

She could see nothing was contrived or an effort to impress. She realized she had tapped his knowledge as though it had been trapped inside him, waiting.

She asked his background. He hesitated. Simple things: a poor family, a mother that drove him to be more than a boxer, his winning a football scholarship to the University of Maine. His feeling out of place. When drafted, he was relieved, although being Military Police in Vietnam was tough duty.

Ken told her it was only recently he was happy doing a job and studying any subject he liked. No pressure. His job was enough, yet he intended to be the best. Kind of like Polo, he said. His words were conflicting and obvious. To Emily, he was still trying hard.

She tried to put together the pieces of Ken's life; He said he didn't fit even though good at sports. What athlete would feel out of place in an athletic environment? He didn't want pressure, but accepted being drafted and getting into the worst type of it in Vietnam. Now he studies anything he wants, although he took a job as a cop. Well, she thought, his being a cop in a small town must seem a dream compared to being an MP in Vietnam. Now, not that he realizes it, he's turned around and wants to be the best, like Polo: one hell of a goal to set for himself, if he didn't want pressure.

They enjoyed each other. She agreed to another date in a week or two. At present, Emily couldn't get free from her past. She still needed time to keep herself together.

During the third week of January, Tom Crane called. Before she met him on the following Saturday, Emily knew she and Polo had to talk. When Polo called, saying his leg was acting up and he wouldn't be able to take her dancing, she caught him off guard, "That's okay, Ray, I'll be right over."

Conflicted, Polo knew nothing he could do would avoid the meeting. Yet, he wanted to see her, only not under these circumstances. She sat beside him. The glance that passed between them blended into her words, and brought sadness to his heart.

"Ray, please don't deny it, I know you like me more than a friend, and no matter how hard it is for me to say, that's all I can be. We'd be foolish not to face up to that fact. You're my best friend. If you were thirty years younger, we could have really hit it off, but, you know ..."

He stopped her, "That's not true Emily. Thirty years ago, I was a big, ex-jock rookie cop pounding a beat in Kenmore Square. You would no more have looked at me than jump off a cliff. The only reason we're here now is fate dumped us together. You were messed up, and I thought you were just another willful, college brat used to having her own way.

When I finally realized you were a really a great kid, I was up to my ears over you. I couldn't help it. I was what you needed. As you said, I was your rock, and I loved it. Now you're getting it back together. That's not to say you don't still have a way to go, but its coming. I can see you beginning to stand on your own two feet again. I knew it would happen. I just wasn't ready for it to be this soon ..."

Now, Emily stopped him, "I'm not as ready as you think, Ray. I still need you. Am I unfair? God, I'm begging you to forgive me if I am. I need you, Ray. I do. I can't offer you more than friendship, but please, don't take yours away. We mean too much to each other. If you take that away I'll ... I don't know ...."

He didn't speak, trying to decide what to do, and then rose. Tears streaked her cheeks.

"Okay, Emily, you should leave now. Let's go on the way we are. Understand this; you must promise to tell me when it's time for me to go."

She walked to him, "That day will never come, Ray."

He held her gently in his arms.

145

Lieutenant Collin happened to be driving past Polo's house at that moment and saw Emily's Mercedes in the drive. Slowing, and looking through the picture window, he saw two shadows merge into one, "What in hell's name is going on here?"

Tom Crane took Emily to the same lounge, sitting in the same booth. He didn't ask her to dance, instead, he seemed resolute, "I've not been truthful with you, and I want to get things cleared up before we go any further, which I hope we do."

She was quick to respond, "I knew it! I knew it! You're divorced with five kids."

"No," He laughed, "Not that bad. It's that I don't work for Thorton Academy. I knew your brother Paul, and I met you a long time ago."

Wide eyed, she smirked, "Oh, is that *all?*"

"Now, Emily, just give me a chance."

When she failed to answer, he asked, "My last name, Crane, does that sound familiar?"

"A little, I can't place it though."

"Okay, here goes. Your father, my father, Bradford Crane, and two others are principals in a charitable corporation called The Quad Trust. My father has a seat on the New York Stock Exchange. The investments the members make, plus their dividends, are managed by my father through the Trust. It then donates the dividends and a set percentage of the principle each year to various charitable causes. In this case, they supply the funds to support ten Academies, which help children, such as the one you work for. They're located from southern Connecticut, Massachusetts and over to upper state New York."

"I knew Dad had some interest in my Academy, but what's that got to do with you being at my school New Year's Eve?"

"I'm employed by The Quad Trust. My job, as a CPA, is to inspect and qualify all ten Academies, checking the accounts follow our specifications. They must demonstrate eighty percent of income they receive from Quad Trust goes directly to supplies, medical assistance, and education of the children. The remaining twenty percent covers administration expenses. The Trust doesn't mind donating money; it does mind wasting money. It keeps me extremely busy. To keep costs down, I'm the only auditor. It takes upwards of two days for each Academy on a five-week rotating schedule. So, add driving everywhere, I'm always on the go."

She gave an insolent smile, "If you're this busy, I won't keep you."

"I don't think I'll ever be too busy for you, Emi."

"You called me Emi, the only other person to call me that is my brother."

"You mean Paul, that's who I picked it up from."

"How do you know Paully?"

"That's one of the other things I mentioned about meeting you. Twenty years ago, your father, mother, you and Paul came down to our summer home in Newport, Rhode Island. Your family stayed four days. You were such a brat, it felt like four weeks. I remember your mother took you aside and smacked your butt. I'll admit I cheered every slap, quietly of course, but I cheered."

"How can you say that?" However, Emily knew, "I remember how I was, Tom, I was spoiled for a long time, right up until Paully started getting into trouble growing up. I tried to help him so much; I finally became a pretty good kid."

"I'd say you are. So what's Paul up to now?"

"Oh, he's away. He likes to travel."

"I remember he left Brown University a lot."

"So you knew my brother after Newport, I mean when he was going to college. I didn't know that. Paully never mentioned you."

Tom was uncomfortable, "Yes, I would see him now and then when he stopped by the house. Tell me, Paul aside, how's your father doing?"

Emily noticed the abrupt subject change and found it unsettling. Strange. She couldn't recall Paully ever mentioning Tom Crane. She let the subject of her twin lapse, "Dad's doing well considering. He's teaching English courses in reading at the Correction Center. He's actually quite good."

"That's great, Emi. I know our fathers stay in touch almost every week. Father wanted to go up to see him, but your father said he preferred not to have visitors, other than his children. Father understood."

Excusing himself, Tom headed for the men's room. It gave Emily a little time to think. Her brother talked over everything with her. It was odd he never mentioned Tom Crane. When did he see Tom? When he was at Brown? When Paully had a drug problem? Tom called her Emi, just as Paully. So, he must have talked about her. There's a story here, she was determined to hear it.

When Tom returned she asked, "I don't understand, what do you mean when you said you saw Paully now and then?"

Tom was ready for the question, "It's not complicated. When Paul was at Brown and I was at my parent's place, we would get together for a few brews and broads. That's all, for Christ's sake."

"All right Tom, no need to get testy. I only thought it strange. Paully never mentioned seeing you."

"Hey, you know Paul. I don't think he was too outgoing about who he saw or where he went. And to be truthful, we had a little falling out and that was that."

"Over what?"

"That's kind of personal, Emi, I'm sorry."

The subject dropped clumsily. Although they managed to find other interests to gloss over, the unanswered question loomed between them. Gradually, a few drinks and dances eased some discomfort.

Still, a cloud of doubt lingered as he took her in his arms, "I'd like to see you next week."

His goodnight kiss swept through her.

"God," she thought, "I really like this guy. Why am I pressing him about Paully? Tom says he saw Paully a few times and they had a falling out. Let it go. Am I so insecure it's making me paranoid?"

Another goodnight kiss. She had to see him again.

Over the next two weeks, Emily immersed herself in her work, seeing Tom three nights, liking him more.

Ken Collin was getting too deep for her. It wasn't an act. When they were together, he was too serious, not just over her, about life. He didn't know how to lighten up. He spoke too seriously of *Chekhov's Plays* or *Faust, Milton* and on. She didn't want serious right now. He was too intense, seldom away from town affairs except when seeing her. With the town, he was being too meticulous over minute details, which he felt only he could address.

She saw Polo and went with him to see her father. There again, they talked the business of the town. She listened, interested, adding her thoughts. They were a relaxed threesome.

Chapter

Seventeen

Expecting the ringing phone to be Tom Crane, she answered lightheartedly.

"Emi, it's Paully."

Unprepared, her voice constricted in her throat. "Emi, is that you? It's Paully."

"Paully? Where are you? Are you okay? What are …?"

"Take it easy, Emi, I'm all right, I'm fine. Tell me about Dad. What happened?"

She calmed, giving the story of their father's friends, Detective Polo's help and the farce of the sentencing where their father had received a prison term of four to six years. He was doing well, helping other prisoners. Emily expected their father would get out in three years for good behavior, according to the detective.

Paul sounded relieved and asked how she was doing under the circumstances. He admitted he ran because of the pressure. Emily forgave him as always, asking again, where he was. He was vague, saying northern Maine. That was the reason for the call. He was working as a waiter in a lounge near some college and his Chevy couldn't navigate the snow. He needed money for a four-wheel drive Jeep. The whole reason for the call boiled down to Paul needing ten thousand dollars from their father. He'd meet her in about a week, when he could get to Portland and catch the Portland to Boston bus. He would call with the timetable when he was leaving so she could drive to Portsmouth, New Hampshire. He'd get off the bus there.

Emily asked if he was all right, meaning off drugs. The reply was of course, which, by the sound of his voice, was not convincing. He said he'd sneak home some day, when their father was released. He'd busted parole and damned if he was going to serve time.

She mentioned seeing an old friend of his, Tom Crane. Paul was vehement, "Stay away from that bastard." It was an order. Paul never spoke like that.

"Why Paully? What's the matter with Tom?"

He was sullen, "Just do what I say!"

The rest of their conversation was worthless. Emily could get nothing more out of him. She thought perhaps when they met there might be more she could do to help him as well as find out about Crane. How? It was difficult to imagine.

Visibly upset, meeting with her father, she had no idea of his reaction as she told him about Paul calling, needing money.

"Why did he leave Palton House? He promised to stay."

"Dad, I was so upset, I didn't think to ask him. I don't know why he left. We're both just mixed up."

"Emily, don't include yourself in with him."

"Are you going to help him, Dad?"

"Everything I do will only prolong the agony of my son. What choice have I? I can't turn my back on him, which means there is no choice, I've got to do what he asks."

Sinclair took Emily into one of the prison offices and called his bank, a direct line to Alice Evans. He gave her two account numbers, telling her to withdraw eight thousand dollars from one account and seven thousand from the other. The bills were to be no larger than one hundred dollars, and put into a manila envelope. His daughter would pick it up the next day. Mrs. Evans did as instructed, though knowing breaking the fifteen thousand dollars into two withdrawals was a common process as not to provoke Federal oversight. Any deposits or withdrawals of ten thousand dollars or more must be reported. Evans was also smart enough to know it was not her place to question the man who had made her Chairman of the bank.

"Dad, Paully only asked for ten thousand."

"I know." Sinclair resigned to the fact his son would need more, and probably more after this.

Paul found Emily waiting at the bus station in Portsmouth. Both were in tears and hid in a corner like two parting lovers.

"It wasn't right leaving Palton House, Paully. You promised Dad you'd stay."

"I know, I know. I can't be confined. You know that, Emi. I can't help it, my problem I mean. I can't shake it. You know I've tried to stay there."

"Not hard enough."

"Don't get me arguing and angry, Emi, I'm not going back. They'd put me in jail and I'd never survive. We talked about that before, if you remember."

"Don't you realize this means there's no end to it?"

"I'm reconciled to that."

She knew it was no use, "Dad sent fifteen thousand."

"Tell him thanks, and I'm sorry for the grief I've caused."

As the Portland, Maine bus pulled in, they moved to it, Emily still crying. She knew it could be the last time she saw him.

"Emi, I'll slip back someday to see you and Dad. Don't go looking for me in Maine, because I'm just going back to get my car. A friend up state told me about another job out west, I'm going there."

Paul then became agitated, "One other thing Emi, Don't see Tom Crane again. He's not for you. Don't ask why; just trust me on this, please."

With that, Paul was on the bus and gone. As heartbroken as she was at her twin leaving, she couldn't help wondering what he had against Tom. Why such an intense reaction?

Paul didn't leave Maine, only moving southwest to Bridgeton, where he bought a used Jeep and rented an isolated cabin well outside of town. The new job Paul had found was perfect for his plans. Delivering his employer's produce to most of the restaurants and lounges, he got to know all the service employees and waiters and waitresses. After he made the contacts he needed, he took a trip to Boston. There, through a contact, he bought eight thousand dollars worth of cocaine, using most of the money his father had given him to buy a car.

"What does the town think of Sinclair's light sentence?" Polo asked the three selectmen having coffee with him. They looked back at him indifferently.

"Didn't really get a handle on it, Polo. There was so little feedback, it's hard to say."

Malcolm Slocomb chimed in, "I don't know what to say either. It's been over four months and I wonder if most of the people remember, or if they do, do they care."

Mary Wells thought a bit, "I think it's like; if Mister Sinclair did it, there must have been a good reason. The light sentence proves it, so forgot it."

Polo shook his head smiling, "I can't believe what I'm hearing. I don't mind it falling off the radar, yet it's surprising after the ruckus it caused."

"Look at it this way, Polo, you're sure as hell not going to have farmers with pitchforks beating down the doors wanting to hang Sinclair. You've got to realize most of them are pretty much in debt to him. Like us."

At that, they laughed, finished their coffee, and went about their business.

Emily updated her father about Paul. Parker was in a quandary, helpless. Private Investigators finding Paul would not solve the problem. Bringing him back would only remand him to jail. There was no answer.

In her difficulty letting go of Paul, Emily turned to Polo once again. Even though hard pressed to explain the meeting with her brother, she needed advice and had to meet with the detective. She knew she also wanted to see him.

Polo was of no help, nor tried to be. There was no sense in giving Emily false hope. He was not surprised at her meeting her brother, knowing if there came a chance, she would go to him. Polo's concern was more serious, and he did not couch his comments. Brother or not, if she were found meeting a parole violator, with a package containing fifteen thousand dollars, the *very least* that would happen would be negative publicity. Polo was adamant, frightening her, "Don't you understand the chance you've taken? You cannot allow anything to damage your father's reputation when he is subject to the good behavior clause. What you have done is God damn serious. A parole violator receiving thousands of dollars from a convicted murderer who's *in prison* would ruin any early release program and add another sentence."

Polo's comments were scathing. She shivered at his comments. He did not let up.

"From now on, no matter how difficult it is to refuse, nothing suspect can impinge on your father's reputation, or yours, for that matter."

"I wasn't thinking, Ray. I'm sorry. It was my brother. He needed help."

"If he calls again, I'll handle it. This is your father's freedom for Christ's sake."

"Okay, I promise I'll call you first. Take me to lunch?"

At lunch, Polo mentioned he discussed the townspeople's apparent disinterest in condemning her father for what happened. Emily wasn't surprised. She felt that the benefits, charities, and good deeds her father had done were the reasons. Polo smiled inwardly. The observation to be careful, no good deed goes unpunished, could fit here, considering her brother.

155

Emily told him of Paul's dislike for Tom Crane, a person she was dating and conversely, Crane's silence concerning her brother bothered her.

Polo, who knew she had been dating someone, asked, "Paul must have some reason, do you want me to look into it?"

"No, it wouldn't be right to snoop on a boyfriend."

"I'd argue that point, Emily. Let's talk about Paul, instead."

"What about him?"

"What was he like when you two met? I'll bet he was half in the bag, because the pieces don't fit. Before you say anything, Emily, listen. Why didn't Paul show up at Dedham? You said Paul's shouldering the blame for ... ah, what happened. Paul's making that up. People in his condition don't take the blame for anything. That's why the destruction of the orchids is perfect for him to hide behind. That way he's off the hook. He can blame that instead of his drugs ..."

"I don't want to hear any more, Ray, let it go."

"Just let me finish."

"I don't want to hear anything more. I'm sorry, I can't listen to this."

Chapter

Eighteen

The month of February was typical for New England. Raw, gale swept snow blew down from the plains of Canada, chilling New Englander's blood, even below Connecticut. It's called The Montreal Express.

The Georgian home on Great Hill was swathed in ice crystals from freezing rains. The rain froze in great windswept icicles along the edge of every roof and downspout.

No one looked out at them or marveled at their beauty. No longer a home, the house stood against the gale. Silent, dark, empty.

Federal Census did his rounds faithfully, and then retired to his rooms in the garage to huddle by his potbellied stove, vainly trying to ease the chill in his bones. He was lonely. There was no master or mistress in the home, no children. Only Polo or Emily coming to cheer him now and then. He thought back on two decades of pleasant years. Gone now, he despaired, knowing all to well they were gone. Forever. That he was aging poorly, stared him in the face from the mirror. Seventy-six years old, nursing his pained body for fifty-two of them, had taken a toll. The shrapnel wound, which had torn open his leg, distressed him more each day. "Blast the AEF, blast France, blast the War to End All Wars, blast the Second World War, and blast this weather." He cursed, "And especially blast this damnable leg!"

He missed Paul Sinclair. In the past, when the pain was most unbearable, Paul, God bless him, would supply him cocaine

157

so he could carry on his duties. The drug was gone now, however, and nothing else helped. No over the counter pills, no prescriptions from the Veteran's Hospital and no amount of whiskey helped. Only the drugs Paul slipped him secretly eased the pain.

When Polo or Emily stopped by, they were used to the limp and he gritted his teeth, not letting on. He was too proud. He was keen on her company and Polo's as well. He smiled, never thought he would want to be with that cuss.

The problem was, in this type of weather people hunkered down. Polo would be handling winter problems around the town. Emily cozy in her condominium, going from there to school then straight back, due to the roads being too icy for travel with this wind. FC didn't tell them how much he needed their company. Another thing he was too proud to let known. Without company, he had too much time to think, and that was not good.

The storm lasted erratically for over a week. During it, each day, FC did his rounds loyally, limping from his garage, into the blowing snow, to the house. Stairs were hard for him. He struggled from room to room, checking windows, testing water faucets against freeze ups, thermostats for cycling, cellar leaks and a half dozen other items listed in his mind. Satisfied, he locked the front door and trudged down to feed Emily's horse, which of course, had to be outside in this weather, packing a path around his paddock before going into his stall.

FC liked the horse. It brought back memories. He always gave it a couple of extra flakes of hay, warm mash twice a week, a few rubs and carrots before he climbed up to the garage. He sat close to the stove, shaking. His leg so agonizingly stiff he could hardly move. As the warmth eased the cold, a throbbing, relentless pain replaced the stiffness. No question, it was worse than ever. Grabbing his bottle of whiskey, he took a long swig and glanced out at the wind driven snow, now drifted halfway up his window. The whiskey did nothing to ease the pain and worse, it no longer tasted good. The last straw, he grumbled. When even whiskey doesn't taste good, what's left? Crying out from pain, he dragged his leg to his chest of drawers and stopped, again looking out at the blowing snow, unable to see the house. He knew it in his heart; the house would never be a home again. There was no longer a reason to put up with the pain. Federal reached into his drawer and brought the WWI Enfield revolver to his head. "Goodbye."

The cemetery ground was too frozen for the backhoe, so Federal Census was cremated. Hardly any mourners attended the non-denominational service, as few knew him. No one knew his religion, or even if he had relatives. Parker Sinclair attended along with a Detention Center supervisor. Polo, Emily, Ken Collin, one selectman and a handful of the curious rounded out the service.

Polo had told the Sinclair's he went up to the Hill to drop in on FC. As he drove up the unplowed drive he noticed there were no footprints or smoke from the garage's chimney. Guessing something was wrong, he had to kick the door to pieces and there found the floor a thick sheet of ice from a burst water pipe. FC was face down, frozen in five inches of ice. Polo contacted the Fire Department to chop him out, then called the coroner, morgue, Parker and Emily. Polo also called Zimmerman's Plumbing to shut off the water to the garage and to check the main house for the rest of the winter. That done, he pushed through the snowdrifts to feed a stomping, whinnying horse.

At first, all involved thought FC had a heart attack. As the ice thawed around the stiff body however, the coroner found the head wound. From that discovery, more ice had to be hacked away to find the weapon and make sure the gunshot was self-inflicted. The axes chipped away, the revolver found and all was resolved; FC had committed suicide. Plain and simple the coroner said.

Polo, Parker, and Emily sat back at the Detention Center after the service, the mood somber. Although Polo had known FC for a short time, for some reason he liked the old coot and sorry for his death, especially his being despondent enough to take his own life. Emily's loss was deep. She had grown up with FC since she was five years old and had never known Great Hill without him. It was Parker who felt the bitterness of loss—the emptiness, the most. No one would have dreamed the confidences the two shared. Money when FC needed it, no strings attached. Always paid back, mostly in services. The support FC provided Parker when problems erupted with Paul. When no one was around, Parker and FC would sit in the XKE for hours, swapping tales of Pacific islands and France at war.

They never spoke of the battles or their medals, only their experiences, the excitement, the shocking loss of friends, and Parker's homesickness for his wife and children.

Even when Sinclair asked, FC didn't give advice. He gave various beliefs, ideas, tattered proverbs and what ifs; but refused to give advice. This convoluted process would have annoyed others. Not Parker, he had cracked FC's code. Parker would let FC ramble on seemingly thoughtless, without point, until a viewpoint emerged, helped along by FC's facial expressions. Nevertheless, FC never gave advice.

Parker smiled in remembrances, his eyes watering. An era had ended. Never again would The Hill be the same. Parker thought of his wife, also gone, Paul probably lost forever and Emily in her own condominium. There was no reason to keep the house on the Hill.

No reason, simply memories clinging to him—so painfully.

Chapter

Nineteen

By the beginning of May 1967, Paul Sinclair's business expanded more than he had ever dreamed. With twenty-five outlets for his product throughout North Conway and the Mount Washington Valley, his cash flow easily afforded the increasing demand for the terrible drug. Expansion into the high school was a simple matter. It only took one student, which led to many more. The original student went on to the University of New Hampshire in Durham, opening the floodgates there.

Paul was no fool. He understood the dangers involved. Using intermediaries, he distanced himself from multiple contacts. Changing his name to Peter Stanford, he avoided the displays of affluence he acquired. His business plan, cash only, enabled him to move small amounts into five banks outside the valley, without disclosing one cent to any government agency, notably the Internal Revenue Service.

Strangely, the more mired he got into marketing illegal drugs the less he used them. Money, and acquiring more, became his drug. He became adept at playing the game, yet knew he had to establish an Out Clause. His personal goal was one million dollars.

If he had stayed clean and with his family in Barretton, he would have become a multimillionaire.

But Paul only saw the now, and knew if he sold his business to his Boston suppliers and combined it with his bank accounts he could realize that million. The problem was, he knew if he offered his business to Boston, any meeting for the payoff, considering their total lack of ethics, especially to a white, Anglo Saxon, Yankee, could be fatal. He didn't intend to disappear, quickly and permanently. So, how to do it? His other worry was the sheer volume of his purchases must have sparked unwanted interest by the Boston suppliers. For this reason, Paul explored acquiring product from New York. He knew this move could put him in a difficult situation. Acquiring drugs from New York would then arouse *their* interest in his outlets, and if Boston found out what he was doing … well, he didn't want to think of it.

The plan he eventually formulated was to buy as much product as he could afford from both suppliers for two months. Move it as fast as possible, then sell the business piecemeal to his suppliers—somehow. According to his calculations, he figured to make well over a million dollars, *if* he moved as quietly and as quickly as possible.

Ray Polo was irritated. The man holed up in the house wouldn't come out, no matter how the police tried. It had started with a family argument, which escalated to a slap, resulting in a wife running from the house. Now the man was brandishing a pistol, refusing to come out. A Special Weapons and Tactics team from Worchester was on its way, along with State Troopers. Barretton's police force was there, staying behind police vehicles, waiting for the big guns, or Polo, to arrive.

Getting there first, Polo could tell the man in the house was frightened enough to freak out once the other police forces arrived. He had seen it before, a dozen times in Boston.

Overreaction killed people, and he knew this whole situation would get out of control. That was sure to happen here. The man's wife said when her husband drank beer it was like taking a stupid pill. As long as it was booze and not drugs, where people go crazy, Polo felt he could handle the situation. He stood where the man in the house could see him and took off his jacket. He slowly removed his service revolver and shoulder holster, placing them on the ground.

The man couldn't see the snub-nosed automatic tucked in the small of Polo's back. As his officers watched in disbelief, Polo walked within twenty-five feet of the house. The man waved a gun from the partially opened door. Polo waited. Nothing happened.

"Look, you stupid, God damned idiot!" Polo shouted, "I don't know if you've been drinking or not, but your wife says you've got a stupid pill in you, so you'd better sober up fast and listen. Right now, all you'll be charged with is domestic violence and resisting arrest, armed. If you wait any longer the SWAT team will be here and they'll riddle your home, fire in tear gas, break down your doors and if you're not dead, they'll drag your sorry ass out of there and you'll spend the next twenty years in prison."

As Polo spoke, he inched up the pathway until he reached the steps leading to the house. No response. He noticed the man shaking.

"Think, you stupid jerk, I'll tell you one more time, when you hear sirens, I walk off. You can have a couple of months in jail, or take your chances with what's coming. My bet is you'll either be shot or get twenty years. Most likely you'll be shot because SWAT guys don't have a hell of a lot of patience."

The door opened more, the gun still pointed at Polo.

"You're Ray Polo; the big shot cop around here, ain't ya?"

Polo nodded, he had his man. Yet that damned gun pointed at him was a distraction.

"Yes, I'm Polo. Now drop that gun and get down those stairs before it's too late."

"You give me your word, Mr. Polo?"

Polo nodded again and, as if on cue, in the distance, the sound of sirens. The man heard them and started down the stairs, still holding the gun.

"Drop the gun for Christ's sake or my men will shoot you!"

The gun dropped, Polo grabbed the man on the last step, swung him around, his fist crashing on the man's jaw. knocking him down in a heap.

"That's for scaring the shit out of me."

The Barretton Police carried the man into a police cruiser as Polo instructed, and sped off without a siren.

The State Police was unhappy. The Worchester SWAT team was unhappy. Polo was happy as hell. He had stopped a possible tragedy and he hadn't been shot. On the Police Band he apologized to all the parties, saying the Barretton Police Department handled it professionally; the subject had come out and arrested. End of story.

By the time Polo got to the stationhouse, the man had been charged and placed in a cell to sleep off his drunkenness and the punch. Polo gathered his police officers, ignoring the congratulations, "I'm going to tell you this just once. If anyone ever, *ever* does what I just did, *I'll take their badges*. No if ands or buts. What I did comes from Boston experience, which none of you will ever get out here. What I did was also *stupid,* and if you can't see why, you shouldn't be on the Force. I could be lying up there in a pool of blood. That guy in the cell could be shot or charged with murder. Either way, a tragedy could've been avoided. Collin made the right decision. He called for backup with experience, then called me. I'm the one who fouled up. I was lucky. Lucky and stupid. Do anything that dim-witted, and you won't live to see your pension.

My only other comment is this; when that guy came out of the house with a gun pointing at me, *why in hell didn't someone shoot the son of a bitch?*"

Polo walked out, leaving everyone shaking heads. Another Polo tale would do the rounds.

The letter arrived like a bolt from the blue. Parker Sinclair never received letters. He stared at the envelope, not recognizing the precise script. The cancel stamp showed a date of Sept.8.67 and Amherst, NH. Addressed to,

Mr. Parker R. Sinclair
Northeastern Correctional Center
Concord, Mass. 01742

There was no name, only a return address. Parker tore it open.

Dear Parker,

I have no doubt this letter will come as a surprise. I hope you will remember me from the distant past. If you do not, please destroy this missive and I promise, I will not try to contact you again.

Parker stopped reading and went to the end of the letter.

'Yours Fondly,
Ruth (Thomas) Carvel

My God, Parker thought, Ruth Thomas. I remember her; we met at Hampton Beach and dated before the war, before Nancy. I really liked Ruth right up to the moment I met Nancy; strange, her contacting me.

A few more memories slipped through his mind, then he continued reading:

This is difficult to say outright, but I have lost my husband Jeff from cancer and have found myself passing the hours thinking back to happier times. You may remember Jeff Carvel as being one of your father's managers when you visited the factory before leaving for the Navy. He and I met shortly after your wedding in Hawaii and we married about a year later. He was a wonderful person, too young to go at sixty-nine, but as they say, God takes the good first. I have two boys and a girl who unfortunately have moved out of New England.

Excuse me for dwelling on the past but in truth that is the reason for this letter.

Please accept my deepest sympathies over the loss of your wife and what has happened to you.

To be brazen about this, I would like to correspond-there I wrote it! (We'll see if I have the nerve to mail it). If I do, perhaps we can recall our times together and help each other to while away the hours that must drag on you, as they do me.

If you do write, I promise to be much more upbeat- this one was to put the past behind.

My address is Mrs. J. Carvel, 11 Franklin Ct., Amherst, Mass. 01002

Yours Fondly,

Ruth (Thomas) Carvel

Emily Sinclair's life smoothed into a pleasant routine; work she loved, each week seeing Polo for lunch, Ken Collin for a movie and conversation, her father every Saturday. Then it was Tom Crane at least twice. She liked them all, but Tom was the one she waited impatiently to see. On the twenty-eighth of September, her birthday, Polo gave her a card and flowers at lunch. Ken Collin didn't know it was her birthday. Tom called, sent flowers and when he arrived shocked her with a gold link necklace with a stunning deep blue sapphire imbedded in gold. Her birthstone. Surprise gave way to smiles; she felt she was finding happiness and Tom seemed that way as well. Emily hoped she knew where they were heading, yet still held herself back, reserved. Tom accepted her reticence and gave her the leeway she needed. He knew she liked him and saw no reason why he couldn't let nature take its course.

On Friday 29th, the day after her birthday, Emily and Polo went to see her father. Polo knew they wanted to have personal time together and stayed in the visitor's area.

After the happy birthdays and a card, her father spoke half-seriously, "I now bestow on you the key to your Trust," and handed Emily a symbolic key. "My God, Dad, I completely forgot! I receive my Trust! I now become the richest woman on the east coast!"

"Not by a long shot, although you'll never want for anything."

"I don't want for anything now, Dad, except to have you out of here."

"Thank you dear. Nevertheless, have you decided what you want to do?"

"I want to leave it where it is. I have a great car and an allowance, thanks to you. I have a nice condo and salary from Thorton; I love my job. So I'm comfortable the way things are right now and would like to let the Trust stay as it is."

"That's fine if that's how you want it. By the way, speaking of your school, how's everything there?"

"I love it again, Dad. Lot of work because we're short two teachers, but the rest of us pitch in and get things done. They're great kids trying their best, and we help. It's rewarding."

"That's great, but strange. How long have you been short teachers?"

"Actually, as I think of it, I would guess for over a year, but I'm not complaining, the Quad Trust has been wonderful. Anyway, speaking of the Trust, I met Tom Crane, who does the audits for you. You know his father. I didn't tell you before, but now that I'm dating him, I thought ..."

The look that crept across over her father's face caused Emily to catch her breath. "What is it, Dad? You all right?"

Sinclair held up his hand for her not to speak. He walked off, leaving her sitting there dumbfounded, at a loss as to what was wrong.

When he returned, he sat and took her hands, "Don't ever see Tom Archer Crane again. You know I would never ask this of you if I didn't have a good reason. I'm asking you to promise me you'll not see him."

"Why? Paully said the same thing. Why don't you and Paully want me to see him? You've got to give me a reason."

"Emily, Tom's father is a good friend of mine and one of the four partners in the Quad Trust. For me to accuse his son of what I firmly believe he is guilty of, would destroy our friendship. I believe he is guilty of something, and hearing Paul warned you also, only confirms, my beliefs. I'm asking you not to see him again. Ever again."

167

"Dad, without a reason? I can't do that. I can't ignore a person I like so much. What if you're wrong? What if you've made an error? I don't know what to say. What would I tell him? Someone says you're guilty of something, I don't know what, so I can't see you anymore?"

"I'm not just someone, Emily."

"You know it's not meant that way, Dad, it's just that …."

Parker Sinclair studied the floor. Emily stood near the window. Polo, outside, saw something was seriously wrong and stayed out of it. A father daughter quarrel was not something to step into.

Her father broke the silence, "All right, if I tell you I'll loose Tom's father, Bradford Crane's friendship, and this will probably cause the breakup of the Quad Trust. Do you feel enough for this person to have that happen?"

"Dad, I can't believe anything could be that serious. I know I'm being selfish, except this is my happiness, I need a reason."

Sinclair's sad eyes saw his daughter as a little girl, having her dreams dashed, "I think, no … that's wrong, I know, Tom Crane started your brother on drugs."

At first, Emily couldn't comprehend what was said; then her body tightened, her breathing labored. She barely caught the arm of a chair before her legs weakened. Everything blurred to nothingness.

When she came to, she was in the infirmary. With Polo and Sinclair still shaken, the doctor assured them she would be fine in a half hour or so. The men settled down onto a couch. Neither spoke at first. Polo seeing Sinclair perplexed, in grave thought.

At last, he looked at Polo, "Thank you for not questioning me, Ray. So now that I've got my wits about me, I'll tell you; I told Emily her boyfriend got Paul onto drugs."

Polo looked away, "Are you serious? Christ, that's one hell of a charge to lay on anyone, much less your own daughter."

"I know, still, I don't regret it, despite what just happened. It was the only way I can get her to stop seeing that drug dealing son of a bitch."

"Do you think she will, Parker? Stop seeing him I mean."

"I don't know. If she believes me, she will. She loves her brother. I can't prove Crane did it and Paul won't admit it. Some stupid druggie's code of honor."

"If I can talk to him, I'll get him to admit it."

"No doubt, Ray. Thank you, but Paul's gone, God knows where."

"I don't mean talk to Paul; I mean *talk* to this Crane guy."

Sinclair stared at Polo for most of a minute, "No that won't work, as much as I would like to have you *talk* to him. It's unfair to you. If Emily does, or doesn't believe me, she's going to see Crane at least one more time. You can bet he'll be ready with a slick answer about her brother. Although my Emily is levelheaded, who knows what a person in love will believe? Could you snoop, please excuse the word, and get to the truth, short of breaking a few of Tom Crane's bones? Because there *is* something else I want to share with you in confidence."

For an instant, Sinclair paused, unsure of his next words. He knew there was no alternative, "Ray, for some time now, actually two years, ever since I suspected Crane had initiated Paul's drug problem, I've had a detective follow him. Even though I acted surprised when Emily said she was dating him, I already knew from my contact. I couldn't let on because Emily might question how I knew. She's smart enough to put two and two together and come up with the right answer. Anyway, to get back to my story, aside from his dating other women here and there, still is in fact, it appears Crane has a designer drug habit. He parties heavy, and, this is the key part, he pays cash most of the time and burns money like it is going out of style. He has a condominium smack in the middle of Newport, runs around in a new BMW Seven Series and has a forty-foot yawl at a slip at the main dock. With that knowledge, I hired another detective who is also a CPA, dealing in white-collar crime. He came up with the facts Crane earns thirty-two thousand a year, which I knew, and he has a Limited Trust from his father he cannot touch until he is thirty-five. A Limited Trust, Ray, means he can only draw down so much each year, in Crane's case, only fifteen thousand. Can you imagine a father who cannot trust his son to handle money until he is thirty-five? Even then, it is limited. The kid's a wastrel."

Polo smiled to himself, Parker's own son fit that description. Sinclair continued, "Now, this is where it gets more interesting. The detective tracking Crane told me he is erratic in his duties to the Quad Trust and is often on his boat through the week. It has been this way at least since I hired the detective. In other words, he's seeing my daughter, and other women, when he should be in other cities or states doing audits. Now, listen to this, when I contacted one of my friends who's supervising the expenditures of the Academies for the Quad Trust, he reports, every audit comes though on time, every month."

Polo could see Crane was not doing his job. So what? Happened in every business. Parker would have to come up with more than this to hang something on him.

"Ray, here's my point. Something Emily said today struck me. She said her school was short two teachers. *That is not true*, at least not on the forms from Crane's audits. Which means the Quad Trust is paying two salaries which do not have teachers attached, as well as paying expense vouchers for them and expenses for Crane's mileage, which never happened."

Sinclair now had Polo's full attention.

"Let me continue this a bit further. We hire teachers as needed. For the sake of argument, let's say one Academy has a shady Comptroller. That person says he needs two teachers. The auditor, Crane, confirms the need and two phantom teachers start getting paid four hundred dollars a week, which totals eight hundred a week. Now, we have ten schools. If there are three Comptrollers who don't give a damn about the children, we can extrapolate twenty four hundred dollars a week. If that's split between the Comptrollers and Crane, they more than double their incomes. That, Ray, spells grand theft.

On top of that, you can bet Crane isn't paying taxes on one cent of it. The Trust tried to save money by making the Comptroller, the Manager as well. We thought having an Auditor's oversight would be adequate. It would be if the Auditor were honest. I went along with Crane's father Bradford, for hiring his son, but that was before I started to suspect him about *my* son.

One last thing, Ray, Emily and Paul's Trusts are tandem with the Quad Trust. My contact at the Quad stated Crane, as auditor for the academies went through all the titles in the Trusts about a month ago. I'll admit he has somewhat the right to do that in his contract, but not the *need*. You can see the point I'm making. Crane must know Emily's Trust is now available to her. Ray, just to let you know the importance of what I'm telling you, her before tax yearly *dividends* from the Trust could comfortably be set at half a million dollars."

Polo leaned back in his chair, amazed; Parker had laid out a scenario both well thought out, and shocking, if correct.

"Okay Parker, lets break this down. You think Crane got your son on drugs and you want to get even *and*, get him away from your daughter. The second story line is you think Crane is a crook. He spends more than he earns. He pays with cash. He has too many expensive toys. You have a school that he, in essence, supervises and they're paying for more teachers than they have. That scenario is plausible and you're right, it very well could expand to other schools. On top of this, you have a bastard, who you think may be after your daughter's money. Do I have your permission to do something about it?"

"Help me here, Ray. Crane will find some way to weasel out of what I told her. If he's the sly fox I think he is, Emily will believe him. I don't have any facts to back me. That's how he'll get her to believe him."

"Let me think a minute."

In the silence, Sinclair looked close to crying.

"Okay, Parker. There's no sense in my going and beating a confession out of him because you could be wrong, am I right?"

Sinclair nodded without conviction.

"So there's nothing I can do on that end, but, here's what we'll do about Crane's wild ways. I'll clue in a friend of mine with the IRS about what we think is going on. He'll pull Crane's tax return. If it shows he's only claiming his salary then, with your written permission, as a partner in the Quad Trust, we will do a little night audit on Emily's school. If you're right in your assumptions we'll find where the phantom teacher's checks go. If you're wrong, I'll be in deep trouble with my IRS friend."

Polo looked up, "Talk to you later about it, Emily's walking this way."

She had recovered from her fainting spell and did not want to continue the conversation, saying goodbye to her father. The parting strained, she saying she would speak to Tom Crane. Sinclair gave Polo a knowing glance. On the way back to her place, Emily guessed her father had spoken to Polo about Tom and kept her thoughts to herself. Polo was equally silent, other than asking her to coffee in a day or two and she agreed.

To get Crane out of his head, Sinclair thought about Ruth Carvel. She was lonely, that was obvious. She did not have to write him. She reached back into happier times and found him. She heard what had happened, yet still wanted to correspond. He wondered if she thought of him in the past, then found it to be highly unlikely, also highly conceited. He mused over what he would say if he did write. He dismissed the notion and went on to other things. Then came back to her. Finally, he left and taught his students English pronunciations.

He went back to his cell and wrote.

Dear Ruth,

I must tell you your letter was the surprise you thought it would be. In all honesty, I had not thought of you for all the many years that have passed. However, your missive became more and more welcome as I remembered those days with you. I would like to be a friend of yours again, although I am poorly positioned to be so at my present address. If you can put up with accepting where I am each time and write, I will certainly respond.

As a starter in memories, do you recall the time at Hampton when we walked along the beach one night and fell into that ditch? If memory doesn't fail me, the bottom was all mud and you lost a shoe. I also seem to recall that you took it well—you were like that.

I'll let it go at that for a beginning.

Yours,

Parker

Not a week passed, another letter came. He knew the return address.

Dear Parker,

Your letter was most welcome and made my day. I had thought of you now and then as the years passed, but frankly it was only when I read of your 'problems' that memories poured forth. And, speaking of memories, it must have been some other young lady you were walking with that time. I would never walk alone with a boy on a beach at night in those days!

Parker stopped reading. The wrong woman, my God! He felt terrible at his blunder, then continued, feeling the fool.

Parker, I'm teasing you. It was I! Although, please allow me to elaborate.

You had your arm around me and you slipped. A gentleman would have let go, but you dragged me in behind you. Shame!

You are correct when you said I lost a shoe. I also had mud all over my dress and a sprained ankle. You carried me all the way back to the B and B where I was staying and I just now started to laugh at the memory of the owner's look, how she glared at you for bringing me back in such condition.

You sent me two boxes after that. One was a lovely pair of shoes, my size, how did you know? In the other box was a pair of rubber boots, plus a note asking for another date— AFTER my sprain healed! You made that clear. Of all things! The nerve of you!

Anyway, after that we did have more fun.

173

Then you were honest, and told me you had met someone you cared for more, and you were gone from me.

Now we converse again. Strange world, Parker.

Fondly,

Ruth

When Emily opened the door, it took only a split second for Tom Crane to see something was wrong. She was visibly agitated as she asked him to come in and sit down.

"What's wrong, Emily?"

"Tom, I want a straight answer. Did you turn my brother on to drugs?"

"What are you accusing me of? Why would you even ask me ask such a thing?"

"I asked a question, Tom."

He closed his eyes, then tilted his head to the ceiling, "That story went around a long time ago, and I guessed you would hear it someday. I simply didn't know how to bring it up. I swear I did not start, or give, Paul drugs. You're upset and I understand why, but listen to me, please."

She sat on the sofa, her nerves unraveling. She loved this man and what he said now could decide their future.

"When I met Paul again, he was going to Brown University. He'd come down to my parent's home in Newport when he didn't feel like going to classes. He was a little young for me to hang out with, but he was a character and I enjoyed his company. I'd see him maybe once a month. Then, as the year went on, I noticed a change in his personality to where he was getting more and more jumpy. I didn't know that much about drugs, so I didn't know whether to face him down about that possibility, or what to do. I told you before, he and I had a falling out and I didn't want to tell you the reason."

She was restless, nearly shaking, trying to focus on his words.

"Please be patient with me, Emi. It's not easy to tell you what happened. One evening he was moody and I was fed up with him. Next thing, he jumped up and said, "Let's go to Fall River. I've got to see someone." I asked why he didn't see him on his way back to the university; it was right on his way. He mumbled something about his not going back to Brown and he needed to pick up something before this person left the state. To get rid of him, I said okay and I drove while he looked at a note with directions. We parked beside a tavern, and I know, it was dumb of me not to see what was going on. When it finally hit me, he jumped out and ran inside before I could say anything. I couldn't leave him there, so I waited."

Tom rose, rubbing his hands together. He sat on the sofa near her. Emily looked at him, perplexed, waiting impatiently for his story to continue.

"This is where it becomes difficult for me, Emily, and I'll look bad. Except you have to know. While I was waiting, I rolled the windows down and smoked a cigarette, getting angrier by the second. Fifteen minutes later, I saw him in the rearview mirror. As he came to the car, he threw a plastic bag onto my seat, and then walked right past me ... and *kept* walking! I was no fool; I saw the bag contained white powder. Paul had walked off, waiting to see if the police or some hoods jumped me. I was shaking. I grabbed the bag, opened my door, and threw it under the car. I hit the ignition, starting to leave. Paul ran back and jumped in. When he asked for the bag, I hit him in the face with a backhander."

Tom stopped. He had been so involved with the story he failed to notice her crying.

"Emi, all I can say is I'm sorry."

She put a hand on his arm, "Please Tom, go on."

"I don't want to put you through this."

"Please, I've got to know."

"God, Emily I hate telling you this. I told him I threw the bag under the car and he cried that it was all the money he had. I didn't care. Emi, I've got be honest, I hated Paul that moment. Some punks could have beaten me up, or if it had been the police, my reputation and my family's would have been ruined. By the size of the bag, I could have gone to prison. He whimpered about my throwing the bag away. His nose was bleeding and he cried all the way back to Newport. I didn't give a damn. I was focused on what could have happened. I've never forgiven him. Anyway, when we got back I grabbed him, pushed him into that little Jag of his, and told him never to come back. I imagine that's when he started the story blaming me. Getting even, I guess. He said I was the person supplying him drugs and I've never lived it down. That was the last I ever saw of him, Emi. And that's the truth ... I'm so sorry."

Neither spoke. Emily choked up, Tom talked out. She moved closer to him and put her hand in his, "Thank you for telling me. It hurts. I can see why you didn't want to tell me before."

"Tonight, I was going to ask you to marry me. Not now, you have a lot to forgive me for, if you can. I know I didn't help Paul when he needed it."

"Jesus, Tom, just give me a little time. I need to face what my brother was like. In a few days, please remember the question you were going to ask."

Tom got up, said goodbye. Emily didn't want him to go, although she understood. She could see he had laid himself open and needed time to himself.

She kissed him lightly as he left, "Call me tomorrow ... please."

Tom sat in his BMW, knowing it was the perfect moment to leave. The smile widened across his face. He had laid out a plausible story and she bought it. That Goddamn father of hers must have told her. Well, whatever. They can't prove he turned her wacked out brother onto drugs. Though now, he'd have to move on her faster, before anything else could go wrong. Next date, push ... give her a diamond, tell her they should elope. A good idea. That diamond would get him her multimillion-dollar Trust and, she's good looking. Not the best personality, still, he could put up with her, at least for a while.

As Tom drove off, he reached under the seat, picking up a tin, prying off the top. A couple of pinches between his thumb and forefinger, he sniffed. He couldn't be more proud of himself. He'd dodged a bullet, and had a plan.

The story Tom told was true, only it hadn't happened between he and Paul, but with two other people he knew. And, it did fit perfectly.

Parker wrote again to Ruth. Letters passed between them. One day a phone call came to her home. Calls became common. Then, one day, Parker stood at the front door of the Center, and welcomed his visitor.

Chapter

Twenty

I RS agent in charge, Kevin Sullivan, sat in his office with Ray Polo, Parker Sinclair, and two other agents.

Four days earlier, agent Sullivan laid out his documentation stating Tom Crane's tax form claimed his sole income derived from his salary from the Quad Trust and a personal Trust. Sullivan also confirmed Crane lived well above his means, *exceedingly* well, and must have a supplemental income not listed on his tax form.

Following this information, the next move was to get into the Comptroller's office at Emily's School and dig into expense and payroll records. Sinclair had the legal right to go into any academy controlled by the Trust, but they wanted the survey discrete so as not to alert other academy Comptrollers. Because of this, they used Polo to flash his badge at the sixty-eight-year-old night security guard at Emily's school, saying there had been a report of someone prowling around the building.

The security guard, finding comfort in Polo's size, obliged to shut off the alarm system, and the two started their search the furthest distance from the offices. Sinclair supplied a master key to the building and Agent Sullivan along with two IRS CPAs carrying their own master file keys, thumbed quickly through two years of checks. Once they matched two payroll stubs claiming one name and the cancelled checks to Tom Crane, it was obvious not the least attempt to obfuscate the fraud was attempted. Next, they

179

made copies on a copier without a counter, returned every item to its rightful place, and slipped out, signaling Polo by flashing their car lights. He told the security guard all looked okay and ordered him not to inform anyone in the office or the teachers about a break-in report. He explained it could be a disgruntled employee and the police had the building under surveillance. Despite the lame reason, Polo hoped it would keep the man quiet for a few days. That would be long enough.

So now, sitting in Agent Sullivan's office, they listened to a litany of two weekly check stubs made out to false names and one check made out to, and cashed, by Tom Crane. The other, by the Comptroller. Parker Sinclair's educated guess was right on the mark. The Comptroller and Crane were pocketing sixteen hundred dollars a month each, going back seventeen months. Twenty-seven thousand, two hundred dollars, was stolen from this one Academy. How many more were there?

The first step was to draw up a brief on the charges and a warrant for Crane's arrest, which would be served the next day. At that same time, nine CPAs and eighteen agents would enter the remaining nine Academies to review the accounts payable, salaries, and any other bookkeeping arrangements possibly used to hide illegal activities. Guilty parties would be arrested at that time. If any more Comptrollers were charged, Sinclair authorized the Office Manager placed in control until reorganization.

As Polo and Sinclair drove from the IRS office, Sinclair commented, almost to himself, he should call Crane's father the next day. He didn't know what to say. Sorry Bradford, your son is a crook and I caught him. Whatever he said, nothing was going to come out right.

Tom Crane had done more than steal money; he had ruined a thirty-year friendship, and that would break up the Trust. Sinclair felt he had no choice. Stealing is reprehensible under any circumstances; to do this to children for greed is despicable. Sinclair would do it again if he had to, but a sudden consternation came upon him painfully. Emily, he had not thought of her! What could he do?

"My, God, Ray, I've totally forgotten about Emily!"

"I haven't, Parker. As soon as I heard about the checks I knew she'd be terribly hurt."

"I can't tell her, Ray, I just can't. You've got to do it … please."

Polo nodded. He had already thought it out, and knew it was impossible to put Parker through the agony of telling his daughter the person she loved is a thief. There was no one else to tell her. The following day would be Saturday October, 21st. Polo knew the IRS would make the arrest sometime then.

Emily's father had been incarcerated for one year, Polo thought, as he headed for her condominium. The changes since then baffled him. How did he wind up having to tell the woman *he* secretly, or not so secretly loved, the person *she* loved was a crook, not a cheap one to be sure, nevertheless, a crook.

When Polo asked to meet her, Emily could tell he was serious about something and told him to come down in the morning. She did not mention she and Tom had planned to meet at noon and drive across to the Mohawk Trail to see the foliage, despite the lateness of the season. Tom only said he wanted to go for a drive. To her it was so different, his wanting to drive there, she felt something momentous was going to happen, and easily guessed its significance. Emily was sure of her answer.

When Polo entered, she gave him a kiss on the cheek, "Okay, Ray, what's the grave look about? You've had me curious since you called. it can't be all that bad."

"I'm afraid it is."

She tensed, "God! It's not Dad?"

"No, it's not your father or Paul. Please sit down."

Doing as told, she stared at Polo.

"Emily, there is no easy way to tell you this. If it hasn't happened already, Tom Crane is being arrested today for …"

She went dumb, "What are you saying, Ray? What the hell are you saying?"

"Please Emily, sit back and I'll tell you."

All sorts of thoughts raced through her mind, drunken driving, in a fight, caught doing something wrong with his rowdy boat friends. Polo was too serious for that. She inhaled, and huddled in her chair, frightened of what she'd hear next.

Polo watched her intently for signs of fainting, "Crane has been arrested for conspiracy to commit larceny and grand larceny. In his case, over twenty-seven thousand dollars and possibly many thousands more."

Emily's breathing became shallower, her eyes roamed the room, "You must be joking, that can't be true. It's not. It's not, it's *just* not."

"Emily, listen to me. This is another of those hellish things you have to face. I know it's tough and I know I can't feel what you are going though. Try to stay calm, and understand."

"What did you say he did? I mean, whom did he steal from? It's got to be a mistake!"

"It's not a mistake. Crane stole it from your school."

"From my school? That shows it's crazy! We don't have that kind of money there!"

"I can't go into this step by step; but you know your school was short two teachers. Nevertheless, the Trust was paying for them. An investigation revealed your Comptroller and Crane split the money for seventeen months."

"Who said he did this? I mean who said this happened, who accused him?"

He had to tell her, "You told your father about being short two teachers, and he knew that wasn't right since the Trust was paying for them. Your father, not trusting Crane because of Paul, asked me to help, so I contacted IRS friends and it went from there."

"So you and my father conspired to get Tom?"

"What are you saying, we *conspired to get Tom*? Money was stolen. We got the thief."

She recoiled at the word thief. Her face became fixed, her body rigid, "My father was wrong about Tom giving Paul drugs! Tom told me what happened. You're probably wrong now, too! The two of you are out to get him only because I love him!"

Polo stood, "I don't care what you've been through. I will not take that kind of talk! You have no right to say that about your father, or me. You ought to hear yourself, a starry-eyed little girl in love, ready to fight anyone for her lover, and won't believe he is a damn crook no matter what. For Christ's sake, Emily, he stole from your kids! Someday when you're really in love, you'll look back and realize how stupid and cruel you are right now."

Polo threw open the door and headed for his Buick. Rammed into Drive, the tires spun, stones pelting his fenders and bodies of the vehicles around him. The owners of the vehicles lucky they didn't catch up as he tore down the street.

Angry, despondent, he couldn't rationalize her words. Stupid women in love, brainless. She hurt him more than when his wife left. He believed in Emily so much, thought he knew her. Now she too had turned on him, over another man, again, like his wife. His anger subsided. Hurt replaced it. He was not accustomed to despair, his concern for her for over a year, replaced by emptiness. Even all he had accomplished with the police, paled to little or no value without her in his life.

He entered his house studying her touches: the drapes, a lamp, dishes, even food in the refrigerator. She was everywhere. He cracked open a beer, fell into a chair and sulked.

Another beer found him wallowing in self-pity. Three more drove him even lower.

The doorbell rang.

"There's no one here. Beat it!"

The bell, again.

"God damn it! Get the hell out of here or I'll put a slug through the door!"

The door opened slowly.

183

"Emily! God damn it! What in Christ's name are you doing coming here?"

She came closer. He could smell fading perfume, "Please, Ray, please forgive me."

Polo said nothing, doing his best to sober up. She was tear-stained, wretched; pain etched her face.

She shook slightly, "Please, Ray, I didn't know what I was saying. It wasn't me talking. One minute I thought I was going to be proposed to, the next I was stunned by what you said. I retaliated without thinking, everything crashed down on me. I couldn't help it. I'm sorry, I'm sorry."

He stood and put his arms around her. He felt her quivering, "You don't know how it feels, Ray. My heart's broken."

He knew how she felt, only too well. Yet even though drunk, he couldn't let on, "I do know how you feel, and I want to help. But you can't do this to me again, Emily. No matter how I … feel about you, I can only take so much."

"I promise, with all my heart, I won't. You're the last person I want to hurt. What should I do? I need help. Please tell me what to do. You're the only person who can help me."

She started to fade and sagged in his arms.

Carrying her to the couch, he guessed that, aside from the shock he put her through, her mother's pills were in her system. He called Connie Johnson at the station, asking her to come over when her shift ended at noon. Then, to make sure Emily would be all right; he called the police doctor and told him to come over.

The doctor didn't question the circumstances, only checked Emily and found she had the appearance of sedatives, barbiturates he said. After checking her breathing, pulse and eyes, he stated she would be fine, once she slept it off. Connie arrived at that moment and agreed to take Emily to her house until she woke. They got her into Connie's car and left. Polo squirmed his way into Emily's Mercedes and put it away in his garage, hidden from prying eyes. He almost had to call someone to get him out.

Connie brought Emily back late the next morning. She had slept for sixteen hours and only now was becoming fully awake.

When Connie had left Emily was afraid, "Wasn't a bad dream, huh?"

"I'm afraid not."

She closed her eyes, "Anything more?"

"Crane was arrested, denied everything. The Comptroller was arrested at home, admitted every charge."

"How bad will it be for Tom?"

"I want you to know it may get worse, and you've got to face it. On Monday the other nine schools will be audited and I think some of them will add to his problems."

"So you think he's done something very wrong?"

"Very wrong? Call it a simple case of white-collar crime if it makes you feel better. He cheated your schools handicapped kids, and that makes him stinking scum in my book."

She managed a smile, "Same old Polo, everyone's only black or white."

"That's not true, Emily. Originally I thought your father was black in my book, yet now, he's almost white as far as I'm concerned."

"I'm sorry again. Please, take me for coffee and tell me you forgive me. I've got to hear that, Ray."

She didn't want to go into the coffee shop, too many people. They sat in the back seat of Buick beside the dumpster and stared at a gnarly old oak in front of the hood.

"Something else is on your mind."

"Ray, I'm coming apart ... mentally."

"Help me here, give me a for instance."

"Well, a for instance is, after you stormed out, I went ballistic. Cursing you and throwing things, I was hysterical. Then suddenly I stopped, sat there and calmly reasoned things out. If you said Tom was a crook, then he was a crook. Then, I was going to call him, warn him. Yet, if he weren't a crook, what would I be warning him about? Then I started on a rampage again, cursing a blue streak at Tom for having me love him ... and then, all at once,

185

I didn't love him. What kind of false love is that? I must be so desperate. I swore at myself for being so blind and stupid, to believe he wasn't the person that hooked Paully. I'm on a seesaw, Ray, I'm happy, I'm sad. I take a pill to help me sleep and I go berserk for an hour, then I sleep. I was this way before I met Tom, and now again. Help me, for Christ's sake."

"Number one, stop taking those pills. They were for your mother and you don't really know how they affect you. Number two, and forgive me for asking, are you pregnant?"

"No, no chance of that."

"Now, you're beyond my ability. You've been through too much and there's no shame in seeking professional help. I can find you someone who should be able to help, if you want."

She knew what he meant, "Okay, let's call that someone a shrink. I'm ready. Only please do it as soon as you can."

Tom Crane's troubles compounded on Monday. Four additional Comptrollers, listing phantom teachers were caught in the IRS blitz. In the seventeen months Crane had his operation functioning, he raked in an estimated two hundred, fifty thousand dollars. Along with his yearly thirty-two thousand dollar salary and fifteen thousand from his Trust, it was certainly enough to pay for his lavish lifestyle. He spent it all, excluding a checking account with twenty-two thousand dollars.

The IRS confiscated his condominium, yawl, BMW, Bentley Flying Spur, Harley Davidson, checking account, and miscellaneous other items.

When the dust settled, Crane's father, Bradford Crane, reimbursed the Quad Trust for the total amount stolen, then removed himself from the Trust altogether. He paid his son's unpaid taxes, and Bradford never spoke to Parker again, stating that Sinclair should have kept his son's transgressions between the two fathers. Especially so, considering Sinclair's son Paul was no angel. The fact the felony couldn't have been discovered without contacting the authorities, fell on deaf ears. Although five Comptrollers had stolen money, the Court found Crane seduced them into the crimes. They received six months imprisonment, four years probation with the mandate to make full restitution. The best attorney's money could buy represented Crane against the IRS and other Federal agencies as his crimes had crossed state lines. Since his father made restitution, Tom Crane, received only three years in federal prison and five years probation. Yet, he was infuriated with his father for not getting him a better deal. In response, his father was irate enough to remove his son from his Trust and dispersed the monies to his three other children. The removal was sure to cause legal and sibling problems down the road, but Bradford didn't give a damn. He had enough money to handle any problems he might have with a convicted felon.

Chapter

Twenty One

By the beginning of December, it was apparent to everyone the town was growing. A fifty-eight-unit condominium was under development where the Miller's Farm and FC's old trailer once stood. Seventy-three single-family building permits were issued by the end of November, not including three multi-apartment complexes.

The voters had chosen a Charter form of government and the Manager had designated a tract of town owned land as mixed use, light industry. This move was designed to draw employment for younger people in hopes of keeping them in a town that, although growing, it's population was aging at the same time. The new town office multiplex, encompassing all the town agencies including the police and fire stations completion dates were on schedule.

Professionally, Ray Polo was satisfied. The new police station would answer the town's estimated needs for at least the next fifteen years. The staffing, now at sixteen officers, was the best-trained, professional force in the state. Other town committees often called Polo asking if he were available to help them. He offered advice on the phone, but, with his mind fixed on retirement, he was unwilling to offer more.

Collin became Captain, the other officers moved up a notch. Ken proved up to the challenge and expected to become Chief someday. Polo backed off from the every day, down and

189

dirty management, giving the new Captain full authority. The fleet of new Dodge Chargers, meeting Polo and Collin's performance specifications had been delivered. Per capita crime was the lowest in the Commonwealth. The town Manager was pleased with Polo's performance, average townspeople congratulated him and Parker Sinclair felt his judgment justified, his money well spent.

Polo's personal life was another matter, and remained in flux. Emily's problems ran deeper than anyone realized. It turned out she had been taking far more of her mother's pills than she let on. Was there any permanent damage to the psyche? That was hard to say, but the doctor's didn't believe so. Time would tell, they said. Her psychotherapist indicated she was harboring grief and guilt, intertwined with her brother and father's tribulations. This had biased her values, made her question her life. With the proper balance of drugs, a stable life, friends, and bi-weekly meetings to help her face her devils and get them out in the open, the doctor felt she would respond positively. Nevertheless, Polo and her father were made aware Emily could go along as normal as the next person. Yet, a traumatic occurrence, or flashback to some deep-seated episode, could prompt sudden emotional turmoil. The severity? The doctors couldn't predict.

Other doctors confirmed the diagnosis, leaving both men concerned for her future. They resolved to be careful, which meant nothing, since they didn't know what to be careful about. Still, while they trod gently around her, Emily, with nominal pills, went on with her life, just as she had in the past.

The holiday season came, a few gifts passed between the three of them, along with wishes for a better New Year. The twelve months of 1968 slipped into the mist of fading dreams.

The tourist town of North Conway, in the Mount Washington Valley of New Hampshire was a magnet for students looking for service industry jobs when college semester's end. As the student workforce grew throughout the valley, cocaine was the insidious poison trapping their minds, and Paul Sinclair's business grew exponentially with it.

Paul had become paranoid with good reason. The deal he was waiting to close was going to set him up for the rest of his life. Three hundred thousand dollars was the final figure agreed upon by his new Montreal supplier. When that deposit was confirmed, he would be gone. Added to that amount, he had five hundred thousand tucked away in various banks. He smiled; it was all tax-free, as long as he moved faster than the IRS.

His nerves were stretched. If his suppliers in Boston or New York heard about the deal he made with Montreal, he could be fitted for cement boots. For the past three months, he had lived on edge. He practiced pistol shooting in the woods and watched for people who might be following his Jeep as he made his rounds. He kept a .38 revolver under the vehicle's seat, and .45 automatics in each of the cabin's three rooms. He slept in his clothes, even with his boots and jacket on at times. Photocells were mounted on the trees at the entrance to his dirt road; if the beams were broken, an alarm would sound in the cabin. The trouble with the damn alarms, he cussed, was deer or moose wandering down his road would set the alarm off, causing him to leap to a window. Six times, it had happened, four when in fitful sleep.

This January night, when it squealed in his ear, he got up and turned it off. On his way to the bathroom, he glanced up the road. A car, stopped, lights out, two men struggling down frozen ruts toward his cabin. This was *it*; no one knew where he lived. These men after him do bad things. Paul grabbed a .45 off the couch and, when he turned back to see the men, one was climbing through a snow bank, obviously headed for the rear of the cabin. The moonlight glowed off his pistol. Paul understood, there would be no conversation. He was prepared. The other man crept slowly up the three stairs, the dry, cold snow squeaking under his shoes. His body filled the glass pane in the front door. Paul aimed chest high, firing four shots. Glass and wood exploded under the force of the slugs and the man, thrown back off the stairs, crashed to the frozen ground. Paul forced open the shattered door, taking a quick look. The assassin wore street shoes and no gloves. City hit men he thought, no brains. That was important. He ran beside the ruts for twenty yards then jumped over a snow bank, pulling woolen gloves out of his jacket. A quick glance confirmed the car at the end of the drive was vacant. Paul's heart pounded, knowing the man out back, in shoes, without gloves, wouldn't last too long.

After ten minutes, he heard the man shout, 'Tommy, Tommy'. The voice sounded scared. Paul was sure the man was shivering. Most importantly, he hadn't gone in the cabin. Paul waited.

It had been a cold winter and then, five days earlier, the temperature had dropped even lower. The gusting wind behind the cabin must have brought the chill factor to five degrees, Paul guessed. The man must be freezing. Paul saw a movement at the side of the building, too far for a shot in the shadows. Patience, patience. He was tense, waiting; the man stumbled through the snow to the front. He looked at the house, saw no one up at the car, then saw the body. Panicking, he started to run up the drive. Paul stood and fired three times into his chest.

The man, hurled into the icy snow bank, slid down, lying in the ruts, gurgling blood, and died.

Paul shook from released tension. After checking the car at the end of the drive, he walked unsteadily back to the cabin. Crouched by the stove, shivering, he sniffed white powder from a plastic bag. That would help him decide what to do.

Leave? Run? No. Hide. Hide everything so no one would ever know, and then run. He stared at the problem, deciding his next moves. His plow was mounted on the Jeep beside the house. He cleared a path to the frozen lake. Finding the keys still in the Lincoln, he brought it down and dragged the men into the trunk.

Two questions remained for him; would the ice hold the Lincoln long enough for him drive out onto the lake and then, could he jump out of the vehicle before it broke through. Well, he thought, won't know without trying. He put the Lincoln into gear, letting it slowly roll down the embankment and onto the lake. The frozen sheet was cracking under the load while Paul kept the door open and the car in gear until it barely moved. When the ice couldn't withstand the weight longer; he jumped out and watched the vehicle sluggishly break through, then begin to sink beneath the fractured field. Paul had the foresight to open the windows and when the water reached them, the Lincoln disappeared in seconds. He tossed in his assassin's guns and his three .45 automatics, keeping only his .38 revolver.

At the cabin, he pried away most of the splintered front door wood, shoving it in the wood stove, then patched the door with a piece of plywood. He thought the snow would cover the glass and blood on the steps and driveway until spring. By then it wouldn't matter.

He took the plow off the Jeep, packed some clothes along with his last packet of cocaine and a shopping bag containing seventeen thousand dollars. At first, he regretted not putting his clothes on the smaller of the two thugs and burning down the cabin. Too late now to consider that. Then again, in all probability, even with a charred body, even a myopic coroner would find the slugs. Besides, this was a better solution; a fire would have brought response from the Bridgeton Volunteer Fire Department. Now, however, it would be two, perhaps three months before the cabin's owner came looking for his rent. Still in the throes of winter, the landlord would find nothing other than a broken door and Paul no longer in residence.

Satisfied nothing remained to incriminate him; he turned the Jeep around and drove away. Before reaching the New Hampshire border on Route 302, he pulled over. Shaking badly, he reached for the plastic bag under the front seat. A few minutes later, he relaxed, energized over what he had accomplished. Now, the question was, who fingered him? He stopped at an all night diner in Conway, ordered a burger with fries to go, and then called three numbers from a pay phone in the rear of the store.

His Montreal contact was not surprised to hear his voice and Paul said he would send the names of his down line of distributors when Montreal sent three hundred thousand dollars, in English pounds, to the Royal Cayman Bank, Grand Cayman

Island, deposited to the account of Paul Sinclair. Montreal was surprised at the name; they knew him only as Peter Stanford. Paul hated giving his real name, yet there was no choice, it was the only way to get the money.

Maxie, in Boston, was surprised to hear his voice and recovered too late to hide it.

Paul was now certain Boston had tried to get rid of him. To get even, Paul told him his hit men, Tommy and the other punk, were gone for good, and he was coming for him next. Maxie was screaming as Paul hung up. He had spoken foolishly. Maxie couldn't be frightened, or ever give up the chase. For good reason.

Paul went south on Route NH16, then to Interstate 93. Before the Massachusetts border, he turned west driving along route 125 until he found a worn motel to plot his next steps.

Chapter

Twenty Two

On Tuesday, February 24, Polo received a call from Parker Sinclair asking if he was available the following afternoon. When they met, there was small talk, such as whether Polo thought Albert DeSalvo was the Boston Strangler. Sinclair thought he was, but Polo reminded him, DeSalvo's conviction was for rape only, not murder.

Their chatter ended. Sinclair told him he'd been informed he could have weekends at home, part of his pre-release program. Polo smiled inwardly. Parker was sentenced to only four to six years for killing his wife. He'd served around fifteen months and now he'd have weekends at home, the only restriction being no travel out of state, or driving. The deal keeps getting better, Polo smiled.

Sinclair wanted to go home for the afternoon without anyone knowing and Polo, a police supervisor of sorts, received permission to leave with him. Heading for the Buick, Sinclair stopped short, "What in the devil is this thing, Ray? Please don't tell me it's one of our police cars."

"Yep, I ordered seven of these Buick, two twenty five chase vehicles. I figured what the hell; you were picking up the tab, so why not go first class."

Sinclair laughed, "I'd love to see you going around a corner chasing some crook in this thing."

"I bet I could make it around."

"In control? Doubtful. My Jaguar could go around you twice while you were trying to go around once."

"Seriously Parker, I thought this visit wasn't official, so I brought my own car and as it turns out that's probably best. The Buick's been seen going up to the Hill any number of times. People seeing a police cruiser going up there could cause flap."

As they drove, Sinclair talked about his student prisoners, his hope the effort would help some of them get a job and stay away from their past lives. Polo didn't want to dash his passenger's hopes, so kept quiet. When Sinclair mentioned having a woman friend visiting him, Polo swerved, almost running off the road, causing them to laugh.

"That's great, Parker, can I be best man?"

"Why not, Ray? You're my best friend now that old FC is gone."

They fell silent. Polo thinking that here he is, a Boston cop and FC, the crippled old man, were a multimillionaire's best friends. Strange, and why?

Sinclair thought of Federal Census, and remained mute as Great Hill loomed in front of them. The wind was gusting, the temperature hovering around twenty-six degrees. Both men hurried inside. Polo turned the heat higher.

"I'm going to leave you for a couple of hours, let you have some time by yourself. I think that would be wise, Parker."

"That's good of you, Ray, it's what I wanted. Thanks."

Sinclair had tried to prepare for what was going to happen. It didn't help. His eyes watered as he walked slowly through the lower rooms feeling the memories, at times sad, at times smiling. His eyes overflowed. She was gone, gone forever. Could he ever be happy here again? He had to be here for some unfathomable reason. Fate put him here. Is it because this is where Paul would find him when he came back? He didn't know. When Emily comes, she would make it a home again. So he hoped. She's got to, she must.

The atrium was empty except for a new couch, table, and two chairs. So sterile, All his orchids gone.

At last, he summoned his courage to mount the stairs to the bedroom. He stood looking through the open door then, a step at a time, entered. Completely altered, the room was renovated from floor to ceiling. The color scheme different, every piece of furniture new and repositioned. Sinclair stared blankly. He entered, as he knew he must. Still, he couldn't focus. His mind told him he was utterly sad. He sat, crying. Nancy K was never going to be there. He still couldn't accept, couldn't comprehend. She wasn't here, and was never going to return, never going to smile, never say another word, never laugh again. At last he knew; all left now, were the countless wisps of memories, wrapping around, pressing on him. Memories in time fade, they hadn't yet and would never leave. Whether in prison or Great Hill, they would never be gone.

He took a key and went through the cold to the garage. On his way, he glanced down at the forlorn, snow-drifted paddock. Emily had mentioned Bismarck was at winter quarters in Saratoga. Even the horse was gone.

He unlocked the door knowing the rooms had only been cleaned, not repaired from the water damage after Federal's death. He went through the room, opening the inner door to the garage and stood looking at the car cover. Pulling it back, he smiled at the Jag. The vehicle was up on jacks, immaculate. He realized someone taking constant care of it. Slipping behind the wheel, he sat on the cold leather. His eyes flooded again. The times Nancy K and he would cruise over the back roads in the summer and fall evenings, listening to the bark of the exhaust as he geared down for a curve, then the howl of the twin cam motor in full acceleration as he powered out of the turn. In the fall the windows would be rolled up, top down, crisp air, heater on, and they'd share a cup of coffee.

His thoughts changed; no more FC sitting with him, conversations about everything around them, life, laughing at one of FC's obtuse comments. FC always saw through him and got to the crux of any matter. He only let four people into the core of his life. Now his wife and FC were dead and his son gone, probably killing himself with drugs. Only Emily was left, though certainly not well emotionally. Who could blame her? Who was left to

197

blame anyone for anything? Thank God for Ray. Where would the two of them be without him right now? Couldn't stand the man when he badgered, trying to find out what happened, or rather the why, of what happened. Insufferable, that's what he was. Now we wouldn't do without him, a big, honest, tough cop. He obviously loves Emily, yet knows that's out, still, he watches over her like a guardian. He's not only great for us, he's great for the town. I don't have to worry about Emily while he's ...

A knock on the door, breaking Sinclair's thoughts.

"Come on in, Ray."

"I don't want to intrude it's just that it's so damn cold out here, I wanted to see if you were all right."

"You're not intruding and I am cold. Come on, sit in the Jag with me."

"I'd never fit in this Tinker Toy, Parker, and if I did, you'd never pry me out."

"Good point, Ray." Parker wished Polo could have fit.

Parker left with thoughts of FC and Nancy K.

Back at the house, Polo made two cups of coffee. Parker said he had the difficult part of his return to the Hill out in the open and now was ready to spend weekends there. As he was not allowed to drive, he had arranged for a limo service to drive him both ways, not in a limo of course.

He asked two favors of Ray; would he please tell Emily her father would be at home on weekends and he hoped she would visit? Also, and this was important, tell her that he was seeing a woman he knew from the past named Ruth Carvel. Be sure and point out Ruth will not be there the first weekend.

"I hate to ask this of you, Ray, but I'm having difficulty in communicating with her and you seem to handle things better. This is a terrible thing for me to admit. I never had a problem talking with her before."

"Don't worry it into an ulcer, Parker; it will all work out if we give her time to heal."

"I don't want to lose her; she's all I have left here."

"Okay, Ray," Emily asked, "what's so all fired important for me to here at 9:00 AM?"

"Have some coffee?

"Whoa, hang on! This must be *big*, you here before me, and making coffee."

"It is, sit. I'll tell you there's good news and there's news I don't know how you'll respond."

"You're making me leery, let's have the good news first."

"Your father is in a pre-release program at the Detention Center, which means he'll be here on weekends, until put on probation."

Happiness filled Emily's face, "Damn, Ray, damn, that's great. It seems so long since he left, like years. I'll be here every weekend and drive him so crazy with attention he'll want to go back to the Center every Monday. Gosh, I've got to get the stuff he needs in, I've only got a day."

"Just so you know, we were here yesterday that's why there's two dirty cups."

She looked at him sternly.

"I'm just kidding, kid. I left him here a couple hours, let him wander around and get his emotions straightened out. I found him sitting in the Jag and he seems okay. God awful sad, but that's to be expected."

"Sure it's to be expected, I know first hand. Funny, he used to do the same thing with FC. Just sit in the Jag, shooting the breeze. Never leave the garage."

She stopped, staring at Ray's expression, "Okay Mr. Polo, your minds somewhere else. Hit me with the bad news."

"I'm not saying its bad news, just something I was asked to tell you that you don't know. Your father and I don't know how you'll take it so he asked me ..."

"Good Lord, you're beating around the bush, Ray, I've never known you to be devious. Let's have it."

"Your father has a lady friend."

199

Emily stayed calm, although empathic, "What does *a lady friend* mean, Ray? You're not suggesting the *lady friend* is a woman in the same jail with him, are you?"

Polo gave a nervous laugh, "No, no. The only thing I know about her is that your father went out with her before the war, before your mother. I don't know anything other than that, so please, don't grill me."

She went to the window, studying a few snowflakes dancing along the driveway.

"I'm glad, Ray. Naturally, I'm shocked. It's a good thing I had a pill earlier. But I think I'm glad."

"You sure? I mean I did lay it on you."

"Ray, for you, that was subtle. You know, the more I look at it, someone Dad likes will help him. Not to forget, we'll never do that, yet someone to talk to as he did with mom. I wonder how they met again, with Dad in prison. Anyway, want to meet her."

Emily's eyes were moist. Ray could see she was happy with her thoughts.

"Not this weekend. Your father said it was going to be just you and him."

Although Parker had not said that, Polo was sure the comment could only help make her feel good. He was right.

Mid-morning on Saturday the following weekend, found Emily and her father at Great Hill. At first, their meeting was uncomfortable. They were awkward around each other.

Eventually pleasant memories overcame the terrible. The father-daughter relationship found itself despite what went before. No panacea could ever gloss over what had happened. The past lived with them, always would. They moved in and out of those recollections until, finally, difficult memories were urged to the background, never gone, accepted by both they never would. Father and daughter knew they had to go on with their lives.

"Dad, Ray tells me that you have a lady friend. Tell me about her."

Parker was sheepish. She had never seen him that way and couldn't hide a smile.

"When I knew her, her name was Ruth Thomas, now it's Ruth Carvel, her husband died. Before I met your mother, I went out with Ruth a number of times. She was a great person, lot of fun, still is. Of course, once I met your mother no one else mattered. Ruth is quite a few years older now so you have to take that into consideration."

"Take what into consideration?"

"Well I mean it was a long time ago, she's aged."

"We all age, Dad, and why are you blushing?"

"I am not. The fireplace is throwing too much heat."

"Dad, the fireplace is two rooms away."

Neither could stop laughing.

"Seriously, Dad, I think it's great you've met a woman who likes *jailbirds*."

"Why you spoiled little horror. That settles it; I'm taking you to the orphanage right now."

"You can't scare me with that anymore; the law won't let you drive."

"Then I'm going to put you over my knee and give you the paddling you deserve."

With this, Parker jumped up and Emily quickly took a few steps back.

"See, I can still make you jump."

They both ended up laughing again. They were getting back together.

"Say, Dad, why don't you ask her over next weekend and I'll ask Ray. We'll double date. I'll cook dinner."

Parker gave her a mischievous look, "You're not planning to poison her, are you?"

Emily smiled sweetly, "Daddy, Daddy, how could you think such a thing?"

***

Irritated by the lack of response to the deal, Paul Sinclair called his Montreal connection.

"Why haven't you wired my money to the Grand Cayman's bank?"

"Well I'll be damned, if it isn't Peter Stanford, or should I say Paul Sinclair?"

The voice dripped with sarcasm. Paul abruptly went from irritation to concern, something was going on, still, he wasn't going to be cowed.

"Look, if you want my list of distributors you're going to pay, or I'll go somewhere else and you'll be out."

The voice on the phone growled, "Paul, Paul, Paul, you little jock strap, you've got nowhere to go. Let me tell you something. We're not as stupid as you think. We have our own network between suppliers, which means we stay within territories, it's better for business, less trouble between us. When you came to me, I figured you were some little smartass trying to con me, so I went along with you.

Then I contacted Boston. I told them your proposition and your real name's Paul Sinclair. They were interested in you, and I mean *interested*. So, that opened a numbers of options. Just so you know, the guy you know as Maxie in Boston figured you got rid of the two guys he sent for you. I don't understand how a little jerk like you did it, but one of the guys you whacked was Maxie's eighteen-year-old son. Follow what I'm saying, kid? You're walking dead. Maxie figures you hit his son and he doesn't even have a body for a big splashy funeral.

"Right now, he has all sorts of contracts out to track you down and he'll find your ass and your local distributors. That won't be hard. He already knows you're a parole violator so if you surface anywhere, even in prison … let's just say I'll get a kick out of reading your obit in the paper. Oh, and kid, just to let you know, he figured you had money stashed in banks, so our friends in the financial business queried all the banks in the area about you, or a Peter Stanford, and guess what? Your name came up with five banks for a total of around five hundred thou. Not bad for a whacked out little shithead. Anyway, your money's frozen, just the way you're going to be when Maxie catches up with you. I'll guarantee that."

The phone went dead. Paul was leaning against the booth, soaked in sweat. He had to get back to his motel. It was obvious they didn't know where he was, but he couldn't get at his money.

Safe behind his locked door he knew he had to think. First however, the plastic bag.

Lying in bed at Great Hill, Parker was awake, thinking of Ruth Carvel and dinner the next day. Then he sighed, his heart aching. Nancy K. What would she think? She'd be happy for him, no question, that was her. Nan. Her long dark hair, lying on her shoulders, flecked with gray. Nancy's smile, her taking his hand as they walked, messing his hair when he kidded her over some nothing, surprising him at the bank with lunch, giving him a no-reason gift, enjoying a laugh over one of his silly remarks.

She wore a pale blue blouse and white pleated skirt when they met. He thought her voice so wonderful. He was in love with her then, and for the rest of his life. She was so athletic; whether swimming, skiing, golf or showing their daughter, when a child, how to ride English saddle.

Her light kiss on his cheek … how it affected him. He once heard someone use the expression a person moved with grace. To him, that was his Nan.

After the war, when his Navy cruiser docked in San Diego, he stood on the bridge looking for her in the middle of hundreds of other wives and lovers. Then, a tall woman with a child holding each of her hands, stood out. They met, said nothing, staring at each other. The V mail letters came alive. She, unchanged, he, a man aged, a scar across his eyebrow, a poorly set broken nose. None of it mattered. He was home safe, and still loved her. She could see it in his eyes. Words would be a waste.

The children. He laughed aloud, remembering. Not four years old, wide-eyed, frightened. Their mother was crying. This strange man made her cry. So why was she hugging him?

Parker shivered under the blankets, then rose and sat in a chair by the window. To talk to her. She never answered. That was all right, didn't matter. As long as she knew he would always keep her alive within, was enough. Tears confirmed his thoughts.

Though he was not allowed to leave the house, he decided to go to the cemetery in the morning. It would be his first time there, to say goodbye. Polo could drive him, after which, he would help his daughter make their home ready for his guest.

Polo volunteered to pick Ruth up at her home. He waited while she bought flowers, and when they arrived at Great Hill, the weather had turned cold and windy. They hurried up the stairs, the front door opening before they rang the bell. Parker made the introductions to his daughter and from there the conversation seldom lapsed. They sat by the fire for a drink. When Emily said she must see to dinner, Ruth went with her to help.

"Well, Ray, what do you think?"

"Gosh, from the moment I picked her up she's been a delight."

Parker was pleased, but teased Polo, "A delight? Good Lord, Ray, what's a gruff ex-Boston cop doing using a word like delight? What going on? The Barretton Police giving courtesy lessons to smooth your rough edges?"

They laughed so loud both women hurried back to the room.

"Okay, you two," Emily asked, "What's so funny?"

Polo was self-conscious, but Parker had to tell them, "Ray thought Ruth is a delight, and I was baffled where he acquired this newfound style."

The women smiled, Emily remarking, "Don't go making Ray embarrassed, Dad, because that's the only word that could describe Ruth, delightful."

They returned to the kitchen, arm in arm. The men grinned like Cheshire Cats drinking cream.

Polo had one disturbing thought: Emily might have another pill in her.

For the next four weekends, Polo would pick up Sinclair from the Correctional Center on Fridays and Emily would pick up Ruth at her home Saturday morning, then drive her home Saturday evening. As Emily's car was small, she had to take Polo's Buick when picking up Ruth.

By the end of the forth weekend, plans changed. Emily or Polo would use the Buick on Friday nights, pick up Ruth and her overnight case, then drive south to get Parker from the Center and head to the Hill.

Emily said it was all right for Ruth to stay overnight as she, Emily, considered herself a very stern chaperone and any transgressions would be met with ruthlessness, meaning, she told her father, that he would be Ruth-less. Parker smiled, although not amused.

February gave way to March winds; they also brought warmer air to melt the remaining muddy snow, which then turned to slush and made the ground soggy. By the middle of the month, daffodils and crocus forced themselves through any remaining ice, blooming now in the slush; nothing could stop the inevitable.

On Great Hill, the inevitable also came to the older couple strolling among the budding trees, coat collars pulled up around their ears.

"Ruth, I'm asking you to marry me."

"Parker, from the moment we met before the war I'd have married you, and I've never changed through all these years. I still want to. Yes."

"I must be honest Ruth, and tell you something you must never mention to a soul as long as you live."

205

When he finished, she was weak, crying in disbelief. She held him close as they returned to the house.

When they sat by the fire that evening, she smiled, watching him in a minor argument with the television news. What a wonderful man, she thought. To have survived what he's been through, yet still carry on, and be able to love again.

Emily and Polo had congratulated them, and left hours ago.

Chapter

Twenty Three

Paul removed the number plates then pushed the Jeep into an isolated pond near southern New Hampshire's Loudon Raceway. He thumbed back to a nearby dealer, where he bought a nondescript 1960 Pontiac sedan. Now, the Jeep, sunken, could not be traced to him. However, he had no plans, and only nine thousand dollars left to survive. He couldn't withdraw his money from the banks since they'd frozen his accounts.

His Trust was due him. Like his sister, he turned twenty-five. How to get at it? What if his father had disowned him? The Boston gang, would they trace him back to his home? Without drugs to help over the rough spots, it was too much to grasp. He had barely enough, *if* he didn't go overboard using them. What to do? Where to go? He took another sniff, to help him think straight. At least, that's what the drugs told him.

Maxie, his former Boston dealer had indeed traced Paul to his father and his wealth. Maxie puzzled over the best approach for using that knowledge. He was confused; Paul was a drug addict, on the run for parole violation. His father had murdered his wife, less than two years ago, yet he's home on weekends. What in hell was going on?

There's money to make here, he thought. Maybe he wouldn't have Paul hit once they found him.

Maxie needed revenge. Still, if there was money involved, get that first, then kill him.

The wedding was held on Sunday, March 31 1968, at Great Hill. At first, the minister was hesitant about performing the ceremony between a murderer, serving time for the death of his wife, and a widow. After soul searching, and consulting his bishop, he united them—Emily, the maid of honor, Polo, the best man.

A major crisis loomed prior to the wedding. Ruth had two sons and a daughter from her first marriage; all were now in their middle and late twenties with spouses and children. The daughter could not accept the fact of her mother marrying again, wanting Ruth to remain single the rest of her life in reverence to her departed husband. The daughter was adamant, trenchant in her remarks concerning Parker, whoever he was. Ruth would not hear of it, telling her the marriage was going to happen and hoped her daughter would accept that fact, and attend. Her daughter hung up.

Ruth's two sons gave the opposite response. Happy for their mother, they would fly in to attend. Ruth did not want her boys thrown into turmoil by misinformation concerning Parker's past. Therefore, once again, Ray took on the impossible task of fully disclosing the details. He would inform them who Parker was, his past, and, to top it off, the fact their mother's new husband was a pre-release prisoner. Polo played up how distasteful the job was, but he had an idea, and, if he had an unlimited budget, he said he would do it. Although it raised eyebrows, it was agreed.

He had introduced himself to Ruth's sons by phone and knew the brothers, though living in different towns, were close to Charlottesville, a Virginia airport. He told them to be there with their wives on Saturday the 30th at 9: 00 AM, and someone bearing a sign would meet them. The two couples arrived, given VIP service and boarded a twelve person Lear jet for the trip north.

Landing at Worchester Regional Airport, they then toured the countryside by helicopter, where Polo pointed out Sinclair's bank, other buildings and holdings, then the Georgian house on

Great Hill. They landed in the paddock below the home, Parker, Ruth and Emily there to greet them

Parker took over the proceedings and presented a side of him Polo guessed was there, only hibernating in prison. Courteous, the perfectly casual host, initiating conversations and subjects, bringing out each guest, having them relax, finding their interests. Parker was a natural. It was a successful introduction. Ruth's sons were delighted with their mother's choice of another husband. Private rooms, catered dinner, fine wine, rounded out most of the evening. Then, Polo asked Ruth's sons and wives into the atrium. Ruth looked at Emily and Parker. Nervousness showed, perhaps Polo was not the person to explain the circumstances after all. Well, the die was cast; only hope remained.

Settled into comfortable chairs, Polo began, "Your mother, and mother in law," inclining his head to the son's wives, "and Parker want you to be aware of a circumstance that will more than likely never become knowledge where you live, but one of which you should be made aware."

Jeff Carvel spoke up, "Mr. Polo, a question if I may. Are you a friend of Mr. Sinclair's, or an employee?"

"I met Parker in my official capacity as Captain Detective with the Boston Police Department, working under directions of the Commissioner. When I retired from the BPD, I was hired by Parker as a consultant to create a professional police force for the town of Barretton. During that period I became friendly with both Parker and Emily."

"Just so I understand, Mr. Polo, you met Parker professionally and are now a friend. Are you no longer involved with him *professionally*, whatever that means?"

Polo saw that Jeff Carvel was sharp and getting ahead of the pace he wished to control.

"That is correct, other than the Barretton Police position. But please," he said firmly, "hold your questions until I've finished. Parker Sinclair was married to his first wife, Nancy, for more than twenty-four years and was devoted to her. Unfortunately, she began to suffer from early stages of

209

Alzheimer's and although the family did all they possibly could to stop the progression, Mrs. Sinclair got worse and, of even more concern, she became violent. It went on for months. Parker gave her all the help he, and the doctor's could, but she couldn't be helped. She was irrational, nothing would help, and she would not take prescribed sedatives. The room you're sitting in was covered in orchids at one time. Mrs. Sinclair destroyed them all. That night Parker's wife …"

Jeff Carvel stood, glaring at Polo, "He shot his wife! I read about him when I was in Boston!"

First was silence, followed by disbelief, when Polo did not deny the statement. There were gasps. The family members stared at each other, wordlessly turning back to Polo.

"It's true. Parker did end his wife's life. He did it to end her months of pain and mental suffering. He was found guilty of second degree murder, with extenuating circumstances, temporary insanity over his wife's condition."

"How long ago was this?"

"About fifteen months ago."

"Fifteen months? How can he be out, at home, after only fifteen months?"

That question opened a floodgate of questions with Ruth's sons pummeling Polo with concerns.

"Everyone *SHUT UP!*"

The group was intimidated. Someone that large and angry gave good reason.

In the dining room, they heard Polo shout, and cringed.

Polo began again, "Excuse me for shouting, *but just listen.* I was given Parker's case because he would not say why he did it. Outside of Parker, his children and the doctors, nobody knew Mrs. Sinclair's severe condition and he wouldn't say why he shot her because of his misplaced pride in trying to protect her dignity. He was willing to go to prison for thirty or forty years to protect her honor because he wanted people to remember her as she was, not who she had become.

It wasn't until I got the reason out of Emily and Paul, their son, to why he did it, and what had happened here, that the Court understood and granted leniency. Your mother is marrying a decent man, driven to his limit by a woman he loved, a woman who had entered a hell where she could only lash out in her agony. She destroyed the only thing he had left, his orchids. She would have never done that had she been in her right mind. Think! Put yourselves in his position. Your spouse does not know who you are, her brain degenerating into insanity and violence. What would you do? Have her drugged into never, never land as the doctors wanted? Put her in an asylum? Parker said people were only stored there, and chose not to. He tried to nurse her because of his love for her. It overwhelmed him; he couldn't understand that he couldn't help. He sought help from the best men, nothing worked.

It drove him nearly crazy, until he snapped for one moment. And she was gone. Before I met him, I wanted him imprisoned for the rest of his life. I learned from his children the hell he went through and changed my mind. I'm proud to say I became his friend. He doesn't deserve the hell he put himself through and I hope, if I ever came to that condition, someone would have the decency to put *me* out of my misery. That is how the Court judged the sad state of Parker's wife, with compassion and grace. All of you should understand and feel that way as well. Look how his daughter loves him. Do you think she would, if what he did was wrong in her eyes?"

They said nothing. Polo left and walked into an empty study, drained from raw emotion. Was what he said true, or made up as he spoke? He couldn't even be truthful to himself, yet he had to make them empathize. He had done his best.

Jeff Carvel spoke to his brother and their wives after Polo left, "It comes down to this. Mom's no fool, she's knows what she's doing. This Polo person changed his mind about Mr. Sinclair and he's obviously no fool either. And look how Mr. Sinclair's daughter loves him. I say let's back mom. Only for God's sake, don't tell our sister. If she got wind of it, she'd raise holy hell."

At length they agreed and moved awkwardly back into the living room.

From the moment Ruth, Emily, and Parker heard Polo yell shut up, they feared disaster was upon them, so when the group returned, smiles returned, then handshakes and hugs all around. Jeff Carvel summed it all up, "That Ray Polo guy sure is one hell of a convincing speaker."

Emily found Polo alone in the study. She sat on the arm of his chair, reverting to a little girl, her head on his shoulder, "Why aren't I older, or you younger?"

Before the wedding, Ruth and Parker requested there be no gifts. After the wedding however, Polo had one gift from Judge Butts: Parker's early release. Of course, there were still five years probation, which, considering all, was easily acceptable.

On April 4, 1968, on the heels of Martin Luther King's assassination in Memphis, Commissioner Kearney asked Polo back into the Boston Precinct. His special assignment was to direct coordination policies of police riot squads. The intension: to prevent or suppress any possible increase in gang activities. Assigned a sector of Dorchester, Captain Collin and two other Barretton officers volunteered. They wanted to gain experience with anti-gang operations.

The sector assigned to Polo's team of twenty officers was quiet until after midnight, when sporadic violence flared up. Most of the hostility wasn't in response to King's death, only an excuse to loot storefronts of televisions, stereos, watches and other items of value. Some police officer's were later charged with dereliction of duty, standing aside while looter's smashed and grabbed what they could and ran without interference. Polo would not allow that.

He separated his force into two groups. Ten men on foot with three police dogs were in areas he considered critical. As Polo had only a small group and, wanting it to appear as an overwhelming force, he kept five marked police cars with two men each, as flying squads. These squads screeched into hot spots, blue lights flashing and sirens blaring. Most looters scattered, which was what he wanted. Those dumb enough to be caught were handcuffed and placed into the rear of the police cars with the interior door handles removed and grates separating the front and rear seats.

Seemingly endless, the night wore on—sporadic gunfire in the distance, car windows by the dozens smashed, alarms going off, and average pedestrians, white or black, who lacked the sense to stay inside, chased or beaten.

Terror ultimately struck. Polo's group came upon five youths walking along Auckland Street at three in the morning toting an assortment of electronic gear. Polo's cruiser was the last in a motorcade of three, as two of his other five cars were responding to another call. The first two police cars pulled over and the officers in the first car confronted the looters.

Polo slowed, then pulled over to the curb and watched. As three police officers, one a woman, approached the group, two of the youths ran down a driveway empty handed and disappeared. The police let them go. Polo approved, but noticed none of his officers had drawn their weapons, as he required with his show of force. He made a mental note to correct that.

Without warning, one of the young men dropped his plunder, pulled an automatic, shouted *run*, and fired on the three officers. One officer went down, wounded in the shoulder, another officer dropped, hit in the chest. The third officer jumped behind the car and shot one of the men in the leg. The officers in the second car barely had time to react before the shooter shattered their windshield with two shots and, with his friend, dashed past them down the sidewalk towards Polo, not realizing he was there.

Polo slid across the seat to the passenger side, shouted, stop or ... and shot the gunman point-blank in the chest, twice. The youth lurched back into his friend, sending him sprawling on the pavement. Polo jumped out, picked up the shooter's partner, and slammed him into a chain link fence repeatedly, before one of the officers ran to stop him.

The youth Polo shot was dead. Telling the officer to cuff and throw the injured youth into the cruiser and then call for an ambulance and backup. Polo ran back to the wounded while another officer called in for an ambulance. The wounded officer was a policewoman, struggling with her pain and being tended by the officers. Polo turned to the other wounded police officer.

"He's dead, sir."

Lying there was Captain Kenneth Collin.

Polo fought to concentrate, bewildered, looking from left to right, helpless. A cloud of recrimination enveloped him. Everyone was tired, too casual. Perhaps they, he, didn't instill in everyone to follow proper police procedure despite the chaotic circumstances. A police officer died because of it. It should not have happened. He lost an officer, his first in thirty years. The burden crushed upon his shoulders. It was so unnecessary. A stupid, momentary error, and a dedicated officer, a living human being, died.

The person Polo killed was a nineteen-year old parolee, let back on the streets on early release five weeks earlier to ease overcrowding. Boston's police oversight committee absolved Polo of any procedure infractions.

Captain Collin received full Boston Police Department honors and the department commendation for meritorious service. With a contingent of the Boston Police Honor Guard, his body was transferred to Barretton for local services, prior to interment. The town mourned, flags at half-mast. Collin, well liked, was the town's first police captain.

Emily was heartbroken. Sinclair dismayed. How could a person, after adversity, become so successful, only to have their life taken so indifferently?

On Saturday, April 13, 1968, under a blustery, sunny sky, Polo gave a brief eulogy.

"For those of you who don't know, Kenneth Collin was a Vietnam veteran who received the bronze star and two purple hearts. For those medals, he lost a leg and three years of his life fighting for his country, the country he believed in.

This time Ken gave his *life* for what he believed. He wanted to create, in Barretton, a town safe for anyone to walk around day or night, a town safe from the very type of person who took his life. He had succeeded in what he wanted, but then confronted a person who put no value on life. Collin met that type many times in Vietnam and survived. Still, he was too disbelieving and trusting to realize it could happen here in America.

Ken and two other Barretton officers had volunteered to help Boston in what could have been a serious confrontation with looters after the tragic and needless death of Martin Luther King. After sixteen hours of facing down and dispersing many probable looters, we were tired. Because of that, we dropped our guard for one moment and Barretton lost a decent, dedicated human being. Barretton now has our first heartrending and untimely death … and I have lost a friend.

That we caught the people who committed this crime does not ease our grief, and let us pray this never happens again for Barretton and her officers.

At this time, I would like to announce a benefactor has come forward to assist us in creating a memorial park on town owned land beside the new police station.

We're asking everyone to submit ideas and designs and attend informational meetings so that all people will have a part in the park for Ken, and future town heroes. Further information will be posted in the county newspaper. Thank you."

Polo stepped down from the makeshift podium. Collin's parents had flown in from Colorado and he presented them with the Barretton town flag, the American flag, and the Barretton Honor Medal, newly created for the occasion.

Then, for no apparent reason, he walked off across the cemetery. The minister spoke; the bagpiper played Amazing Grace as has been done countless times for lost police and fire officers. And Captain Kenneth L. Collin went to eternal rest.

When his mind once again began to comprehend the present, Polo had no recollection, his memory a blank. He was dazed. The last strains of the pipes had long quieted. The mourners, officers and friends, everyone was gone. He found himself leaning against a tree, staring at the open grave repeating, "You shouldn't be here, Ken ... my fault ..."

He felt her before he saw her, and turned. Emily stood in the distance. He moved to her, she was the lifeline he desperately needed at this moment.

"You all right, Ray?"

"What happened? What did I do?"

"I don't ... we don't know. After you presented the flags to Ken's parents, you walked across the cemetery. I started after you, but Dad said no, best to leave you alone. Everyone was concerned because you just stood there, watching us. Dad shook his head and told everyone to leave you be. So, the service went on and everyone left.

Dad told me to stay, that was all he said, stay. I watched you walk back to Ken's grave and you stood there mumbling something I couldn't understand."

"I don't remember a thing after I spoke to his parents."

"It will probably come back to you; your mind just doesn't want to accept this. I guess that's it."

"It won't come back to me; it never does, going blank."

"I've never heard about this."

"It isn't the first time. It almost happened when Ken was shot, but somehow I stayed aware. A doctor I spoke with in the past called it something like transient memory loss. It often happens under stress he said, your mind doesn't want to remember. The bigger problem is I never have recall. It never comes back. Anyway, thanks for staying."

"I wouldn't have left without you."

Emily was concerned. Polo never mentioned he had seen a doctor for anything.

He turned and looked at her, "What I said doesn't get repeated, okay?"

With no one on the town's police force qualified to be Captain, and Polo unwilling to assume the position, he temporally accepted responsibility until a suitable candidate appointed. There was no lack of applicants. Barretton now had the reputation as being one of the finest small town police forces in New England. In short order, Polo reduced the candidates to two police lieutenants and one captain from other police departments. Sinclair and three town officials reviewed his recommendation and interviewed the men.

Polo's preferred candidate was approved and the new captain brought up to town standards.

Polo then turned his full attention back to the details of Ken Collin's memorial.

Chapter

Twenty Four

Paul Sinclair had every right to be paranoid. His drugs were running out. They no longer brought comfort. Fear clung to him like a damp cloak, his every thought laced with dread. He drove west the length of Massachusetts' northern boundary and on to Troy, New York, north to Saratoga Springs on Route 87, then back over to Bennington, Vermont. He had no idea where to go. He pictured his pursuers in the rearview mirror, hoping to lose them by using backcountry roads. He stayed only one night, or at most two, in one motel after another. Without question, he knew they were after him. He had to stay ahead.

Paul believed he had been on the run for months. Where could he go? Call Emily he decided. She'd help him. First though, drive more, stop their following him, get away.

The beginning of May, Polo watched Emily and Ruth planting flowers along the front entrance to the home on Great Hill. They were happy together, he thought. Thank God. He turned from the window and sat across from Parker.

"You were quiet at lunch, Ray, and now you're restless. What is it?"

"I'm thinking my job here," he hesitated, before continuing, "has run its course."

219

"I felt that had been on your mind for a few weeks now. As far as the town and me, you always have a position here."

"I know and thanks. But we both know the job you hired me for is finished. The town has an excellent police force now, and to be honest, I'm tired. Too much has happened, and Ken's death was a blow, the final straw."

"You've shouldered the blame for that too long, Ray. It wasn't your fault, yet for some reason your mind has that trapped inside."

"You're not a cop, Parker, you couldn't understand. It's not only that, it's about his funeral. I told you about going blank. Not knowing what was going on or afterward."

"I'm sure there's an answer."

"Possibly, however, as I told Emily, it's happened before. Three or four times I've been in a jam with some crook or murderer," he regretted the word, "and blanked out. Kept right on doing what I was supposed to and nobody noticed the difference. Yet I've had no recall, then or ever. Tension causes it, I'm sure. The problem is I don't know when it's going to happen and that's not a plus in a police officer, you must admit. What if I ever had to testify at a trial? Sorry judge, I don't remember a thing."

"Aren't you interested in knowing what it is that happens?"

"Nah, I'm stubborn. I was told a few things about it, but I don't want anybody crawling around in my brain."

Parker smiled, he knew Polo had made his mind up.

"I feel bad you've decided to do this. Ruth and I will miss you, not to mention, Emily. It will be very hard on her."

"I know, except it's got to happen sometime. It's best for the health of both of us. You know that, don't you?"

"To be honest, I do, Ray."

They sipped their coffee, lost in their own thoughts, staring at the two women enjoying themselves.

"Do you have a date set?"

"Some time this month, in a week or two. My friend, Sal Fanara, he's the Sheriff in Dade County, Florida, has asked me to come down and do some consulting work and train new detectives.

Said he can get me a teaching position in the Police Academy down there. It sounds good. I enjoyed teaching our recruits. I think I'd like to continue doing that sort of thing."

"That does sound good, Ray, except right now you'd be going right into a Florida summer. A big person like you will feel it. Why don't you wait?"

"Fanara mentioned the heat. Although he said you go from an air-conditioned house to an air-conditioned car to an air-conditioned office. That's how he stands it in summer."

"That could be true, I suppose. When are you telling Emily? You must have given it some thought."

"Well, remember when you asked me to tell Emily about your getting weekends off from the Center and tell her about your lady friend?"

"Damn it, I do. Please, don't ask me to tell Emily you're leaving."

Polo was dejected, it; was his obligation.

"I guess you're right. I'll tell her soon."

"Ray, you've got to give her time to say goodbye over a few days."

"That's what I don't want. It will hurt both of us too much. I don't know, I guess I'll start by taking her to lunch next week. See what develops from there."

By the time Emily and Polo met for lunch he had firmed up the offer with Sal Fanara in Miami; Polo would start teaching in the new officer recruiting class at the middle of June. Fanara wanted him to be down at least two weeks before the start for orientation. He also wanted Polo to assist in two murder cases, which had frustrated police investigators.

The luncheon with Emily started well, then, as Polo described his move to Florida, her tears welled up. Polo expected it. It wasn't fair to tell her by phone, and now, it was hard on him as well. The last thing he wanted was to say goodbye, perhaps forever. Deep inside he wanted Emily to meet, love and marry a decent person who would make her happy. She was still fragile; this was his concern. Leaving would not help. What else could he do? He had to rebuild his life as well.

Halfway through the meal she stopped eating, opened her purse, and washed down a sedative, "Ray, I'm not trying to be dramatic. I need this right now."

"I understand, you've had everything thrown at you this past year and hurting you is the last thing I'd ever want, you know that. But your father is home now, and Ruth's a great steadying influence on you. You're going to get through this. Don't worry, we'll talk on the phone and I'll be back now and then ... or maybe you could come down some time."

Polo had no plans of returning because of his feelings for her, and didn't want her to come down to see him. It would hurt, not help either of them. The pill began to take effect. He reached in her purse, taking her car keys. She didn't protest.

The Buick droned along route 202 past the Quabbin Reservoir. Not talking, she fell asleep. He went on for another hour before turning back. He liked her beside him, knowing it would never happen again.

When she woke, Polo left her at Great Hill. Ruth spoke of her concern and hopes for Emily, saying she would do whatever was required to help her when Polo left.

He spoke more with Parker about his move to Florida. Sinclair no longer tried to talk him out of going. He stopped by the police station, gave the keys to Emily's car to Connie, and told her to have two officers pick it up and deliver it to the Hill. For a while, he drove aimlessly around town, then headed home to pack odds and ends. Sitting down, he had a couple of beers. Thoughts of her almost made him cry.

At last, after three more weeks of dodging his enemies, Paul Sinclair had a plan; go to Mexico. To do this would take money. The only way he could get money was his Trust. That would solve his problem. It became simple. His father must give him his Trust money. With that, he'd be a top dog in the midst of peasants across the border.

To shake off his damn pursuers he began heading for Great Hill in the most round about way. He drove straight south from Brattleboro, Vermont on route 91. He knew he must be careful going into Massachusetts, even with his fake Peter Stanford driver's license.

On the southern border above Connecticut, he took a backcountry road to Palmer, Massachusetts. There, stopping at the Monson State Hospital parking lot, he went inside. After looking out a window for ten minutes making sure no one was following him, he used a pay phone to call Emily's condominium. No answer. He panicked and called Great Hill. Ruth answered.

"Is Emi, Emily there?"

"Who's calling please?"

"Who's asking?" Paul did not know the voice.

"My name is Ruth."

He couldn't make sense of the name. Housekeeper, relative, who?

"If Emi's there, tell her a good friend is on the phone and wants to surprise her."

Putting the phone down, Ruth called Emily on the intercom.

"Emily, there's a man on the phone wants to talk to you. Called you Emi. He sounds strange though. Do you want me to say you're not here?"

Emily knew it wouldn't be Tom Crane as she picked up the phone. Before she answered, she spoke into the intercom, telling Ruth she could hang up. When Emily heard the click, she answered, tensing.

"Emi, its Paul."

"God, Paully! Are you all right?"

"Yeah, I'm okay. I had some problems in New Hampshire' I'm okay now. Really, really I am!"

There was no question drugs had him.

"Paully, where are you?"

"It doesn't matter. I'm going to see you in a few days."

"That's great. Where will I meet you?"

"I'm coming home. You've got to get in touch with Dad at the prison for me."

Of course she thought, he doesn't know, "Dad's home now Paully, he got an early release. The story we told Detective Polo got him out early."

"That's great because I need money and fast!"

"Are you in trouble? Tell me!"

"Look, Emi, I can't talk too long. I'm in enough trouble that I've got to get away. That's why I need to talk to Dad."

"Is it over the parole violation?"

Paul giggled, "No, that's nothing. It's some other people don't like me, seriously don't like me."

"Why?"

"I don't know, just take my word for it."

"Do you want to talk to Dad now?"

"No. You soften him up; you were good at that. He can't be too happy after I broke my word about staying in rehab."

"You shouldn't have."

"Don't start, I've got enough troubles."

"When will you be here?"

"I'm not sure. I've got some driving to do first. I'll call when I know. I've got to go, I'm in a hurry."

"Be careful, Paully, I love you."

"I love you too, Emi. Trust me."

Emily shook with fear. Whatever is wrong, she thought, her father and Polo will get him out of it. She knew they would. She couldn't tell her brother his Trust was dissolved, there was nothing left, other than what father decided. What on earth was she going to say to him before Paully called again?

It only took a few seconds before the subject reared. She walked into the kitchen. Parker and Ruth took one look at her. She was so flushed, they thought she was going to faint. All Emily wanted was a pill, it wasn't to be, she had to tell them. She looked at her father, murmured, "Paully."

Ruth knew little of Paul Sinclair, only that Emily had a twin brother and he traveled. The rest, Ruth felt was unsaid, and not positive. She stood to leave. Parker asked her to stay, explaining as much as he knew about his son and his problems. He had nowhere near a full understanding of Paul's troubles.

From listening to Emily, it was obvious Paul was not going to return to face his parole violations. Sinclair sensed there was more wrong than either knew. Paul was looking for money to get away. His Trust was dissolved; Parker reminded Emily. What was the right thing to do? Give him what he wanted and let him go? Find out the problems and resolve them? Or turn him down? Paul had broken his word over a most serious agreement. He couldn't be trusted in word or actions. Ruth was asked her thoughts, but said it was their son and brother, their blood. She felt she had no right to voice her opinions, although holding some privately.

Parker decided he would pay Paul to enter the finest, most qualified rehabilitation facility in the country. Included in the offer, Parker would pay all legal expenses to help his son straighten out his life and pay his debt concerning the parole violation. If Paul agreed to this, and succeeded in rehabilitating himself, then his Trust would be reinstated. If he refused, and this was the part that made it the most difficult decision, Parker would not give him further financial assistance. Ruth and Emily agreed, knowing how demanding Paul's efforts in rehab would have to be.

They did not let Polo know about the call, the decision, or that Paul would be arriving sometime soon.

Paul didn't call. Other than that, life began to normalize for the family. In the course of a conversation, Parker learned Ruth had been chairwoman of a beautification committee for the town of Amherst's village center, her former home. Better than that, the resulting grounds had won an Arborist Award, Small Town Category, for New Hampshire. Parker jumped on that information as he often noticed Barretton's town square was too shabby for a growing town. He and Ruth initiated action through the town leaders, garden groups, arborists, land planners, and average townspeople to improve the three acres involved. Parker underwrote the project. Ruth Sinclair was elected Chair, whether due to the offer, or that she was the most qualified was not a concern. She began with an excellent concept for the overall design, and then acquired participation from all concerned onto the plat of the property. With Emily's assistance, and to everyone's surprise, Ruth had a consensus from the divergent parties within two weeks.

Parker and Emily were proud of her. The two women worked together as sisters and it made Parker feel they were a family once again. It also made him think of Nancy.

Since Bradford Crane, Tom Crane's father, had ended his involvement in the Quad Trust, Parker Sinclair reinstituted it as the Tri Trust with the two remaining members and continued funding the ten Thorton Academy schools. As the Academies were to continue, Emily withdrew part of her Trust to fund five more teachers with Master's Degrees for special needs children. These teachers were to float between the schools giving hands on skills to both students and their teachers.

The only other minor, and humorous distraction at this time, was a letter Emily received from Tom Crane, still in prison, asking Emily to forgive him and stated his undying love for her and his hope that some day they could meet again and ….

Emily smiled, shaking her head at Tom's chutzpah. She tore the letter in two, while laughing to Polo how Tom just would not give up trying to get into her Trust.

Paul Sinclair had driven around secondary roads in central Massachusetts for two weeks, staying in state parks, sleeping in his car on dirt roads, not shaving, seldom washing his face … always however, with a revolver on the seat or tucked in the back of his pants. At last, hidden in a darkened phone booth, he called Emily's condominium.

"Emi," His voice was strained, no hello, "I need Dad! Did you soften him up?"

"I've spoken to him Paully, it doesn't sound good. He wants you to go back into rehab to get over what's wrong."

His voice became shrill, "It's too late for that, God Damn him! Don't you understand for Christ's sake? I've got to get away. What the hell's the matter with you?"

"Paully, calm down, we'll work it out. I can get three or four thousand dollars quickly, will that help?"

"I'm talking *money*! The money due me from my Trust! Christ! I'm going to the Hill now!"

"Wait, Paully, please, just wait. Let me talk to Dad again tonight. I'll convince him. You come for breakfast tomorrow morning. When the bank opens, we'll get you money then. How's that sound?"

"Damn it! That's right; we have to wait for his bank to open, don't we, don't we?"

She had to baby him, "Yes, Paully, he never has much money in the house. You know that. We have to wait for the bank to open, okay? Come by at nine tomorrow, we'll all have a good breakfast, then go to the bank together. Dad will get you some money, and then you can ..."

"Okay Emi, I'll wait until then, but Dad better give it to me, he'd better."

"He will ... I know he will ... Okay?"

"Okay, Emi, I'll be there tomorrow ... what time? Yeah, yeah, nine."

Emily hung up. This was not the brother she loved. This was a terrifying stranger. She had to go to Great Hill this night and talk to her father. He must change his mind; there was no telling what Paully might do. She had no experience in a confrontation like this. Call Polo, that's what she'd do, he would know how to handle it. No, don't call him, he doesn't like Paully, he'd arrest him, we can't have that. What if Paully gets violent? He sounded angry, or was it fright? He's been angry before, he could fly off the handle, then what could we do? Call Polo.

227

Only a recording; she struggled to get her voice under control, "Ray, Emily. We have a problem that came up. Could you come over to Great Hill tomorrow morning at eight? It's important we see you. Talk to you then."

That was the thing to do, she felt. Have Ray get over there early. Then, if her father said they didn't need him, they could say it was a false alarm and have him leave before Paully got there.

Emily decided to go to the Hill. If her father and Ruth were still awake, she'd explain Paully's phone call and discuss what they should do in the morning. If they were asleep, she'd overnight and tell them early. She stayed calm. Good, she thought, she had a plan. Thinking over how to convince her father, she was slow in packing her overnight case. Resolve gave the answer; she headed for her car.

Polo heard the message at eleven that night. He called Emily's phone, got her recording, figured she must be at Great Hill, and didn't want to wake the family. Whatever it was, she sounded okay, so he felt it could wait until he got there in the morning.

Chapter

Twenty Five

Polo finished shaving, still wondering why the Sinclair's, or at least Emily, wanted him at Great Hill so early. Driving to the Hill, he gave it more thought. He'd bet they planned to take him for a ride in the country, then lunch. Sort of a going away get-together, probably a couple of funny cards, maybe a small gift or two. He liked the thought; it was something his family would never have done.

Turning up the drive, he noticed Emily's Mercedes parked by the garages so he drove up to the front of the house. It was easy to smell spring. He felt good. He had made his decision. Although he would miss all the Sinclair's, it was for the best.

The door was ajar, but he rang the bell anyway, no answer. He was expected. They must be busy and left it ajar for him.

No one in the hall or den, "Hello? Where is everybody?"

He walked through the dining room into the kitchen, no coffee … nothing. This was strange; surely they weren't hiding and going to jump out at him. Don't be ridiculous. Walking back past the dining room, heading for the study, he glanced toward the second floor. He saw her halfway up the stairs … sitting … her blouse covered in blood.

His mind went blank, denying the scene.

Sitting on a couch, head back, he looked to his left, seeing one of his police officers, and then to his right, a man, staring at him.

He recognized where he was. The Sinclair home.

"What are you doing here, Captain, and who's this?"

"This is Doctor Simon, Chief. You called us."

"What are you talking about? I didn't call anyone. What's going on?"

Doctor Simon came up to him smiling gently, and tried to shine a light in his eyes.

"Get the hell away with that God damn light! What's going on here?"

"Take it easy, Chief."

The doctor turned to the officer, "You see; it's like I told you, Transient Global Amnesia. I've seen only one other case of it in forty-five years. No memory of what happened. Obviously, he retained his personal identity, and did all the things he should have, such as calling you. Yet, he doesn't remember a thing."

The officer asked, "You're telling me he doesn't know what happened here?"

"Up to a point he does, yes, then there will be a blank, probably after he saw her. He knows what's happening *now*. Yet his mind will probably never recall the blank. You must realize, Captain, the mind is a delicate miracle. There are horrors it refuses to accept."

"You mean we've got to tell him?"

"Unfortunately yes, I'll give him a shot first."

Polo half listened to it all, responding, "What the hell are you two talking about? Stuff your Goddamn shots. Tell me what's going on Captain, and be damned quick about it! What in hell are all these people doing here?"

The doctor sat on the coffee table in front of him, "Chief Polo, I'm terribly sorry. There has been a tragic crime committed here and I have to tell …"

A sight came to Polo … Emily on the stairs, covered in blood, "Oh my God! Don't tell me Emily's dead!"

"No, she's all right, in shock, but all right. You must have seen her covered in blood and thought she was injured. Do you remember that?"

"I remember going to her."

"Do you remember holding her in your arms?"

"No"

"Look at your shirt and jacket."

Spotted with blood.

"Do you recall anything else, Chief, anything else you did, such as calling the station?"

"No."

"Not ordering Connie Johnson to get your men up here with an ambulance and doctors?"

"No, this sort of thing has happened to me before. A few times under stress, I blank out, even though I keep doing my job."

Was it seeing Emily covered in blood? Then, if it wasn't hers, who's …?

He feared the doctor's next words.

"Jesus, Chief Polo, I hate to be the one to tell you this … Mr. and Mrs. Sinclair are dead."

Chapter

Twenty Six

Numb, impassive. They inserted a needle into a vein, he didn't notice.

"We're going to put you out for a while Chief. You'll remember what I'm going to tell you now, however. When your police responded to your call, they found you sitting on the stairs holding Miss Sinclair. You wouldn't let her go until they said they wanted to find where she was bleeding. Her blouse was covered in blood, yet she wasn't injured. Then they saw spots leading from the bedroom. I'm sorry again, Chief, as I said, the Sinclair's were in bed, shot dead."

The comprehension, the utter dismay on Polo's face caused the doctor to hesitate.

Barretton Police Captain Rudi Thorn took over, "Chief, the room was ransacked. Someone was apparently looking for money, not jewelry. Miss Sinclair's in shock, otherwise unhurt. We think she came in after the killer left, because she wasn't harmed. The coroner will give us an approximate time, although it looks like it happened last night or real early this morning. I guess when she came in and found them; she tried to help and got covered with their blood. That's why you saw her bloody like that. We're losing you, Chief, so I'll be quick: Miss Sinclair's in shock. At first, she kept repeating ... Lee or Leigh ... that's all. It's a name, doesn't mean anything to anyone right now. We'll track him or her down, so that's it, just Lee for now. Unfortunately, Doc Simon had to put her under heavy sedation due to her condition, so she's no help to the police right now. Do you know a Lee?"

Polo didn't answer; the injection put him out. Doctor Simon took over, "He's gone. Get him to the infirmary, let him sleep it off. I doubt he's going to sleep much for a long time after this mess, if he's as close to this family and that girl as you say, Captain."

The doctor turned to Thorn, "He'll be all right, but a hell of a lot to get over. Any other thoughts on this?"

Captain Thorn, now in charge, was a veteran police officer, having joined the Barretton Police from the Holyoke PD after Ken Collin was murdered. Thorn rubbed his forehead thinking of the sequence of events, then called the other three police officers over.

"Okay guys, this is how I think it went down. I'm going to assume, unless we hear differently from the coroner, that the break in occurred sometime late last night. I'm going by the fact that some of the blood is dry. So, one or more perpetrators come in, because the door wasn't jimmied, and start creeping around and then see lights on upstairs."

"How do you know a light was on, Lieutenant?"

"Because a light is on up there, and there are two books on the floor; the Sinclair's must have been reading. I'm guessing Mr. Sinclair heard something and started to get up, his body position would suggest he was half out of bed when he was shot, then fell back on to it. Then Mrs. Sinclair was taken down. The killer ransacked the room looking for money, as he left the jewelry. Whether he got money, is unknown. Whatever happened, it doesn't appear the killer or killers looked anywhere else. The rest of the house is apparently untouched, so they took off. As I told the Doc, Emily must have come in after they left; I cannot see any other scenario because she's still alive.

So, where are we? Emily comes in, finds her parents shot, grabs them, hugs them, whatever … gets covered in blood. She makes it to the stairs and walks or falls half way down. The Chief comes in X time later, finds her, finds her parents, calls the station, goes back and holds her, and here we are. The doc says the Chief has Transient Amnesia or something like that. It means the mind can't take the stress and blocks the memory, so even though a person keeps doing things, like he did, they can't remember.

My guess is, in his loss of memory stage, he pulled his revolver and went through the house looking for the perps. I'll bet they find his fingerprints everywhere, then he came back and put his gun on the stair and held her until we showed up. I doubt we'll find prints. I think the killers went in and out the front door, and don't expect to get much from that; there must have been a dozen people grab that doorknob by now. Anyway, start looking around without disturbing anything.

We don't have a murder investigation team, mainly because we don't have murders. At least it was that way before this family. One more thing men, Emily said one word, a person's name, Lee or Leigh. We don't know if it's a first or last name; it could be nothing or it could be important. If any of you know someone around by that name, even remotely, let us know. To repeat myself, we're basically nowhere. Keep anyone other than authorized personnel off the premises. Arrest anyone who won't leave or tries to sneak in. Those of you not on duty go home and get some rest. When this hits the fan this afternoon, it's going to be hell. Doc says the Chief will be back to normal tomorrow.

Right now, he's doped up, so we'll have to wait until morning for orders from him, or the State Police."

It all started over for the town, and this time worse. People shocked, disbelieving, television trucks half-blocking the drive leading up to the home. Jeff Pike was back again, still impressed with himself, getting in everyone's way, making sure the TV cameras were lingering on him talking to people with shocked faces, tears if possible, as he asked the same stupid questions, "How do you feel about this? What do you think happened?" Newspaper reporters everywhere, endlessly interviewing townspeople. Previous employees of the Sinclair's telling how nice they were, helpful, generous, what could have happened? Who was going to pay for the new police station? Some lunatic must be on the loose. What are the police doing? The reporters rushed everywhere after any morsel of gossip, asking the mundane from the dull; anyone with the slightest hint they may know some worthless tidbit.

Polo groped awake, someone was screaming, "If you find anyone," the man was choking, barely able to speak, "If you find anyone, kill … kill them".

Choking back the bile rising in his throat, tears stung his eyes. There was no one else in the room. Lee … Lee flashed through his mind. Emily said Lee.

Why? Where is she? How is she? And Parker, and Ruth?

Polo stared blindly at the wall, "They're dead, my good Lord, they're dead."

He had to see her, to find the murderers. He struggled out of bed, trying to stand and fell into the armchair. The nurse came, scolded him for shouting and left. A few choice words chased her down the corridor. He called the police station, telling Connie he was all right and to send a squad car to his house, get pants, shirt and skivvies, then pick him up. In addition, she was to have whoever on the force knows anything about the Sinclair murders, at the station by the time he got there.

The nurses said he couldn't leave without the doctor's release, and put in a call. Polo said he was leaving. The orderlies were nervous; Polo was a big, angry person, and definitely not likely to listen to them. The police car arrived. He dressed, and the confrontation began just as the doctor called back, "If Chief Polo wants to leave, let him."

Although weary, Polo brought together his team, "Have you sealed off the area?"

The Captain stated they marked it off, but the area was subject to the coroner, forensics, the ambulance, and undertaker, and the reporters and photographers had been scrambling all over the place. Then the County Sheriff's been around and the Chiefs of Worcester and Springfield have been over, giving advice as well.

"So, in other words, the whole site is contaminated?"

"Fraid so, Chief and worse, the State Police are supposed to be taking over, so all I've done is have our men guard the site until you decide what to do."

"Where'd you hear about the Staties?"

"The TV." The Captain said sheepishly.

"Fine, police work via TV."

The phone rang for Polo. He took it in his office

"Ray, how are you doing?" asked Commissioner Kearney. "I heard about the Sinclairs; it's a blow to a lot of people."

"Yeah, especially to the Sinclairs."

"You know what I mean. How's the girl?"

"She's under sedation. As soon as I get everyone organized on this I'm going to see her."

"That's what I want to talk to you about, Ray."

"What do you want to talk to me about that hasn't already been on TV?"

"Jesus, Ray, I wanted to tell you first, but you weren't at your house or the station and I didn't want to say who I was, so I kept calling. Like I'm doing now, for Christ's sake."

"Okay, Walt, my error. Sorry. Now tell me what all this crap is about."

"Giving it to you straight, the Governor wants his own people to take over."

"Governor Volpe? You're saying the Barretton Police is entirely off the case?"

"That's what I'm saying, and it's an order from on high. Anything your force can do to help is fine; only don't get in their way. Sinclair has friends, and they're going to throw every resource at it."

"This is a slap in my men's face. I'm resigning in protest this minute, damn them all to hell."

"No you're not, and you know it, so don't go flying off the handle. They've far more resources than you."

237

"That may be true, but no one wants to catch the bastards more than me."

"I know, and that's one of their points, you're too close, too angry, you won't think straight."

"That's bullshit and you know it."

"I know it, you know it, they don't know it, and they're the ones running the show. Look, Ray, you can't fight City Hall. If anyone should know, it's you. And this is the State guys, which is ten times worse. Take your time quitting, go see the Sinclair girl; you can probably help her more than anyone. One other thing, don't think you're fooling me."

"What?"

"Don't what me. I know you're going to keep sniffing around, you're a bloodhound, and bloodhounds don't give up unless someone pulls their chain. Be careful what you do, don't make someone yank it."

"I hear you, Walt, I'll be a phantom."

"Yeah right, a six foot, three, three hundred pound phantom."

"That shows what you know, I only weigh two-fifty."

Emily Sinclair was kept under deep sedation. Each time she started to come out of the medically induced coma she would writhe and scream with recollection. Polo held her in his arms, but her mental state was past chaos. He couldn't help. The present was unknown; a massive void had spirited her away.

The doctor's knew she couldn't be kept under sedation too long and decided to ease the medication once more. This time, nothing happened; she stayed quiet, expressionless, eyes as unfocused as a newborn's. Polo's vigil lasted through each night. The doctors were getting nowhere. From changing her medications to lowering the dosages, nothing was working. She was fading before their eyes.

He sat with her for hours holding her hand, talking as if she could hear through the veil blocking the outside world. He feared what would happen if she finally became conscious of her surroundings and relived seeing her father and Ruth dead. However, she didn't return to the present. Something, somewhere in her mind, kept her living in the past, refusing to leave its solace. Several moments she almost regained consciousness, Polo thought, and called the doctors. But she slipped off, her mind dragging her back, back into the past. The doctors brought in the best experts, who guessed at solutions, or if her mind might stay in the security of oblivion and never recover. Judge Butt's perceptively made Polo her guardian until the Court judged her competent.

The publicly unannounced funeral arrangements, also supervised by the Judge, were held out of the area for those invited. This eliminated reporters and the morbidly curious. Twenty people attended. Polo knew only Commissioner Kearney, Judge Butts and Ruth Sinclair's two sons. Those present, Kearney informed him, were the other two members of the Tri Trust, intimate friends and five representatives from Sinclair's Masonic Lodge.

Polo glanced around. Everyone whose eye he caught nodded briefly to him. It appeared the attendees knew whom he was, making him ill at ease. Suits, Emily called them in the past, and she was right, the in crowd. Ruth Carvel's daughter wasn't present, but her sons, still disbelieving, stood off by themselves, ignoring Polo. The service was secular, after which, members of Parker's Masonic Lodge performed a brief service. The Governor was not present, wanting to avoid attention. As Emily was unresponsive, she did not attend.

Polo felt his nerves fraying, chest tightening and, after the final words were spoken, he left, acknowledging no one. The ache became constant, a weight pressing on his chest, then a headache and numbness in this left arm. When he returned to the station, the pain was such that he let Connie drive him to the hospital emergency room. He had suffered a mild stroke. His doctor advised rest; eating properly, taking his medicine on time, losing

239

weight, all of what they were saying they knew went in one ear and out the other.

Surprisingly, Polo *was* concerned. He took the doctor's advice to heart. He vowed, speaking to himself, to change his ways once he found the killer of the Sinclair's and Emily improved.

Not one clue, not a trace of evidence resulted from the murder investigation. Not one clear, unmatched fingerprint. Even if the perpetrator had opened the front door as he left, any possible prints were smeared by the traffic in and out. Prints on drawers and cabinets the bedroom, were smudged. The four .38 slugs came from the same gun, turned up no matches. Even Emily murmuring Lee or Leigh was a dead end. No one knew anyone with that name remotely connected to the case. The police traced back through the Correctional Center for any prisoner called by those names, first or last, which may have taken one of Sinclair's classes, or knew him. Nothing.

While the State Police, and out of state experts, continued to pour over the site, only one possible clue was found. When the TV vehicles parked on the street left, skid marks from spinning tires were found, going from the end of the driveway onto the street. The clue, if such it was, led to nothing.

Until Emily Sinclair comes around, they were working in the dark, was the collective thinking,

The investigators drifted away, embarrassed, only going through the motions despite the Governor Volpe's orders to find the killer or killers.

Polo didn't quit. Although the jewelry appeared untouched, he had it checked for fingerprints. Sinclair's bank indicated he never kept large amounts of cash at his home.

It became more futile each day. No matter how he searched, Polo couldn't find a motive for the murders. Wanted files turned up no suspects. He paced the grounds through the day and slept in the chair beside Emily most nights. He ridiculed the State Police and their experts. When they told him they were overworked, he mocked them, saying not only were they not working, they had no idea *how* to work.

Word got back to the Commissioner, and he told Polo to back off. Polo retaliated by saying his last month with the Boston PD was over, so Kearney no longer had jurisdiction over him. Kearney hung up. The Barretton Town Managers told him to keep trying; the State Police were doing nothing, other than taking up space.

On 23 July, 1968, Polo admitted he was getting nowhere. Still, he held one more meeting with all his officers. He stated this would be the last time he would bring them together on the case. For two hours, he tried every trick he knew to get something, some straw he could grasp. The officers, thoroughly tired of the endless discussions, were fed up, waiting for the meeting to end.

Lieutenant Thorn reiterated his comments, "Christ, Chief, I'm sorry, but we've gone down this road a dozen times. We've tracked down every blasted lead on this Lee or Leigh person. We're beating our heads against a wall. Lee was all she said."

An officer looked up, "She did say pa, a couple of times when I was near her."

Polo turned, "Pa? Where the hell have you been! Why the devil didn't you tell us this before?"

"I was on vacation, Chief. Does it matter? She said pa. It was God damn obvious her pa didn't do it. I just thought she was thinking of her father. Didn't even recall it until now."

"Are you sure it was pa?"

"Yeah, I'm sure, just pa."

"Emily never called her father, Pa. Now we have two words or partial words. Lee and Pa, or Lee … Pa. Lepa… Leaper, doesn't make any sense."

241

No one made anything of it, ready to pack it in. Polo tensed, holding his hand up, putting two pieces together, shaking, "Shut up! Shut up! Let me think! Don't you see it? It's not LeePa! It's paLee! Palee! Paully, it's Paully! It's Emily's brother, his name is Paul. He's a dope head! A parole violator! She calls him Paully! Paul killed them!"

Polo pounded his fist on the table, "That miserable, dope head son of a bitch! That stinking son of a bitch! When I catch him, I'll kill him, I'll *kill him myself!*"

The table cracked under the pummeling of his fist. The police officers backed away. Polo's chest pained. He was still shouting at them to track down the brother while they rushed him to the hospital. Another slight stroke, more pills, more warnings.

The effect on Polo finding Paul Sinclair had murdered his father and Ruth was devastating. It was bad enough he lost two friends, but Paul was destroying Emily as well. How could he? The reason didn't matter. If Polo found him, he *would* kill him.

The initial pain he had felt at the station had deadened. Of more concern to him was the thought Emily must realize *her own brother* committed the slaughter.

It preyed on his mind, tearing at him. No wonder she was deeply troubled.

The State experts felt foolish; Polo had done it again, succeeded where they failed. At first, there were skeptics of course. However, when Paul's drug record surfaced along with his breaking parole, the odds turned to Polo being right. The town was in shock once again.

The manhunt began. Despite it, Paul was used to avoiding people, and disappeared once more.

Polo left the hospital with a cocktail of pills and warnings. A police car dropped him off at his house where he'd been ordered to rest, a visiting nurse would be coming by. After the patrol car left, Polo went to his garage and found someone had brought his Buick back. The keys were gone; he realized they'd been taken purposely. He went to his junk drawer picking out the spare set. What a bunch of deep thinkers I have, he thought.

Driving to the clinic, he wondered how Emily would react when she came around. Did she know her brother did the killings? She must. Would she revert inward forever? Why would Paul unexpectedly reappear and kill them without warning? What drove him to kill his father and Ruth?

As he walked through the door of the clinic, two doctors took him aside. They had been waiting for him and had called Judge Butts, knowing he had made Polo her guardian.

When they realized Polo had health problems, they waited until he could come to the clinic. The doctor's told him there was no change in Emily and they had reviewed her condition with four professionals specializing in treating shock patients. With their recommendations, the clinic doctor's would like to try a combination of two drugs simultaneously in an attempt to jolt her into consciousness. Polo asked the downside, the downside would be the way she was at present. He gave permission in writing; there was no one else who cared.

They administered the drugs, asking him to stay with her. If there were any response, they said, it would be immediate. He was not religious, but prayed. An hour passed. She was restless. He held her hand and prayed. He was close to giving up. Her head turned, bleary eyes struggling to adjust. She tried to concentrate.

Her eyes focused, "Ray." she hoarsely whispered.

"My God, Emily." His tears fell on the hand holding hers.

He waited, he could see her thinking, remembering. Oh God, please keep her here. Her eyes brimmed with tears as she thought of what had gone past. She gripped his arm, staring, recalling, "He ran past me ... coming out the door, pushed me out of ... the way, he was ugly, horrid ... I could hardly recognize him ... he was screaming Dad wouldn't ... give him his money ... Ray ... it was Paully."

"Yes, I know."

"He was screaming ... I knew something ... terrible had happened. I ... ran to their bedroom ... shook them ... hugged, trying to make them live ... begging them to ... speak to me. I don't ... remember ...."

"I know, I know, try not to think right now. Just rest, I'll be here."

He held her hand. Her eyes were on him, yet unfocused, her mind remembering.

"Ray ... Paully murdered ... my Mother."

"I know, Emily. I'm afraid Ruth is gone too."

"You're not ... listening, Ray, listen to me ... God, Ray ... listen."

Her eyes glazed over, reliving an event, monotone, emotionless, "The night my ... Mother ... died, *my Mother*, Ray, not Ruth. Paully came home ... stoned on crack, upset about something. He heard Mother upstairs complaining about his addiction. They didn't know he was there ... Mother's voice set him off ... he went crazy! I tried to grab him ... but he broke away I chased after him ... he ran up the stairs ... I shouted to Dad ... Paul knew the gun was in the drawer ... he shot her ... he shot our Mother."

Polo's mind refused to grasp the words, "What are you saying?"

She fell back on the bed, soaked in sweat, gasping for breath, "Ray ... are you blind? Don't you understand? Paul murdered *my Mother*!"

She was hallucinating, the drugs. What else could it be?

"Listen ... Ray."

She struggled for words, attempting to lift herself up, "Paully shot my Mother, *he* shot her ... *My father didn't do it*!"

Polo sagged back in the chair trying to deny what he was hearing. It couldn't, it simply *couldn't* be true. His chest tightened, he tried to breathe slowly, his mind, overwhelmed. What if it were true?

The doctors hurried in. They had not heard the conversation, although they could see Emily had been speaking, and thought Polo was overreacting. Knowing his medical history, they helped him to another room, giving him oxygen. As he calmed, the doctor's went back to Emily. She was quietly crying, so they didn't impose.

Polo came blindly back. He couldn't, he *wouldn't* believe. Emily looked at him sadly.

"Emily, I can't, I just can't believe you. Parker did it. You're mistaken."

Her breathing was even, more settled, "Let me try to explain. Please, Ray. When it happened, we were in absolute shock. We stood, disbelieving. Paully broke down crying. Through his drugged mind, he knew what he had done and even *then*, he could only think of himself."

She fought for composure, "Paully's biggest concern was he would die in prison. He started to run away. Dad grabbed him. God, Ray ... it's hard to explain. Dad loved Paully. I did too. We had to do something, anything."

Emily was exhausted, shaking. Polo wouldn't let it go.

"So you decided to blame your *father*?" Were you crazy? How could you?"

"It was Dad who thought ... who thought of it!"

"I don't believe you."

"It was! Please, Ray, listen! It was Dad's idea! He realized Paully was right; there was no question he would lose his mind in prison. He *would* die there ... Dad would do anything to prevent that. He struggled over what to do. We stood there for half an hour, crying, Mother was dead ... God, Ray, she was dead ... and we knew Paully would die too, if we called the police. Dad finally said he would take the blame ... but he made Paully swear on the Bible to go into rehab, and stay until he was clean. Dad hoped the programs he had started, you know, the good he had done in his life would be taken into consideration."

She fell back on the bed, soaked in sweat, crying.

Polo began fitting the pieces together, "So, the three of you came up with a scheme, and it worked. Except later, when it looked like your father was going to jail for a long time, you and

Paul couldn't allow that, and figured I could make a difference in your father's sentence. The two of you made up the story. You set me up. You've been lying to me ever since."

She nodded, too choked up to talk.

"The two of you made up all the stories about how sick your mother was. It had to be without your father knowing what you were up to, because it wasn't true. Parker would never allow her name to be dragged down."

"She *was* sick, Ray!"

"Yes, except nowhere near what you and your brother said. You played it to the hilt. Far more than it was!"

"Yes, we did."

Emily was beginning to crumble. Polo wouldn't let up, "And your Mother didn't smash up the atrium, you and your brother did."

"Yes! Yes! Yes! We thought of it when you said you had never been inside the house. I called you, then we smashed them. You never noticed the dirt was wet."

She made him feel stupid with that remark. Glancing up she saw hurt turning to anger and began whimpering.

"You lied to me. I knew something wasn't right, but you deflected me from keying on Paul. You took my mind off my job, off the pieces that didn't fit."

She pulled back, physically shrinking, "He was my brother, Ray! My twin for God's sake! You must understand! I did use you at first ... but not later ... I cared then"

He ignored what she said, "If you had told me from the start, your Father and Ruth would be alive today!"

"Oh, God, please don't say that, please. I didn't know what would happen!"

Polo ignored the pain in her eyes. He sat there, confounded, staring at the girl he loved. He, the great detective, the solver of cases when everyone else failed, the master, the Sherlock Holmes of the Boston Police Department. He'd been played the fool from beginning to end. His pride was crushed.

He shivered, tension rolled over him, thundering into his brain. The pain was coming; he could feel it in his chin. Ignoring it, he reverted to his old self, where there was safety. Only black or white existed. No emotion, no decision to make, no gray area.

He rose from the chair. She grabbed for his arm. He pulled it away, "Ray, don't leave me. Please don't! I beg you, don't leave! You're all I've left!"

Walking away, he turned, "Emily, understand this, I'm not here for you anymore. You might be able to live with what happened, I can't."

She was gone from him, shut out.

Emily's pleas fell on deaf ears.

Chapter

Twenty Seven

A wide-ranging manhunt to find Paul Sinclair ensued. The investigators located the cabin he rented under his own name in Bridgeton, Maine. Yet they failed to find the Lincoln or bodies. They found the salesman who sold him the Pontiac; eventually found in an abandoned Quincy quarry. When hauled out, four bullet holes had pierced the driver's door, and stains on the seat proved out as blood. Ominously, in the trunk was an empty cement bag, the known 'business card' of a Boston drug mob.

A .38 revolver on the floor contained five spent shell casings. Ballistics proved the slugs matched those taken from the Sinclair bodies. After further dragging, the quarry only turned up other wrecks, the search for Paul Sinclair shut down and the case closed, no follow up.

After Emily admitted Paul murdered her mother, Polo wrote Judge Butts stating what he'd been told, adding he believed her, and declared he would no longer be Emily's legal guardian.

The Judge then phoned, "Why aren't you continuing as guardian, she needs you."

"I'm leaving the state."

Butts' pursued for a more telling answer, "Tell me straight out, Polo, is it because Emily lied to you, so therefore she isn't as flawless, as you thought? She loved her brother, tried to save him from prison, and was wrong, so she wasn't your perfect woman?

Polo didn't answer.

Butt's prodded him again, "You know, Ray, I checked up on you when this whole thing with Parker started. Walt Kearney told me you were a great detective, but you would never be more, because of one major flaw; you only saw black or white. I thought Kearney was wrong. I felt you changed when you met Parker, and the two of you became friends while you created that impressive police force. I realize now your flaw isn't seeing only black or white, it's your gray, shallow *mind*. And while I'm at …"

Butt's stopped speaking; he was talking to a dial tone.

The Judge handled the endless legal ramifications. He brought a Court Stenographer and met with Emily. She haltingly reiterated the story told to Polo. Butts had Parker Sinclair posthumously pardoned, then found not guilty of the murder of his wife. Although Parker and Emily Sinclair were now legally accessories after the fact to murder, Parker was dead and Emily obviously not competent. Judge Butts considered pursuing any charges ludicrous. The Court record changed to state Paul Sinclair was the murderer of Nancy K. Sinclair and later, Parker and Ruth Sinclair. The facts were posted in the County Newspapers, the Boston Globe, and Record American. The Barretton townspeople, tired of all of this, were surprised, then it simply didn't matter, and went on with their lives.

The Court NAMED Judge Butts Executor of the Sinclair estate, an estate estimated by consultants to have a market value of fifty-five million dollars. Butts oversaw the separating of the various businesses into product specific units, then had each unit sold on the open market, or at auction. His keeping a firm hand on the processes involved brought the final amount realized to slightly over sixty-two million dollars.

As Parker and Ruth had been married for only a few months, he had not changed his Will. This omission left the entire estate to Emily Sinclair, as Paul was declared legally dead.

Emily also had a Trust in her name amounting to fifteen million dollars. Yet she was judged, by separate Court proceedings, incompetent to handle the estates.

From this ruling, Judge Butts made the decision to keep Emily's Trust solely for her security, welfare, and happiness until found competent, or died.

Out of the funds from the Parker Sinclair estate, Judge Butts awarded ten million each to Ruth Carvel's sons for the loss of their mother.

Ruth's daughter, who, the Court found, rejected her mother, received nothing. She sued the estate and lost. She sued her two brothers and lost. It was incongruous, for it was she, after all, who argued against the marriage from the beginning.

The Judge directed the Sinclair's estate to continue it's commitment to the Tri Trust Parker founded and supported with two friends. The name of the Trust changed to the PR Sinclair Memorial Trust, as his friends requested. Butts continued the funding Sinclair committed to the Barretton town complex.

Finally, when the judge learned of Emily's love for her school and children, he directed two million dollars from her estate dedicated to the disbursement of those funds for the benefit of the Thorton Academy. All other monies and income from the estate of Parker Sinclair remained in his estate, held in trust until Emily Sinclair was declared competent.

Judge Butts directed he not be compensated for his efforts.

Chapter

Twenty Eight

E mily improved to a point. She insisted on staying at Great Hill. At times, she had good days where she walked the grounds, conversed with her servants and former friends from the school, or otherwise read.

She showed no reaction when informed Paul was assumed dead. She did not ask how; she may have thought it was from drugs. In a way, it was. She did not challenge Judge Butts' decisions, or claim to be competent. When melancholy drifted upon her, she sat for hours, seldom speaking, her eyes exposing the sadness in her life. She wanted no help, even when Judge Butts had Bismarck, her horse, brought back to the house. She often wandered down to the paddock, waiting for him to amble over for a carrot or simply a pat. She thought of her mother teaching her to ride and smiled remembering FC saying he would shoe the horse if she wished. She didn't ride the horse, the horse didn't mind.

When Emily was driven to the Thorton School now and then, the children always gathered round, holding her hand and jabbering on to her. The children sensed, as children will, something wasn't right and instinctively understood. She enjoyed visiting, although never asked to teach.

She did stop running her hand along the curve of the red Jaguar. The memories of her father and mother waving as they drove off tore at her heart. The doctors, and Judge Butts, when he visited, saw that as a good sign, although there were few other indicators to give them confidence. A spark was gone, the spark to unlock her mind, an indefinable key.

Shortly after his phone call to Judge Butt's, Polo moved to Florida. He didn't take the position Sal Fanara offered. Burned out he said, and Sal understood. Polo found a one bedroom, fifth floor condominium a little north of Boca Raton in Highland Beach on Route A1A. It faced east for the sunrises, although he seldom saw them. Because of the damp heat, he took to the habits of a night person, staying up into the small hours, walking regularly beside a dark or a moonlit ocean, learning to evade tripping over beach lovers. He walked along the ocean through the day once in awhile, watched the Red Sox on TV, and had a couple of beers.

In his retirement, the stress disappeared, along with the mental lapses. He quit cigarettes. From walking, he felt physically better, no further pains. He spoke to Commissioner Kearney, Sheriff Fanara, or one of the officers in Barretton. He stopped calling, realizing they had other lives, concerns, and less in common with him as weeks passed into months.

He had no purpose and didn't try to find one. In essence, he knew he was simply running out the string of his life, and yet, he didn't know what to do about it. Though apart, he and Emily were very much alike.

He missed Parker and Ruth and thought often of Emily. He had long past come to understand her reason for lying for her twin, and realized she never dreamed of the terrible events that would follow. He regretted his outburst at the clinic.

Still, it was for the best, he decided. She was gone, although not the parting he wished. When he spoke with people in Barretton or Boston, he never asked about her. As he never brought her up, they felt he didn't want to hear of her, so no one ever mentioned her either. Because of this omission, he didn't know she had never fully recovered.

By the end of 1969, the hurt began to ease. Now, he thought of her fondly, hoping she found someone to love, marry find peace, and live a happy life. Deep within, he knew she deserved it. That was his hope, and gave him peace of mind. Despite that, he still thought of her every day, a few minutes here, an hour there.

Strange, his phone was ringing, "Who's this?"

"It's Judge Norman Butts, Detective Polo."

"Two comments, Judge; I'm no longer a detective and I don't want to talk to you."

"Then I'll make two comments back at you Polo; I don't want to speak with you either, but if we don't talk, someone won't have much of a future."

Polo started to drop the phone, stopped, "What the devil are you talking about?"

"Don't hang up on me … it's Emily. She's still not well."

"Then find her a doctor, what's the hells a matter with you? Is that too difficult to understand?"

"Listen Polo, maybe this is the only language you understand; you stupid son of a bitch. Emily is not well, mentally … and not improving. Do you comprehend that? We think you're the only dumb bastard who can help. Okay? Do you understand that kind of talk?"

The Judge's attack was unusual, "What do you want me to do about it?"

"She's at Great Hill. Go see her, you selfish, God damn shithead!"

The line went dead. Polo stayed frozen at the phone. What a bizarre call. Who did Butt's think he was, talking like that? Why didn't he just explain what was wrong with Emily, instead of teeing off on him like some punk?

He knew why. The judge wasn't going to try to coax or wheedle him into seeing Emily. He laid it on the line; see Emily, or

255

you're a son of a bitch, a bastard, or a stupid shithead. Take your pick.

Polo reflected, "I may be all of those things ... except stupid."

Chapter

Twenty Nine

The house glared at him. He could feel it as he rang the bell.

"Yes, may I help you?"

"My name's Detective Polo. Ray Polo. Is Emily in?"

The woman recognized the name, "Detective Polo. Of course, Emily's spoken of you. Come in; please have a chair in the den. I'll inform her."

Before the woman could leave, he heard Emily's voice as she came through the doorway.

"Joan, who was that at the front ...."

Emily froze in mid-step, "Ray."

"Hello, kid, how's it going?"

She couldn't speak for a moment, swallowing hard, "How come you're here?"

"I heard you weren't well, thought I'd come by and try to cheer you up."

"Christ, Ray. I wish I knew you were coming, I'm a mess."

"Yeah, you could use a little buffing up."

Her voice was cheerful, "Now *that's* the Ray Polo I remember, overflowing with compliments."

Emily looked at him, a smile started at the corners of her mouth, then spread across her face. The transformation coming over her startled Joan. She watched amazed as the woman she

257

thought of as perpetually sad, came to life. Emily's smile, a smile the maid had never seen, warmed the distance between two people.

She knew she was an intruder, excusing herself.

"Come with me, Ray, while I do some buffing up, as you so kindly put it."

Emily took his hand as they went to a bedroom at the far end of the house.

"Make yourself comfortable while I try to work some magic in the bathroom."

Before closing the door, she turned, "God, Ray, I couldn't begin to explain how I feel right now."

He saw tears spring to her eyes. He was close to them himself.

He took off his jacket and wandered about the room, past her writing desk. There was a page torn from an English Verse book, a poem by Emily Dickinson called *Parting*. He read the first stanza. *"My life closed twice before its close; it yet remains to see, if immortality unveil, a third event to me ..."*

Knowing he was intruding on her privacy, he started to walk away. His eye caught the end of the last stanza ... *"Parting is all we know of heaven- And all we need to know of hell."*

He went to the window. Had he done the right thing?

A foolish question. He was where he must be, with her. No matter what the future brought. No matter what part he played.

As she came from the bathroom, he searched her face: hauntingly beautiful, more beautiful than he remembered. Dear God, I love her. She came toward him shyly; he took in all of her, her loveliness, her shape, her negligee.

She put her arms around him.

"Jesus, Emily, I was your friend, not your lover."

"Ray ... that's the mistake I made from the beginning."

THE END